BOOMTOWN

ALSO BY A. F. CARTER:

The Yards

All of Us

The Hostage

BOOMTOWN

A. F. CARTER

THE MYSTERIOUS PRESS
NEW YORK

BOOMTOWN

Mysterious Press
An Imprint of Penzler Publishers
58 Warren Street
New York, N.Y. 10007

Copyright © 2023 by A. F. Carter

First Mysterious Press edition

Interior design by Maria Fernandez

Library of Congress Control Number: 2023908397

ISBN: 978-1-61316-453-2
eBook ISBN: 978-1-61316-454-9

10 9 8 7 6 5 4 3 2 1

Printed in the United States of America
Distributed by W. W. Norton & Company

CHAPTER ONE

CHARLIE

You're a psychopath. That's what my father said when he kicked me out of the house for the last time. I was nineteen, still a kid, but I'd always been trouble. Like from birth. No, make that from conception. My mother, according to him, was sick the entire time she was pregnant.

I wasn't ready for independence, I admit that, and I ran from home to the office, where I pleaded my case to Mom. She wasn't impressed. "If it was up to me," she said, "I'd have thrown you out when you turned eighteen."

"But I'm your oldest son." Though my parents insisted that I'd never spoken a truthful word in my life, this much was undoubtedly true.

"First thing, I have three other children, normal children. Second thing, what's wrong with you can't be fixed." She rubbed her hands together. "Good money after bad? I don't play that game."

◆

My parents owned and operated Starstone Imports. The firm imported finished gemstones. We buy the rough material at mine sites all over the world, then ship it to Mumbai where Indian jewelers cut the gems before dispatching them to our offices in New York. They go from there to high-end jewelers throughout the country.

I'd failed at just about everything by then, having already flunked out of the college my parents spent a fortune getting me into, but I appreciated gemstones. Their beauty didn't particularly interest me, only their value, which is why I helped myself on the way out. And I wasn't about to settle for a few citrines and an amethyst with a window in the middle. I needed a decent start in this life I had to live on my own. So, along with a handful of smaller stones, I snatched a forty-carat, trillion-cut tanzanite. The blue stone came with a cert from the Gemological Institute of America declaring it to be vivid, the highest classification for a tanzanite. Vivid referred not only to its perfect saturation, but to patches of violet that flashed whenever the stone was moved. Looking into this stone was like staring into an indigo sky as the last daylight fades. It was the kind of stone that designers sell to their superrich clients for upward of eighty large.

As it turned out, I made a big mistake. I figured my parents would never call the cops on their eldest son. Beep, wrong. If I was more experienced, or even if I'd given it a little thought at the time, I would have known what was coming. That's because unless a theft is reported to the police, no insurance company will accept a claim.

Two days later I was arrested in a Bronx pawn shop where an old man offered me a hundred bucks for what he claimed was an "over-saturated topaz."

◆

I got eighteen months in a minimum-security prison. Partly because my parents wouldn't pay for a decent lawyer and I had to go with a public defender. Partly because I'd been arrested many times for petty offenses like shoplifting or selling small amounts of coke to my classmates. And partly because I refused a plea bargain that would have put me back on the street in five or six months.

I was furious on sentencing day, not that it did me any good. For the first time in my life, I was out of options. But life can fool you. Prison was just what I needed. Call it a great awakening, but my time at the Beacon Corrections Facility led directly to where I am at this moment, driving through a rinky-dink city named Baxter with a dead whore in the trunk and a guinea head-breaker named Dominick Costa sitting alongside me.

◆

The whore wasn't murdered. Overdose, probably, or suicide. Which doesn't matter. What matters is what I found on my plate when I got to the double-wide trailer where she and the girls live (or in her case, lived). The other girls were freaked, but not me. Everybody dies and it's no big deal unless you die in a whorehouse. Then somebody has to get rid of your body. A headache, yeah, but that's what I'm here for. To solve problems. To keep the operation up and running. To maximize the return on my employer's investment.

"So, you think Corey offed herself?" Dominick half whispers. "I mean, why the fuck would she do something like that?"

Dominick Costa has committed murder. How many times I don't know, but he's pure muscle, which is why Ricky sent him to Baxter. *We'll need an enforcer,* he said, and I couldn't disagree. Only Dominick Costa has the IQ of a frog and he's only manageable because he's scared of Ricky Ricci, who's a thousand miles away in New York.

I normally stay in Boomtown, away from the city, but it rained last night and half the dirt-and-gravel roads are knee-deep mud. I can't risk getting stuck, not with the whore in the trunk. So, I'm driving through Baxter in a three-year-old Honda sedan, keeping my speed down. There's a cop in Baxter, a dyke captain named Delia Mariola. She's a real crusader, gonna make her city safe, and I don't doubt her commitment. But she's got exactly zero say in Boomtown, which is in Sprague County.

"Maybe she OD'd," I finally say.

"On a coupla bags a day?"

"And whatever she might have bought on the outside. Or the johns put up her nose."

Technically, our girls aren't trafficked. These women are older, the youngest past thirty, and they've more or less adjusted to the life and the working-class johns they service. They get a piece of every trick they turn, less room and board, and they can leave anytime they want, no hard feelings. As long as they've paid off debts, including the loans they took prior to working for us. Loans we retired before we transported them to Boomtown. And there's the drugs, too, which we are happy to supply.

I have a hard rule. No shooting up. I don't need the johns walkin' away because some bitch's tracks are oozing. Other than that, it's whatever you want, as long as you work your shift and pay for your highs out of your earnings. No earnings, of course, no drugs. One hand washing the other.

◆

Ricky did the original research and set the goalposts on the day he called me in. I assumed that he'd sniffed out my side deals, which could've gone very bad for me. But Ricky had something else in mind. Somethin' much bigger. First, he showed me a map of this little city. You wouldn't give it a second glance, your eyes passed it on a map, but that was about to change.

"Nissan's building a factory there. Gigantic, right? Like three million square feet, I kid you not. Like fifteen hundred acres. So, who's gonna build it? The locals? There ain't enough workers in the whole city to build that plant, even if they had the skills, which they mainly don't." Ricky was talking with his hands, which he does when he gets excited. "They're gonna come runnin', Charlie, construction workers from all over the country, and they're gonna leave their families behind. So, whatta ya figure they'll want after work?"

I responded without hesitation. "Broads, drugs, gambling . . . and loans when they burn up their paychecks and can't send money home."

"How 'bout truckers haulin' the iron, the concrete, the wiring, the rebar? How 'bout them?"

"Same thing."

"I want every cent, Charlie, and soon. The construction won't last that long, and when it's over, most of those workers are gonna head home. We gotta get it while we can."

◆

The speech was typical Ricky in its ambition. Ricky wants to run New York the way Al Capone ran Chicago. He isn't close, and isn't likely to get close. Capone never had to face the RICO act. But reality never dominated Ricky's scheming, and I wasn't surprised until he named me to manage operations in Baxter. This was a big move up for me. I'd been running a hot jewelry setup that bought from high-end thieves and sold to greedy collectors online. A diamond necklace from a top designer is easy to identify. The FBI maintains a database, as does the industry's trade associations. You try to sell that necklace, you're takin' a big risk. Unless you strip out the diamonds.

With rare exceptions, the stones themselves are as anonymous as anonymous gets. I remounted them, then sold the rings or bracelets or necklaces at twenty-five percent below wholesale to private clients who must have known what they were getting and didn't care.

"Corey was all right," Dominick said. "I liked her."

"Okay, so what?"

"We should, like do something."

"What, you wanna buy her a coffin, maybe a wreath, put up a headstone?"

I shouldn't be talking this way. The sarcasm, I mean. It feels good, but it doesn't work. I can't help myself, though. The schmuck's worried about a dead whore, for Christ's sake. Me, when my mother died, it had exactly zero effect on my mood. Like nothing, right? Because everybody rots in the end.

"We could maybe say somethin'."

"Pray, you mean?"

"Somethin', okay? To show that she lived."

◆

Enough being enough, I don't waste my breath with another comment that'll go right over the jerk's head. We've passed Baxter's northern border. Now we're in Revere County and it's boonies all the way. Farms and cattle and pigs, fields sheeted with frost that go on forever. I turn onto a state road, Highway 20, and drive for about a mile until I come to a grove of trees that runs deep enough to hide what's about to happen. It's three o'clock in the morning and the road's deserted, but I'm not wasting time.

"All right, Dom, there's a shovel in the back. I want you to get out of sight and dig some kind of grave. There's somethin' else I need to do."

"Hey, it's cold out there."

"The exercise'll keep you warm."

The moron stares at me for a moment and I know what's coming. Back east, Costa took orders from Ricky and nobody else. Most likely, Ricky sent him to Baxter as a test. Can I manage him? Can I maintain control?

"I ain't gonna stay out here alone, no transportation if I have to make tracks in a hurry."

Anger's not my thing and I'm not angry now. But I can do anger. Hell, I can do rage when it's called for. Plus, I bulked up in prison and I wasn't small to start out. So Dominick jerks back when I turn and poke a finger into his chest.

"I don't wanna hear that." I keep my voice halfway between a snarl and a roar. "You work for me out here and you'll do what the fuck I tell you to do."

When Costa finds his voice, it's half an octave higher than usual. "I work for Ricky," is the best he can do.

"Ricky's a thousand miles away." Now I'm poking as fast as I can. "Out here, I'm in charge. Completely, Dom, like one hundred fucking percent. You don't like that, get on a train tomorrow morning."

Costa leans against the door and stares at me through dark brown eyes that appear black in the dim light. I'm supposed to be afraid of him, right? He's a killer, a hit man, right? But I don't do fear, either, and when the truth finally dawns on him, he draws a breath. Relieved, I think. No more decisions to make.

"Awright, Charlie. But don't forget me. I get the creeps out of the city."

CHAPTER TWO

CHARLIE

I come into Baxter by a side road, eyes jumping from the windshield to the mirrors. Looking for cops who don't appear. No shocker because Oakland Gardens, hard on the county border, isn't the kind of neighborhood cops feel the need to protect and serve. The houses are more like shacks and they're spread out, like they can't stand to look at each other. Most have been abandoned and there are no squatters either, cold as it's been.

All to the good. I drive past one of the few houses still occupied. It belongs to a biker-pimp named Titus Klint, as does the Harley parked in the yard and the mixed-breed bulldog on a long chain. The animal's already torn up a pair of rival bikers and I know Titus feels secure having the dog around. The mutt has to weigh more than a hundred pounds.

The animal's name is Spike, a choice that I'm sure taxed the limits of Klint's imagination. It pulls at the chain and barks loudly, fangs flashing, then shuts down, enemy vanquished, when I turn the corner.

I pull over and park fifty feet from the intersection. The street I'm on must have a name, but there's no marker and the streetlight on the corner is dark. Me, I'm not the hesitating type once I make a decision. I tried to reason with Klint, a pimp by trade, to bring him and his girls into Ricky's orbit. He refused, threatening me with total destruction if I even spoke to him again.

It isn't something you forget, that kind of insult. That we were already set up only made it worse. Our whores work at the Paradise Inn, a double-wide trailer with a bar-lounge in front and rooms to either side in the back. A prefab Quonset hut almost next door also has a lounge in front, but the larger section in the back houses a small casino. The joint isn't much—a couple of roulette wheels, three blackjack tables, a craps table, and a dozen slots—but it's a real moneymaker. The drug part is also running, though in an earlier stage. We have a presence in several bars and we're wholesaling to a few dealers.

For now, each of these operations is managed by its own crew, but I can pull them together, maybe twenty-five men, at a moment's notice.

◆

Klint made his own bed. He could have accepted our terms, could have paid tribute. He didn't. Now he's going to become an object lesson. I pop the trunk release and get out of the car. My weapon is in the trunk; Corey too. She was still pliant when we folded her into a fetal position, but she's stiff as a board now. At the moment, though, I'm focused on the leather bag next to her feet, the bag and the silenced Sig Sauer automatic inside. Silencers are now legal in forty-two states, thanks to the NRA. Mine isn't legal, of course, but once manufacturers began shipping suppressors to gun stores, a certain number inevitably found their way onto the black market. Like the one attached to the .22 caliber Sig Sauer. The pistol isn't very powerful. Or very accurate. Beyond twenty yards, in fact, it's just about worthless. Close in, though, it's a lot quieter than nine millimeters or forty-fives. Even silenced, guns make noise.

I slide my hands into surgical gloves, also in the bag, and slip a surgical mask over my mouth and nose. I'm not trying to prevent infection, only to avoid leaving my DNA at what's sure to be a crime scene.

There are no lights in the windows that I can see when I turn the corner of a half-demolished house next door. I'm facing the back of Klint's house, but I can already hear Spike growling as I cross the space between the two homes to squat beneath a window that looks into an empty bedroom. The window's been raised a few inches, all to the good.

Out front, Spike begins to bark, softly at first, then loud enough to be heard back in New York. The din is impossible to ignore and I wait, pretty much unconcerned, until I hear Klint's gravelly voice, instantly recognizable.

"Shut the fuck up, shut the fuck up, shut the fuck up."

I raise the window and slip inside, only to find a mattress on the floor to my left with someone lying on it, a woman or a small man. With the covers pulled up, it's impossible to be sure.

"Shut the fuck up, goddamn it."

The bedroom door's open a bit and I peek through the gap to find Klint standing with his back to me. He's still yelling and the dog's still barking, so I'm not worrying about making noise. No, I'm imagining Klint finally closing the door, imagining the look on his face when he turns to me. Will he beg? Attack? Try to run out the door? Will he plead his case, swear eternal fidelity and an ongoing piece of his action?

There was a time in my life, before I learned my lesson, when I would have surrendered to temptation. To look into Klint's blue eyes when he realized that his empty promises wouldn't save him, to relish the moment, the power. To hell with the possibility that he'll attack, that I'll miss or only wound him, that he'll get his hands on me. The risk is part of the thrill, maybe the best part.

No more, though. Now it's all about results. I have a job to do, a simple job, and I do it.

◆

Dominick's waiting for me right where I left him, but there's no grave. I'm thinking he changed his mind, that he intends to defy me, but then he scratches at the ground with the blade of the shovel.

"It's frozen," he announces.

"What's frozen?"

"The ground. You wanna open a grave, you're gonna need dynamite."

I take the shovel and give it a try. Dom's not exaggerating. The winters out here are beyond cold and there's no digging through the frozen ground. Not with a shovel. This is something a better manager might have anticipated. In town, between the full sun and the hundreds of vehicles traveling over the Boomtown roads, there's mud everywhere. Out here, in deep shade, winter hasn't let go.

"Let's make tracks, Dom."

I don't have to tell him twice and we drive away seconds later. I have no choice now. I have to get rid of the whore's body and that means dumping it where it's likely to be found. I enter Baxter the way I left it, along backstreets, until I find a block where the few homes still standing appear to be unoccupied. We have to move fast, but I don't rush. I can't anyway, because the whore's body is jammed and we have to ease her out, a shoulder first, then her feet, finally her head. But once free, she's no problem and we carry her to a chimney standing by itself a few yards from the car, then drop her. Time to go.

"She was somebody's kid," Dominick says out of the blue.

"You don't think she sprang, full-blown, from the head of Zeus?" I might as well have spoken Martian. Dominick's eyes become dolls' eyes, blank as buttons. "Do what makes you feel better, Dom, only do it fast."

I get the blank stare for a few more seconds, then Dom's lips begin to move. "Hail, Mary, full of grace . . ."

CHAPTER THREE

DELIA

E very time I look at Boomtown, which is what it's universally called, the same question jumps up to bite me: How did this happen? On one level the answer is simple. In June of last year, Boomtown Enterprises, an LLC registered in Panama, purchased a strip of Sprague County land bordering a Baxter County neighborhood called the Yards. A half mile deep by two miles long, the acreage was purchased from several corporate farmers. Impromptu roads that would never meet code in Baxter were then laid almost overnight and the land divided into lots.

Boomtown Leasing was the first structure to appear. A prefab A-frame, it was built in less than a week. Getting water and electricity to the property took a bit longer, but its outdoor septic system became a model for what followed as specialized construction workers poured into town. Boilermakers and iron workers, heavy equipment operators and electricians, laborers and masons, welders and pipefitters. They came to build a Nissan factory and most had one thing in common. Male or female, they left their families behind.

Long-haul truckers followed, transporting a dizzying array of construction materials, from prefab girders to twisted rebar to portable toilets. They would return to their families, but not before a taste of what Boomtown had to offer.

◆

The Baxter Police Department, where I'm chief of detectives, lacks jurisdiction in Sprague County. We can chase a fleeing suspect across the county line and that's about it. For anything beyond a hot pursuit, we need the permission of the Sprague County sheriff, Pickford Fletcher. Fletcher allows us to make arrests if we can produce a warrant and we're accompanied by one of his deputies. What we can't do is knock on doors or pull in witnesses or anything that resembles a serious investigation.

Worse yet, the worst of the worst, Boomtown is entirely unpatrolled. The sheriff's office will only respond to 911 calls. And reluctantly, even then.

◆

I can't blame Sheriff Fletcher. Except for a few hamlets, Sprague County is rural, with its homes far apart. Domestic disputes are common, and so are meth labs, but the county's bad actors are locals for the most part, and well known to law enforcement. Boomtown is a whole other world, filled with camper vans, single wides, double wides, and prefab structures of every kind, from sheds to Quonset huts to a pair of houses made from shipping containers. There's even a tent city on the southern end, its Latino residents surviving despite the cold.

Criminal activity of every sort thrives in Boomtown, as it always has in American boomtowns, from Deadwood to Dodge City. Loansharking, brothels, the drug trade in all of its manifestations, a pair of rival casinos. And the saddest part? I've spent the past year forcing drug dealers out of Baxter, only to find new dealers operating with impunity a few yards outside the city line. Their only fear is of one another.

Meanwhile, Baxter's town fathers are negotiating with the Sprague County Board of Supervisors for some sort of limited right to operate in their precious county. Or even to purchase the strip and graft the land to Baxter's existing borders.

◆

Boomtown's not on my to-do list at 6 A.M. on this Monday morning. I've got a battered woman under protection in

Baxter Medical Center and a pimp named Titus Klint, who's about to pay for what he did to her. It'll be a first for the department's newly formed SWAT team. The Baxter PD has grown rapidly over the past year. We've added forty cops and a small warehouse of equipment that includes an armored Lenco BearCat that can transport up to eight. This morning, the Lenco will carry a single officer when it rolls up to Klint's front door. Essentially a distraction while the main force rolls through the back door, the object here is to avoid killing a dog chained at the front of the house. A mixed-breed bulldog, the animal's so uncontrollably vicious it'll most likely be euthanized. But not by us.

We're eight blocks away. Me, six cops in black uniforms worn beneath Grade III body armor, and Detective John Meacham, the Dink. The Dink and I won't be there when the team hits Klint's door. I've named Sergeant Cade Barrow to head SWAT operations. Cade's an ex-Marine, a Special Forces type who's proven himself to be cool under fire. He's been training his crew for the past six weeks and he doesn't need a superior officer to undercut his play. But we'll be watching, me and the Dink.

John Meacham easily met the criteria for worst (and laziest) cop on the force when I started with the department. He's improved slightly, enough to avoid being fired. Still, I'd never have had him with me this morning if I hadn't become aware of his special talent.

The Dink is a drone enthusiast. He's been flying camera drones, like the one at his feet, since they first became available to the general public. Thus far, I've not asked him whose bedroom window he peeps through. I'm afraid he might not lie.

Cade Barrow emerges from the BearCat's rear to offer a thumbs-up. I return the gesture and he climbs back inside. As the BearCat pulls away, Meacham takes his drone airborne. It rained yesterday, but the sky is clear now. A steady breeze pushes hard and cold against my down parka. Winter's last stand, or so we're all hoping. Farmers in the region plant anywhere between mid-April and mid-May, the earlier the better. Not this year.

We're operating in a neighborhood called Oakland Gardens. Always poor, it's on its way out, to be replaced by middle-class housing. Most of its current homes are so decrepit, it's hard to tell the functioning homes from the abandoned. Or it would be without the infrared camera. A glow, pink to a faint red, crowns the rooftops of the occupied houses, while five red blobs, probably dogs, lope through a field of debris at the edge of the monitor. Directly below, the BearCat's hood is bright red, the rest of the vehicle little more than a shadow moving through empty streets.

I realize, suddenly, that I'm holding my breath. The BearCat's progress has a relentless quality about it. The red glow makes the vehicle appear alive, a beast in search of prey. Only a few months ago, before my final promotion, I'd be right there, leading the raid, maybe the first one through the door. I'm only an observer this morning, but I'll get to strut before the press if all goes well.

The BearCat stops a block from Klint's home. The windows are dark in the house and there can't be much heat because the roof is a pale pink. But the dog is clearly visible, lying in the open at the end of its chain.

Five cops emerge from the BearCat's side door, one at a time. Between the black uniforms and the gear, only their faces light up. As they approach the back of Klint's house, Cade's voice sounds on the radio.

"All clear. Go."

"Roger that."

The BearCat turns onto Sherman Avenue, stopping in front of Klint's home. As expected, the dog dashes to the end of its chain as five heavily armed cops approach the back of the house. Then Cade's voice again: "Now."

I can't hear the BearCat's siren or the dog barking, and I can't really see what's happening in back, not in detail. But I know the door's off its hinges when the four cops enter the house. At this point, I'm half expecting thermal flares unleashed by gunfire. Klint's firearm collection provided justification for the SWAT takedown. Instead, I see lights come on inside the house, then a long silence until Cade's voice sounds in my year.

"Captain, you out there?" Cade's tone is dead calm.

"I'm here."

"You want the good news first? Or the bad news?"

"The good news."

"The good news is that we've secured the scene and Mr. Klint is present and accounted for."

"And the bad news?"

"He's deceased. One shot. Through the back of the head."

CHAPTER FOUR

DELIA

Two hours later, I'm in the detectives' squad room. An upgrade is in the works, but has yet to happen. The desks remain battered, the walls punctuated by wanted posters dating back to a time when the meatpacking industry was going full blast. Outside, on the other side of the walls, the surrounding neighborhood is beginning to sparkle. The city parents have designated the area surrounding City Hall Park a "destination zone." Restaurants, boutiques, even a jewelry store with diamonds in the window. It's not Tiffany's, true, and the restaurants will never compete for a James Beard award. But it's Fifth Avenue and the Champs-Élysées by our standards.

The walls in the squad room were originally white. Now they're a sooty, uneven gray tinged with amber, a leftover from a time when you could smoke in municipal offices. And while we're not still dependent on manual typewriters, our records haven't been moved onto someone's cloud. No, they're stored on a thoroughly unreliable server in the basement. Never the trusting type, I've ordered my detectives to back up the server with paper copies of all reports and requisitions.

On this particular morning, I'm finding comfort in the clatter of the printers and the keyboards. So many changes have come to Baxter I feel like I'm policing an entirely new world, and brave it ain't. To give just one example—the city's experienced a wave of burglaries committed by perpetrators who flee to Boomtown with their loot. Murders are up, too, as are assaults. As we expand, so do the criminals and the crimes they commit.

Mayor Venn and Council President Gloria Meacham are in a tough spot. Crime has become the city's big issue, too big to ignore with a primary election two months away. At the same time, there's enormous pressure coming from all directions, including Nissan, to stay on schedule.

◆

I've got three women in three interview rooms. All were present when Cade Barrow and his team busted into Titus

Klint's house to find him dead, his body lying in an open doorway. He'd been shot once in the back of the head, the fatal round likely from a small-caliber weapon.

The women claim to have seen and heard nothing. They claim they were asleep. But each has an arrest record for prostitution and Klint was a pimp with a history of assaults. And even dead, his prominence in a local motorcycle gang, the Horde, renders the women's continued subservience likely. The gang has its fingers in numerous rackets and these women are proven earners.

As I'm weighing the various scenarios, my sometime personal assistant, Martha Blackstone, strolls over to where I'm seated at the far side of Cade Barrow's desk.

"I tried the intercom," she informs me, her tone habitually accusing, "but you weren't in your office."

Though sorely tempted, I stifle a sarcastic response. "So, what's up?"

She lifts her eyes to the ceiling. "Boss wants to see you."

Only six months ago, I was slated for the top job, commissioner of the Baxter Police Department. I turned it down in favor of my current position, chief of detectives. I prefer the action and my former partner, Vern, is better suited to the position. That would be Vern Taney, born and raised in Baxter, a high school football star with an engaging smile who seems to know everyone.

Vern and his wife, Lillian, are my best friends, and have been for years now. My boy, Danny, and his son,

Mike, are inseparable, both on and off the baseball diamond where they spend whatever time they have to spare. The boys are super-hyped just now. The high school season is about to start, the first game this afternoon, and they've only now moved from the junior varsity roster to varsity.

◆

Vern's office is one floor up. Unlike my own collection of bare essentials, his furnishings include a pair of navy love seats on either side of a wooden coffee table. His predecessor, Chief Black, decorated the walls with photos of himself posing alongside politicians and celebrities. Vern hasn't been around long enough for that, but he's got football instead. My ex-partner's a natural politician, and photos from the Baxter Tigers' only state championship abound.

I take a seat on one side of the coffee table, Vern on the other. There's a filled mug in front of my seat, for which I'm grateful. I've been up since three.

"So, what's happening with the ladies?" he asks.

"They're marinating."

Vern's referring to the women found inside Klint's house. They're sitting in separate interview rooms, their paranoia building as they evaluate their shaky prospects.

"You think one of them is good for it? Or all of them? Klint was a mean son of a bitch."

I take a moment to organize my thoughts. That's just my way and Vern's familiar with the habit.

"Cade Barrow and his team were first through the door, but I was only a mile away and I got there in a hurry. Klint was lying in front, draped across the threshold with the door open wide. According to Cade, the women found in the house were in bed when he came through the back door. Now, I know that most hookers are excellent liars, but their shocked responses when told their pimp was dead seemed genuine to me. And the handguns we found in the house hadn't been recently fired and were the wrong caliber anyway."

"Enough, I get it. But why didn't the gunshot wake anyone up?"

"Face it, Vern, you can walk into Baxter Guns and Ammo this morning and buy a silencer to fit any weapon they sell." I sip at my coffee and lean back. "Okay, I'm exaggerating a bit. There's a lot of paperwork and a wait involved. But that doesn't change the bottom line. Any citizen without a felony record can buy a silencer in this state."

"You're talking about a professional hit, not a stoned biker?"

"I'm talking about a motorcycle gang with a long history of mindless violence now out to avenge the death of Titus Klint. They have no choice, Vern. It's a matter of honor. As for the perp? We found an open window at the back of the house and a vicious bulldog in front. The most likely scenario has the shooter creating a disturbance that sets off the dog. Klint opens the door to check it out as the perp climbs through the back window. He finds Klint at the front door, facing away from him, and . . ."

"Bang, you're dead?"

"Yeah, bang, you're dead."

CHAPTER FIVE

DELIA

O ur interview/interrogation rooms are even more decrepit than the squad rooms, but there's been a single upgrade at my insistence. Originally, they had one-way mirrors that allowed us to look inside without being observed. We've replaced the mirrors with CCTV cameras designed to record interviews. State-mandated less than a year ago, suspect interviews must be recorded if a confession, or even a damaging admission, is to be admitted in court. But the cameras also let us monitor the interior when no cops are present. Since their installation, we've yanked the mirrors, producing an even more claustrophobic effect inside.

I find Detective Blanche Weber seated behind a desk in the squad room when I return. Three monitors on the desk reveal the women taken from Klint's home this morning.

Blanche looks up as I approach. She's proven herself an adept detective, dogged in her investigations, a woman who takes failure hard. I'm not convinced that she's viable long-term. Not every case can be closed, not every mutt arrested, and you have to roll with the punches. For now, though, she'll do. She has the instincts of a shark.

"So, what's up, Cap?" She gives her red hair a shake as I approach and sweeps her bangs from her eyes. The gesture is distinctly feminine, but I know Blanche to be an accomplished martial artist who doesn't give way on the street. Maybe that's because she was raised in New Jersey, an Eastern elitist (never mind her working-class family) who's cultivated a bad attitude. Don't call her Jersey Girl.

"That's what I was gonna ask you." I gesture to the monitors. "Anybody look ready to confess?"

"You think one of them killed Klint?"

"No, but if one of them wants to confess, I'll write it up and head out for breakfast. A girl can't live on doughnuts alone." When Blanche's eyes widen, I wave off the comment. "Just kidding, Blanche, but one of them might know who did. That's why they're not getting out of here until they decide to share that information. Plus, I know they're working a stroll in Boomtown and we need to gather whatever intelligence we can. Fast, right? And there's the Horde."

The Horde originally named their gang the Aryan Horde. Stupid, really, in a state with a Caucasian population over ninety percent. And right here, out on the prairie, it's closer to a hundred percent.

"This one here, I'd work her first." Blanche points to the monitor on the far left. The Latina inside has bent forward until her head is almost in her lap. She's small and thin, her blond hair showing several inches of dark root. "Her name's Gina Sanchez."

"And the other two?"

"Hard-core. That one on the right? She's thrown a middle finger at the camera at least ten times. The other one's too lazy. She just spits on the floor."

Gina Sanchez finally raises her head. Her makeup is smudged and tear-streaked, and I can see now that she's younger than I first thought. I wonder if she began as a teen rebel out to prove something. To herself, to her family, to society in general. It doesn't matter because at some point it all went bad.

"Okay, let's start with Gina."

"You want me inside, Cap?"

"Yeah, but I'll take the lead, at least at first. You come in after I soften her up."

◆

Five minutes later, armed with a super-caffeinated Red Bull and a bag of ranch-flavored chips, we make our grand entrance. There are three chairs and a small table in the room. Gina's sitting behind the table, her back to the far wall. Blanche takes the chair closest to the door and folds her arms across her chest.

I drop the food on the table and Gina doesn't hesitate. She pops the tab on the Red Bull and empties half the can. "At this point, you're not a suspect," I explain, my tone matter-of-fact. "But I'm gonna read your rights to you anyway."

I proceed with the ritual, to which Gina pays no attention. Only when I finish does she speak.

"I didn't kill him, but I'm glad he's dead."

"Do you know who did?"

"Maybe."

Gina's tougher than she looked through the window, but her exhaustion is still apparent. Her eyes are hollow and her cheekbones run across her face like the edge of a cliff.

It takes a full minute before she finally lets it out. "I want something."

"Like what?"

She looks around the room, at the blank walls to her left, her right, in front. Finally, she draws a breath and says, "I didn't have nothin' to do with killin' Titus, but it don't matter. The minute I walk outta here, I'll go back to the same prison I lived in when the asshole was alive. Just be someone else with a different name holdin' the key to my cell."

"I'm sympathetic, but I can't buy you a ticket out."

"See, that's just it. You can." Gina relaxes a bit now that she's broken through. "You don't think I could have a cigarette, do ya?"

◆

Smoking is strictly forbidden in municipal buildings, but my colleagues are unlikely to write a summons. I nod to Blanche, who smokes, and she leaves the room. A moment later, she returns with a cigarette tucked between her fingers. Just one.

Gina takes the cigarette and leans into Blanche's lighter. She draws the first hit deep into her lungs, holds it there for a minute, finally blows it toward the ceiling.

"I got a sister back home, she'll take me in if I can get to her. Right now, I don't have twenty dollars to my name. Titus made sure of that." She looks directly into my eyes for the first time. "I'm still young, ya know. Twenty-three. But I have no hope, none at all, if I stay here. I gotta get out, and even then, I'll be walkin' a hard road for a long time."

"Where's home, Gina? Let's see the fine print."

"Texas. Waco, Texas."

"And you want what, a bus ticket?"

"No, it'll take three days to reach Waco on a bus. Every stop, there's a chance I'll call it quits. You know, step out to look for something to put up my nose, maybe a john to supply that something." She stares down at the smoke curling off the cigarette in her hand. "I'm not kiddin' myself. I been runnin' wild since I was fifteen. Quit school. Thought I'd conquer the world. Stupid, stupid, stupid. No, I want to go from here to an airport with a ticket in my hand."

There's an airport about twenty miles south of here in Coombs County, but it's small and private. Crop dusters for the most part. The nearest commercial airport is a hundred miles away. That'll change when Coombs Airport is finally upgraded, a project that's still in the design phase. But the price of a ticket isn't a problem. We've got a dedicated snitch fund that should cover the cost.

I nod to Blanche and she takes charge. Blanche would be a seriously attractive woman if not for a thick jaw that's slightly off-center. A problem in a cocktail lounge, but an asset in the box.

"For the record, Gina. You don't know who killed your pimp?"

Gina flinches at the word pimp, then collects herself. "Does that mean you'll buy the ticket?"

"It means we'll decide after we hear what you have to say. And you'd best not lie to us. Seriously, Gina. You lie to me, you'll be wishing you could resurrect Titus."

"I ain't gonna lie. I mean I already told you I don't know who killed Titus, not for sure." She pauses, but quickly realizes that Detective Weber's spoken her piece. "Okay, you remember Connor . . ." She snaps her fingers. "What's his last name?"

"Connor Schmidt."

"Yeah, him and his father. They kinda ran the rackets in Baxter till they went off to prison. Well, the boys—"

"The boys?" Blanche's tone is sharp. "Say what you mean, Gina. I'm not into guessing games."

"The Horde, then. The gang, they kinda took over. They ran a lot of dope and had a few girls, too. Only Baxter was never wide open. Then Boomtown came along and they got there first, at least when it came to drugs and girls. I know for a fact they buy dope and coke direct from a cartel." Gina looks down at her cigarette before taking a final hit. "So, everything's going along great until these mob guys out of New York show up. Competition, right? Only these guys from New York don't want competition. Right in that bar, the Blue Horse, one of 'em tells Titus that he's gotta pay out if he wants to continue operating. Titus, he goes through the roof. Nobody talks to him like that. No, he's the baddest badass in Boomtown, leastways in his own eyes, and he chases the guy out of the bar. That was two days ago."

"You know the man's name? The one who extorted Titus?"

"I heard his name is Charlie, but I never laid eyes on him that I know about. Anyways, the heads-up I'm givin' you oughta be worth something. The boys, they ain't gonna take this lyin' down. There's gonna be a war."

"This is not coming as a surprise to us, Gina. You want that ticket, I need more."

"Okay, the guys . . . I mean the Horde if you want me to say it. They won't ride into Boomtown till they're ready to do serious harm. No, what they'll do is camp out in Knob Canyon." Finally, a smile. "Knob Canyon ain't really a canyon. Ya know, like the Grand Canyon."

"Then what is it?"

"It's like . . . I don't know, like a gully cut by a river that became a quarry. So, there's cliffs, right, where they chopped out the limestone. And a creek that dries up in summer. The boys have taken it over, okay? Nobody else can go there."

"Where is this canyon?"

"In Leland County, about sixty miles east of here. See—"

First rule of Interviewing 101. You don't interrupt when the back-and-forth is going smoothly. I'm satisfied with Blanche's approach and I'm sure there's more to get. A lot more. Unfortunately, Martha Blackstone chooses that moment to knock twice, then walk inside. I know this can't be good and it isn't.

"Sorry to interrupt, Captain, but there's another body reported in Oakland Gardens. Dumped, it looks like."

CHAPTER SIX

DELIA

t's only three o'clock in the afternoon and I'm sitting in the stands at Goldman High. There's some guilt here, and I'll probably go back to work later, but I can't miss Danny's first game. Mike's either. Only problem, the game's in the second inning when I find a seat and the boys are sitting on the bench. This is expected, but still disappointing. Danny and Mike are new to the varsity team and they'll have to prove themselves.

Lillian Taney's sitting next to me. Her new baby, Cora, is sleeping in a mesh carrier that resembles an overstuffed hobo bag. Four-year-old Emmaline, the Taneys' adopted daughter, is sitting on my lap, chattering away. A year ago, I pulled Emmaline from a fire that would certainly have killed her.

"Ya know," Lillian tells me out of the blue. The game's in the fourth inning by this time. "I thought, when Vern took the commissioner's job, that he'd absolutely hate it. A hundred percent sure, right? Vern was always a cop's cop. He loved the streets."

"True enough, but I think he wanted to . . . to lessen the risk. That's because he loves his family a lot more than the street. You and Mike were always first."

"I'm blushing now." Lillian places a hand on my shoulder. "Let's say you're right. That Vern wanted regular hours and to minimize the risks. That doesn't mean he wouldn't hate being commissioner. But he loves it, Delia. He thinks of himself as the Department's advocate when he deals with the mayor and the City Council. He thinks it's his job to stand up for every cop on the force." She leans over to whisper in my ear. "Keep this to yourself, strictly. Four years from now, he plans to run for mayor."

I'm relieved when Zoe Parillo shows up. She gives my hand a squeeze and kisses Emmaline as she sits down. Zoe and I are lovers, but not partners. We're not ready to merge our lives, in part because Baxter isn't New York or San Francisco. It's a tiny city in the middle of the Bible Belt. And while I've never disguised my orientation, I've never flaunted it either.

"You and Danny up for dinner at my place tonight?" she asks.

I shake my head. "I'm heading back to work after the game."

"The woman?"

Zoe's referring to the body found outside an abandoned home this morning. An anonymous tipster, a man, called it in. Whoever he was, he apparently phoned the *Baxter Bugle* first because the *Bugle*'s star reporter, Basil Ulrich, was at the scene when the first responders arrived. Basil and a photographer.

Basil was still on-scene when I arrived, but despite my eloquent pleas, the man couldn't be moved. The *Bugle* would run a do-you-recognize-this-women segment in tomorrow's edition.

◆

"Do you think they're related, Delia? The woman and what's his name?"

"Titus Klint?"

Zoe works for Baxter's Department of Social Services in a unit that investigates child abuse. She has a hard time with most of it, as you'd expect, but it allows us to communicate frankly. Nothing shocks her.

"On the surface, they're unconnected. Titus was executed, but there's not a bruise on the woman's body. And Arshan places her time of death twelve hours before she was found. That means she died before Titus was murdered."

"But the bodies were both found in Oakland Gardens."

"True enough, and I don't like coincidences. No cop does. We're the ultimate conspiracy theorists. But there are other possibilities out there."

"Like she overdosed and her pals dumped her where it wouldn't come back on them."

"Yeah, like that." I squeeze Zoe's hand as Emmaline snuggles against me. At the moment, I'm not obsessing about our Jane Doe's cause of death. Our esteemed coroner, Arshan Rishnavata, won't begin the autopsy until tomorrow morning. Test results from the blood and fluid he collects will trickle in over the next two weeks with a DNA profile coming last. That aside, identifying the woman is the first priority. I showed a photo of her to the three women still in custody and they failed to identify her. They might be lying, of course, but they responded identically. A glance and a shrug: "Never laid eyes on the woman." Later, I submitted her fingerprints to the AFIS system run by the FBI, with no matches.

◆

The conversation shuts down abruptly when Vern Taney arrives. He settles in beside Lillian and reaches for Emmaline as Goldman High's catcher, Howard Generoso, makes the third out. The boy swings so hard he drops to one knee.

I have to stifle a cheer when Mike and Danny pick up their gloves and trot out to their respective positions. Danny's playing shortstop, with Mike in left field. Neither appreciates my enthusiasm and I've learned to suck it up over the years. Meanwhile, my heart soars when either do well.

The day has grown warmer, hour by hour. The pure blue sky above is broken only by a few white-on-white clouds that seem to hang unmoving. I shrug off the jacket I've been wearing all day and fold it across my lap. Now that Danny and Mike are competing, Emmaline perks up. She sits upright, her eyes glued to the field. I don't know how well she understands the game, but Mike's been schooling her. The two boys take her with them whenever they can.

The half inning is pretty much uneventful. The first two Roosevelt batters strike out. The third hits a one-hop ground ball at Danny. He snatches it up, flips it to first, and trots across the field. I watch him pick up a bat, waggle it between his hands, then discard it in favor of another. Barely sixteen, but already approaching six feet tall, Danny's a strapping kid, bigger than most of the older kids on the team. None of that matters. He still has to prove himself, and now he'll be facing curve balls and sliders for the first time.

I want to yell out some encouragement, like, "Beat his fucking brains out," but I've been told, more than once, to restrain myself. Not Emmaline, who yells out, "Hit a homer, Danny." Her voice is loud and shrill enough to pierce armor, but Danny pays no attention as he approaches the plate and digs in.

The first pitch is inside, designed to intimidate, but Danny doesn't flinch. Nor does he flinch when the second pitch, a curve ball that doesn't break, is further inside. He merely turns inward and lets the ball hit him in the back.

My first instinct is to charge onto the field and put the Roosevelt pitcher in cuffs. Not my son. He flips the bat to one side and trots to first base, supremely indifferent.

Vern Taney chooses that moment to lean toward me. "The heat's on. Two bodies in one day? An election on the horizon. The mayor's afraid he'll be primaried."

Unconcerned, Emmaline bolts to her feet, claps her hands and yells, "Go, Danny."

CHAPTER SEVEN

MAGGIE MILLER

The most important, if not the first thing we have to do, me and Daddy, is find a place to lay our heads. Boomtown is beyond crazy. Three bars on every block, a main drag that's anything but flat, cement mixers lined up for two hundred yards, drums turning, engines throbbing. The stink of diesel exhaust fills the car despite the raised windows.

"You ever see anything like this, Daddy?"

"Once, honey, in Texas when I was younger'n you. A new oil find out in the Permian 'bout a hundred miles south of Odessa. Middle of nowhere, baby girl. Jackrabbits and scorpions, sidewinder rattlesnakes. That's what the boomtown sprang up from when they put it together in a couple of months. Buildings so shabby they were ready to fall down before anybody moved in. And the stink? What with the spills and the gas burnin' off, you couldn't get away from it."

◆

By the time we arrived, I'd watched just about every video and read every article I could find on the woman found dead in a Baxter City vacant lot. Last time I looked the cops had yet to identify the woman, but me and Daddy recognized her soon as we saw her face. It didn't matter that her skin was gray and slack, or that her empty eyes were fixed on nothing. Her name is Corey Miller, my sister, my father's daughter.

◆

Boomtown's in no way complex. A long road that runs north–south alongside the construction site for a couple miles. Ten east–west roads dead-ending on farm fields that spill out as far as the eye can see.

"You got four-wheel drive," Dad observes, "you could run through them fields easy enough. Say you had to get out in a hurry."

"Better be a big hurry. Flat as the land is out there, you'd be spotted five miles off."

Dad shifts his weight as he uncrosses his legs. "Good thought, honey. But there's gotta be a road somewhere. We'll need to know where and how far."

"And where it goes."

◆

We drive up and down along what we decide to call Main Street, then explore a few of the side streets, which we number, north to south, from First Avenue to Tenth Avenue. The layout in Boomtown doesn't have much design to it. Like it was first come, first served. You need enough space for a Quonset hut big enough to house a work crew? Put it here. You need a place to park a camper van, put it next door. And a bar was likely to spring up next to the camper.

What I was lookin' at was somebody seekin' to make a lot of money the fastest way possible. And from what we read online, there wasn't any government settin' the rules. We come upon a water tank on First Avenue that has to be drawin' from a well drilled down to an aquifer. Tested water? Chlorinated water? I'm thinkin' probably not. I'm thinkin' I'll be drinkin' bottled water until we get clear.

On Main Street, near Fifth Avenue, we find the only decent lookin' structure in the whole development, a white A-frame. It's two-floors high, with blue trim and gray shingles on the roof. Red and yellow tulips fill the planters out front, but a scrawny sapling looks about to fall over. An American flag near as big as the roof flies from a pole alongside the little tree.

A sign in front reads: TRIPLE-A REALTY. And below: RENTALS AND LEASES.

◆

On Fourth Avenue, about halfway down, a double-wide trailer sits with the front door facing the road. The trailer rests on steel beams in front and its wheels in back. The arrangement's temporary. There's no foundation.

A sign in front, in red letters, reads: PARADISE INN, the nature of that paradise made clear by a woman sitting outside in a lawn chair. She's wearing flesh-colored lingerie and filing scarlet nails that have to be three inches long.

"Think she worked here?" Daddy asks.

He's talkin' about his daughter, Corey, and whether she was a whore. But Daddy's never been one to mince words. Nice ain't what he lives by. And truth bein' truth, Corey never earned an honest dollar in her life. Daddy, either, come to think on it.

Which does raise an interesting question. What are we doing here?

◆

Baxter is near as crazy as Boomtown. Construction on every block, people with somewhere to go crowding the sidewalks, jackhammers and pile drivers poundin' away. My guess, maybe two years from now, Baxter will be middle-class through and through, every gal with a buck in her pocket, lots of baby carriages, lots of strollers, church bells ringin' out every Sunday morning.

Even now I count a jewelry store next to a steakhouse next to a Starbucks. The Starbucks is brand spanking new, like the Hilton Hotel a few blocks away. Story is that Baxter's people were on the balls of their asses before Nissan decided to build here. The young ones counted the days until they could put the city behind them. Or push a needle into their arms.

I've yet to speak a single word to a Baxterite, but I doubt I'll find a pessimist when I do. Through the cold stink of exhaust, and above the roar of accelerating trucks on every block of Baxter Boulevard, I sense hopefulness. I'm guessin' they're like miners newly dug out of a cave-in. They figure they don't have any right to be alive, but they're damn glad they are.

◆

We reach Baxter Medical Center around noon. The city's morgue is somewhere in the building, probably the basement, and my sister needs to be identified, which is what we're here to do. But the city of Baxter can't boast of a medical examiner with an advanced degree in pathology. Probably because they can't afford one, they've settled for a coroner trained in cardiology. His name is Arshan Rishnavata and we find his office on the third floor of the hospital.

Rishnavata's receptionist, a heavyset woman wearing enough eye shadow to decorate a grade-three stripper, shakes her head after we admit that we don't have an appointment. She gestures to a nearly empty waiting room. "These patients made an appointment."

"We haven't come for treatment," I tell her. "We've come to identify the woman who got found three days ago. The dead girl."

"You have, have you? Well, believe me, you're not the first. Only the others had the good sense to contact the police." Two taps of her fingernail on the counter underline her point. "Those identifications went nowhere."

"That's because the victim wasn't their sister." I nod in daddy's direction. "Or his daughter."

The clerk's eyes move to Daddy, who wears an expression so mild it's like he's not here.

"My daddy's havin' trouble with his cognitive abilities," I explain. "Ever since he fell off that ladder." I point to a depression on Daddy's forehead, a narrow crease about a half-inch deep. "There's days when he's still sharp, but they're gettin' few and far between."

There's nothing wrong with Daddy's cognitive abilities except he's about as stubborn as a man can be. And mean to boot. It's that last part that we want to keep to ourselves by appearing harmless, an addled old man and his grieving daughter come to collect what's left of Corey Miller. No threat to anyone.

"Take a seat. I'll let Dr. Rishnavata know you're here."

I don't protest because I know the woman needs this victory. She needs to have her authority acknowledged and raisin' my voice will get me nowhere. As we find seats in a corner, I straighten Daddy's jacket and whisper in his ear.

"Just you keep in mind, Daddy, a little drool goes a long way."

◆

Rishnavata takes us into his office fifteen minutes later. He's a slight man inhabiting a plain-Jane universe. Most of the wall space is covered by filing cabinets and shelves containing medical textbooks, including one bearing the title *Diagnostic Pathology: Forensic Autopsy.*

I don't wait for him to ask how come we're sure his unidentified body is my sister. I reach into my shoulder bag, pull out a manila envelope, and spill a dozen photos onto his desk. When I glance up, he's starin' at my boobs, which I take as a hopeful sign.

"Her name is Corey Miller. Mine is Maggie Miller and this is my father, Aaron Miller." I pull my shoulders back and add, "Daddy ain't right, Doctor, not since he fell off a ladder two years ago. The docs who treated him said he was lucky to be alive, but I ain't sure about the luck part. I was in the military back then, but I come home to care for him. It just happened we was watchin' the news one night when they showed that photo." I gesture to Daddy. "Now, just this minute, I don't think he remembers that she's dead. But there's times when he's almost back to his regular self. Then he knows. Hurts him bad is what it does."

I find compassion when I stare into Rishnavata's eyes. A companion to the lust. "I'm sorry for your loss," he tells us.

49

Daddy's expression doesn't change, but I nod and thank him before starting down the path me and Daddy planned out before we got here.

"Corey ran pretty wild from the day she entered high school. Drugs and boys. Once she got a taste, she didn't have no stoppin' point. So, I guess you could say that I'm in no way surprised by how her life come to its end. But there is one thing I'm hopin' you might clear up. I read all the stories in the *Baxter Bugle* on the unidentified woman. Cause of her death, according to the paper, was an opiate overdose, which is just what I expected, like I said. But I didn't see no mention of the word accidental. And that's the reason we come in person. If there ain't nothin' foul happening, you would've released her body before this. I mean, where we came from near Grissom Air Base in Indiana, we seen our share of overdoses. Our share and more. And I never known one that wasn't marked accidental and the body released in under a week."

I'm expectin' Rishnavata to come up with something like, "I'm not at liberty to reveal the details of our findings. Only the police can do that." But the appearance of those same police, or one of them, shuts him right up.

The woman who enters, a gold badge clipped to her belt, displays confidence in her stride and in the intensity of her gaze. She's an obvious dyke, what with the short hair and the man-tailored pantsuit, not that it matters to me.

"Captain Mariola," she says, extending a hand.

"Maggie Miller. And this is my father, Aaron."

Daddy shakes Mariola's hand when it's offered, but his expression doesn't change. Instead of hello, he says, "I'm hungry."

"Soon, Daddy." I offer Mariola an apologetic smile. "Usually, he's more . . . like more with-it, but the long car ride's left him confused."

I don't add the obvious and Mariola doesn't ask. She does nod, but her eyes are already examining Corey's photographs. The similarities are obvious. Eye color, for example, and the shape of the chin stand out. But death changes a human, movin' from full to empty, and I can see the cop's not all that impressed.

"You say this is your sister?"

"Yes, ma'am. That'd be Corey Miller. We brought her birth certificate."

"Dental records would've been a lot better." She lifts the photos from the coroner's desk and begins to sort through them.

"We did think of that, but Doc Harmon's office burned down eight years ago, along with the whole mall. That's why I didn't phone before comin' out here. Needed to see for myself. To be certain, ya know? And I also wanted to make sure nothin' happens to her body. Me and Daddy, we're gonna take her home."

I look directly into Mariola's dark brown eyes when I tell this fib, but I can't read her. She doesn't nod her head, or shake it either. It's like she's registering my words, my tone, my body language, but saving final judgment for later.

◆

It's Corey, all right, and my failures rush up to greet me, as shocking as a slap in the face. Fourteen months older, I guided Corey through her toddler years. I took her everywhere, mostly to keep her away from Bradley, our older brother.

The only decent thing Bradley ever did was die young, and that opinion, far as I can tell, is unanimous. It's my belief that he drove Corey onto the path she took after I deserted her.

Bradley's far beyond punishment, in this world at least. But the men who exploited her, and maybe killed her?

◆

They don't do it like you see in the movies. Where they pull out a drawer, then pull back a sheet. What they do now is sit you in front of a blank monitor for a few minutes while the techs prepare the body for viewing. In this case, the monitor blinked twice before Corey's face appeared. This was Daddy's big test, and I knew it would be. I'm not ashamed to admit that my sister was his favorite. But I am ashamed to admit that he failed to protect her. Me and him both.

"That's Corey," I say.

"Are you sure?"

"A hundred percent."

"We'll need a DNA comparison before we release her."

"Already figured that."

"We'll do a mouth swab in the emergency room. Shouldn't take long. But the results won't come back for at least a week."

"Already figured that, too. But—"

Daddy stops me cold when he points to my sister and says, "That's Corey. She's dead, Maggie. How did that happen?"

I put my arm around Daddy's shoulders. "It ain't certain, Daddy. I mean the drugs took her, but it still ain't clear." I give Daddy a few seconds to settle down, then say, "We have a right to know, Captain. If this was an accidental overdose, it needs to be said straight-out. The same principle holds if it was suicide. Or if it wasn't neither one of those things."

Mariola takes her sweet time about it, never mind that Daddy's eyes are leakin' slow, fat tears. And I can pretty much figure the cop's askin' herself why we come all this way unannounced. Me, I can't blame her. It don't sit right. It don't relate to the devoted family shocked by findin' a loved one's face on the nightly news. But I've already run with the best excuse we could devise.

"The case is open and we're still investigating," she admits. "I'm afraid that's the best I can do."

We say goodbye, me and Daddy, and make our way back to the car. There's lots of work ahead, the first job bein' to find a place to live. Two places, really. We got to live in Boomtown mostly. But I want a retreat in Baxter, a secret place we can fly to if our plans go fubar. That's military slang. It means fucked up beyond all repair.

"Daddy, do you think I put too much corn in my cornpone?"

"No, baby girl, you done fine. And them tears for Corey, they was genuine. I had a hell of a time holdin' them back as long as I did. Seems like a life oughta come to more than lyin' on a slab in the morgue."

CHAPTER EIGHT

DELIA

"**Y**ou told me you'd be sitting behind a desk."

Danny's tone is accusing and I can't fault him. But it's not so much that I deceived him as I deceived myself. I'd been all but appointed the new commissioner when I walked away from the position. As commissioner, my role would have been strictly administrative, concerned as much with budgets and politics as with day-to-day operations.

When I told Danny that I intended to refuse the commissioner's job, he was reasonably understanding. But only because I added that my role as chief of detectives would be supervisory. For the most part.

I didn't lie to him, at least not consciously, and I don't micromanage my detectives. Yet there are still times when I hit the street.

For Danny, my occasional forays are more than disappointing. He suspects that sit-back-and-supervise was never on the table. Not from day one. And his concerns are very real because a year ago I was shot twice. My body armor stopped those first two rounds. It would not have stopped a carefully aimed third. No, my survival depended on the courage of a fifteen-year-old girl. I could have died right there, leaving Danny to grow up on his own.

"I do sit behind a desk, my son. Most of the time, anyway."

"But not tonight."

"Danny, I spent the first two hours of my tour reworking a list of open cases. I spent the next two hours with an assistant district attorney, reviewing cases headed for trial. Are the witnesses still available? Has the evidence been preserved? Is the chain of custody intact? Are the cops and detectives prepared to testify? Did the defendant make any damaging admissions? Have they been recorded? Talk about brain fog. If I hadn't studied our pending cases yesterday, we'd still be at it."

We're on the living-room couch, watching a baseball game. Danny has a notebook on his lap. He's become obsessed with approaches to hitting, and for a good reason. The umpiring in high school—while still atrocious in this woman's opinion—is a lot better than Little League umpiring. In Little League, as Danny explains it, you swing at anything you can reach because you can't rely on umpires to call pitches. That's changed and he's determined to master the strike zone before he plays in college.

That he *will* play college ball is an assumption I never challenge. Nor will I discuss the obvious. Top baseball programs, the kind that lead to professional contracts, are found in places like Virginia, Tennessee, and California. Not Baxter.

Danny's growing up. He's already learning to drive and he has a sometimes girlfriend named Gretchen. I think, if could stop time, I would. I'd keep him sixteen forever. I can't, of course. I can't stop time and I have to accept Danny's growing independence. Still, I dread the day I walk into the house and find him gone. Like my life just turned over and where do I go from here?

But there's no denying Danny's complaint and I don't try.

◆

We've developed an informant living in Boomtown, a coke dealer named Stanton Jarret. Jarret was holding two ounces of cocaine when he was arrested by an undercover in Randy's, a swinger bar on Baxter's north side. A man with a plan, Jarret didn't have to be persuaded. When Blanche Weber confronted him in the box, he brazenly volunteered to provide "real-time intelligence" on Boomtown's lowlife population.

"And you'll pardon me for being frank, though it's not my place, you're in need of help," he told her. "Boomtown's wide open. Nobody hiding anything."

Unlike most of the mutts we encounter, Stanton's a college graduate. He made this irrelevant fact known early on. I don't know what he expected to gain, but his achievements didn't interest me or Blanche Weber, the primary on the case. Jarret's rap sheet, on the other hand, caught our attention. Although his sheet's fairly extensive, he'd never been arrested for a violent crime. That justified returning him to the community. And by arranging a low bail, that's what we did. We put him back on the street.

◆

As it happens, Baxter's been hit by a series of robberies. Brazen, but lucky, the perps drive into the city between midnight and four in the morning. Maybe they have a target in mind, maybe not, but their MO doesn't vary. They smash doors and windows and display cases with sledgehammers, then snatch and run.

Thus far, they're five for five, each time escaping into Boomtown without being spotted.

The monetary loss has been relatively insignificant and nobody's even been threatened with violence. But this is a truth lost on Baxter's citizenry. As Katie Burke of WBAX and Basil Ulrich of the *Baxter Bugle* never fail to mention, these messy crimes are happening under the Baxter Police Department's collective nose. Incompetent? Lazy? Terminally stupid? Some combination of all three?

In an effort to attract recruits, the BPD's pay scale has risen by a full twenty percent. And my personal bump, when I moved to the chief's job, was substantial. It seems that Baxter's politicians are determined to present Nissan's execs with an efficient, professional bureaucracy. Every city employee, from the custodial staffs at our schools to the clerks at city hall, has received a pay raise. Along with a notice. City employees will be subject to quarterly evaluations. Placement on civil service exams will determine new hires. No appointees at any of the lower levels. No more patronage. Nepotism goodbye.

◆

We assigned the task of rescuing the BPD's reputation to Stanton Jarret. Go forth, Jarret, and find the bandits who plague our fair city. Give us names and addresses.

Eager to demonstrate his value (and remain out of jail), Jarret took it a step further. According to Jarret, the burglary crew plans to hit a three-unit construction project in Baxter between two and three o'clock this morning. I drove by the site after the squad meeting. The workers were gone, leaving the job protected only by a chain-link fence with a padlocked gate. No problem for men armed with bolt cutters.

"They're strictly small time," Stanton claimed. "Two brothers named Barrow and a couple of their friends. Junkies one and all. Their event horizon extends only as far as their next fix." Then he rubbed it in, and not for the first time. "If Boomtown wasn't off-limits, you would have busted them long ago."

◆

Danny knows about tonight's operation. We'll put a uniformed officer across the street from the construction site. We can't act before an attempt to breach the fence or cut the padlock, but once that happens, cops will stream in from both ends of the block.

I won't be one of them. I'll be several blocks away, ready to supervise the arrest process and the interrogations to follow. Vern wants me to show my face at tomorrow morning's perp walk.

"Before Zoe gets here, Danny, there's something I want to run by you. Something that happened early this afternoon."

Danny pauses the game and turns to me. The boy loves cop gossip. "So, tell me."

"You remember the body we recovered a couple days ago? The woman's?"

"In Oakland Gardens?"

"Yeah, the woman we're trying to identify. Well, two people walked into Arshan's office this afternoon, claiming that our Jane Doe is the sister of one and the daughter of the other. And these folk don't live around the corner. They drove from Indiana."

"Without calling ahead?"

"Right. Just showed up with a handful of photos."

"Did they see the body?"

"Yeah, and they made the ID."

"So, what's the problem?"

"First, as you pointed out, they drove more than five hundred miles without calling first. Maybe that's not such a big deal, but . . ."

"But?"

"The sister's in her early thirties and the father appears to be in his late fifties, maybe early sixties. He suffers from dementia as the result of a head injury. Supposedly, he has good and bad days. Today was a bad one and the sister did all the talking. She wants the body released, but we're not ready. First, the photos she brought are more than ten years old, which was the last time either one laid eyes on her. So, yeah, there's a resemblance, but I want a DNA comparison to be sure. The dental records, by the way, were lost in a fire. So sorry. And there's a second problem, which I didn't discuss with them."

I hesitate for a moment as I review the facts I want to present, an old habit that I'm sure Danny recognizes. "Cause of death first. An overdose, no question about it, but not from a single drug. The lab found a mix of heroin and fentanyl. I know that dealers commonly boost the potency of heroin by adding fentanyl, which is a lot more powerful. But the mix here was fifty-fifty, enough to produce total respiratory failure within a minute, even if she inhaled it. Bad luck? Some dealer mixed the drugs carelessly and she pulled the short straw? See, we've had episodes in the past where the mix was too heavy on the fentanyl. In every one, we were alerted to the situation by doctors in Baxter Medical Center's emergency room. But there were no reported overdoses, fatal or otherwise, in the days before and after Corey Miller's body was discovered. Her overdose was a stand-alone event."

"Maybe she got hold of the fentanyl and mixed the dose herself."

"That's possible, true, but there's a third factor that can't be ignored."

"What's that, Mom?"

"She was two months pregnant, despite her IUD."

CHAPTER NINE

DELIA

"He's threatened." Blanche Weber's talking about her new boyfriend. "And it's, like painfully obvious, Delia. Whenever we're around other cops, he shrinks. And don't laugh. I'm not making a sexual reference here. It's more like cops are so . . . so physical. The way they carry themselves. Their attitudes. It's like Owen thinks he can't keep up. Because he's a dentist and not a knucklehead."

Male inadequacy is a problem I'll never confront. In fact, most of the women I've been with are attracted to my cop attitude. Like I'm walking the walk. Not Zoe, though. Zoe has enough attitude for the both of us. That's what comes of dealing with abusive parents who'll fight for the right to keep on abusing.

"Ever thought about dating a cop, Blanche?"

"Hell, no. I want to leave the testosterone thing behind me when I sign out."

It's a few minutes before one o'clock in the morning and our nondescript Ford Focus is parked on Poplar Street, a block south and two blocks east of the construction site on Oak Street. The rest of our team, ten cops in four unmarked cars, are parked in small lots or on the street with other parked vehicles in front and behind.

"I think he's gonna dump me." Blanche raises a prominent jaw, a habit when she's frustrated or seriously pissed off. "It's gonna be me and the cat again. I hate coming home every night to an empty house."

"I'll be joining you soon enough. My boy's growing fast. He'll be leaving for college in a few years." My turn to pause. "I was nineteen when Danny was born. Now I'm thirty-five. That's a big . . ."

"Investment?"

"Too cold, Blanche. It's just that you don't see an end to it while they're young. It seems like childhood's a forever thing. It's not, though, and I sometimes get the feeling that Danny's looking past me. He's seeing a wife, kids and a mortgage. With me on the periphery."

"One day when I get up the nerve," Blanche says, "I'll tell Owen what cop macho is really about."

"Which is?"

"I've been propositioned more times than I have fingers and toes. And not after dinner and a movie. No, more like, let's park the unit in a convenient alley and knock it out in the back seat." She raises a finger. "I was on the verge of quitting when you promoted me to detective. Squad life's different. Competence counts for something."

I have nothing to add and we again settle back. Poplar Street is entirely residential, bordered on both sides by middle-class homes set on relatively generous lots. This is Norwood, prosperous enough to have survived Baxter's ravaging over the last decade. The homes are all dark except for a single lit window in the second floor of a colonial at our end of the block. The respectable residents of respectable Norwood are asleep, as they should be.

I find my eyes closing and I try to rouse myself by force of will. I needn't have bothered because a voice on the radio flips my adrenaline switch and I'm instantly on full alert. We're operating on a private frequency and the only cop authorized to speak is Patrolman Harry Grogan. Grogan's stationed in a house across the street from the construction site.

"A vehicle approaching. A crew cab pickup, a Ford, older model. Coming from Baxter Boulevard. Now crossing Greenway." The radio shuts down for just a second and I'm already fearing the worst. Then Harry speaks again, level and calm. "It's pulled to a stop and all four doors are opening." Another brief pause. "Four individuals, all male, all white, one carrying a bolt cutter, have exited and are approaching the gate. No guns in evidence. The bolt cutter is being applied to the padlock. It's sliced through and the gate is open."

Cade Barrow's voice cuts in. He utters a single word: "Go."

A trap, no escape except on foot with yours truly far enough away to be out of it. Except for one possibility, the least likely in everybody's opinion. In a panic, with the street blocked, the perps might drive through the site. An eight-foot chain-link fence protects the rear and sides of the lot, but it's possible, just barely, to blow through the fence and emerge on Poplar Street. If they turn left, they'll be coming straight for Blanche and myself. In that case, we'll pull out of our parking space and block the road. If they turn right, toward Boomtown, we'll join a hot pursuit that'll allow us to extend our jurisdiction.

"The subjects are returning to their vehicle." Sirens mask the dry-as-dust voice of Patrolman Grogan and I can barely make out the next sentences. "They're driving onto the site. Repeat: they are driving onto the site at a high rate of speed."

Grogan's voice trails off, probably because the pickup is no longer in view. I can still hear the sirens, but they seem stationary. I know what's supposed to happen at this point. The contingency plan is for pursuing vehicles to drive past each other, turn north at both intersections, then block Poplar Street. But there's no sign of that happening as the pickup emerges from between two homes and turns left. It's coming straight at us now and I'm not surprised. Boomtown is pretty far off, almost a mile, but Blanche and I are parked a few blocks from the border between Baxter and

Maryville County. There's not much cover out that way, but if your brain is drug-addled, if the best plan you can devise to maintain your addiction is smash-and-grab, your decisions are very likely to contain major flaws.

I exit our vehicle, move up two cars, and draw my service weapon. Blanche will wait as long as possible before pulling out to block the street. Then, she, too, will exit and find cover behind cars parked on the far side of the road. When we quizzed our confidential informant on the potential for these thieves to be armed, he merely shrugged his shoulders.

"Can't speak to the issue one way or the other," he told us. "I will make this prediction, though. If they want to be armed, they will be. Boomtown is gun heaven. With no police on patrol, it's every man for himself. Every woman, too."

The pickup comes steadily forward, but it's left headlight dips and rises, dips and rises, as it passes through the intersection and enters the block. A flat tire, almost certainly, maybe more than one. No realistic hope of escape, only fear driving them on. I'm expecting the vehicle to stop when Blanche pulls out to block the road, but the pickup keeps coming. Not fast, but relentlessly. Blanche immediately exits, as planned. She crosses the street and takes cover behind a parked SUV. Then she goes me one better. She draws her weapon and brings it to bear on the oncoming truck. A block behind, a line of unmarked vehicles pursue, the lights in their grills winking on and off, their sirens ripping through the shadows. I see lights coming on in windows all along the block. Witnesses.

"Blanche?" I have to repeat her name, yelling this time, before I catch her attention. "Blanche?"

"Captain?"

"Don't fire to stop the truck. Hear me?" I wait for her to nod. "We're not gonna kill anybody to protect private property."

It doesn't come to that. The pickup grinds to a halt thirty feet short of our sedan. The doors open and the occupants make a run for it with the pursuing units almost upon them.

One of the runners breaks off and comes down the sidewalk toward where I crouch behind a Camry sedan. The man doesn't notice my presence, his mind occupied by what's behind him, and he screams when I seize his legs. I'm expecting a fight, but when I scramble to my feet, he remains where he is. Crying.

Two cops, both male, rush up to the perp. I know both of them and it wouldn't surprise me if they half expected to administer a dose of curbside justice. There are knuckle-heads in every police department.

"Haffner, Coyle, by the book. Both of you. Shake him down, put him in cuffs. Nice and easy."

Their names slow them long enough to notice the silhouettes in the bedroom windows. Without doubt, some of the residents are getting dressed in a hurry. They'll be appearing in a few minutes, cell phones raised.

We have all four in custody. Kids, really, the oldest barely out of his teens. Two are crying, but it's not because they're afraid. This isn't how their lives were supposed to evolve. Their childhood fantasies never included a druggie future with arrest on every horizon. Maybe they'll figure it out before it's too late. Maybe they'll be scared straight. Prosecuting burglaries, even spectacular burglaries, isn't a priority for Baxter's overburdened courts. If they don't have violent histories, if this is a first felony arrest, they'll be out in six months.

"Should we bring them into the house?" Blanche wants to know.

"Not yet, Blanche. One last thing to do."

I phoned Katie Burke at WBAX and Basil Ulrich of the *Bugle* as soon as our suspects were cuffed. They'll arrive any minute. Our commissioner, Vern Tancy, is also on his way. The smash-and-grab burglars have been subdued. Peace has been restored to Happy Valley. Credit must be taken.

◆

I arrive home at 6:30, having briefly supervised the paperwork before leaving Cade Barrow to finish up. The bad guys were unhurt, except for a few bruises, and so many good citizens recorded the tender care they received from the arresting officers that any claim of police brutality is off the table. Katie and Basil had their stories by then, stories that included a quick interview with Vern.

Mission accomplished. In spades.

I expect Danny and Zoe to be asleep when I turn my key in the lock, but I find Danny sitting in front of the television, an open school book on the coffee table. Danny has an engaging smile and he displays it now as he rises to hug me.

"You're on the news," he tells me. "You're a hero."

I look down at a tear in my uniform. I told Danny I'd be well away from the action, but that's not how it worked out. Still, if Danny's pissed off, he doesn't show it as he returns to his seat on the couch.

"The main thing is that we made the arrests and I won't have to be asked about the jerks every time I leave the house. They're kids, by the way, not much older than you. Junkies, too, one and all."

"Is this gonna be another just-say-no lecture?"

"Yes, but it's already done. Like the smash-and-grab burglars." I head for the kitchen end of the room as Zoe walks out of the bedroom. She's wearing a red robe, tightly tied, and there's a little girl named Emmaline holding her hand.

"Guess who came to visit last night?" Zoe's grin reaches from one ear to the other.

"Aunt Delia . . . ."

Emmaline flies across the room and jumps into my arms. I'm not the hero I was a year before when I pulled her from the fire, but I'm still a hero. Emmaline climbs down reluctantly, looks up for a moment, then runs over to Danny and climbs onto the couch. She glances at the open book on the coffee table, a text book, then says, "What are you doing?"

Danny stands up. "I'm gonna fix breakfast, before mom goes back to work. Wanna help?"

"I want pancakes."

I'm tickled. Emmaline hasn't answered the question Danny asked, the wanting part being the only common element. "I do have to go back to work," I say, "but only for the press conference. I assigned the operation to Cade Barrow and I trust him to supervise the follow-up."

Danny glances over his shoulder. "Does that mean you'll be able to watch my game this afternoon?"

"That's exactly what it means. And let me warn you, my expectations are high. Three hits, at least, one of them a home run."

"No pressure, though."

"Wouldn't dream of it."

CHAPTER TEN

CHARLIE

We're waiting for the sirens. Me, Dominick, and a gigantic thug named Bruce Angoleri. Bruce is a sensitive type. Talks a lot too. Like right now.

"What could I say, boss. We got a problem with the girls."

The boss in this case is yours truly. The girls are the whores at the Paradise Inn. And maybe I know what's coming, but I want to hear it from Bruce's lips. He runs the Paradise.

"Spit it out, Bruce."

"Well, like Corey? The girls are upset about how she got dumped outside. I mean you left her for the dogs and the rats. The girls, they gotta be thinkin'."

"Thinking what?"

"That maybe they're next."

I glance at Dominick, but he's wearing his great stone face. "Ya know what, Bruce? Maybe if they stopped using drugs, there wouldn't be any reason to leave 'em for the dogs and the rats. Cops, either. Now, you got a nice operation going. A real earner. Am I right?"

"True, boss. Sometimes we gotta turn the johns away. But that's the point. We need more girls, but the way it's lookin', the ones we got are talkin' about a strike. They're sayin' Corey probably has a family and she deserved to be laid in the ground proper. Like it's bad enough the johns treat 'em like meat."

I don't answer right away. We're back in Oakland Gardens, parked a few blocks from where I dumped Corey, and we have a job to do, a job that bears no relation to the fate of an overdosed whore. I don't like workin' in Baxter. On the whole, Boomtown's a lot safer. But this ain't the whole. Tonight, we have special protection. There ain't a chance in hell that a patrol car will happen by at the wrong time. The neighborhood's pretty much deserted, too, and just as beat up as the last time I was here.

The streetlights on this block are out and it's warm enough to sit with the windows down. There are stars, too, what with every streetlight dark, and enough moon to silverplate the decay. I can imagine an overhead shot of the neighborhood as the opening to one of those after-the-war movies. Maybe the last survivors crawling from the ruins. Mutated, right?

It's a nice thought, but it doesn't solve my problems. As for Bruce, I know he's holding back. The man's a pure suck-up, despite the bulk. When you praise him, he purrs like a kitten. When you criticize, he sulks like a beaten dog. Meanwhile, he's paid to handle problems, not pass them up the chain.

Bruce has a fat face with a big nose and bigger eyes. By contrast, his lips are thin red tubes, even relaxed. They disappear when he concentrates, like now. What should he tell me? Will I embarrass him in front of Dominick? How about shoot him in the fuckin' head?

Bruce is riding shotgun with Dominick at the wheel. I'm sitting behind Bruce and he flinches when I shift the rearview mirror so that I can see his face. "Listen close, Bruce. Tell me what's going on. Really going on. And don't leave out the small details. You try to play me, I'll send you home to Ricky with a note in your pocket. Like to the principal's office?"

Bruce chews at his lip for a moment longer, than lets out a long breath. "All right, Charlie. But, like, I got no way of provin' what I'm gonna tell ya. One way or the other. But this is what's goin' down, okay?"

"Just say it, for Christ's sake."

"Right, right. So, we give the girls a little taste, like every night. We charge 'em, of course, but we keep the price down. It's like an incentive. You pull some bullshit and don't work, you go without. Be a good girl and go to bed happy."

"You're tellin' me what I already know."

"Sorry, but last Sunday night was business as usual. We closed up around three and I distributed the goodies. The girls mostly go for oxy, but we couldn't score and I handed out powder. Not much, right? Just enough to relax. Corey got hers, like everyone else, and I don't remember anything unusual. She took her little bag and went off to a room she shares with Rita Lafayette. These two girls, they're thick as thieves, maybe even lovers, so I don't think Rita's bullshittin' me. The broad's devastated."

I lay a hand on Bruce's shoulder and this time he pops up high enough to touch the roof liner. I don't know what he's expecting, but this ain't *The Godfather*.

"Get to the point, Bruce."

"Okay, boss. So, Corey snorted her dope right away, as usual, but Rita left to take a bath, also as usual. Rita likes to get high in the tub. When she came back an hour later, Corey wasn't breathing. We keep Narcan at the ready, but it didn't bring her back. The girl was dead." He shifts around until he's looking at me. "Rita, she has a big mouth and she's sayin' that she watched Corey do her thing and the dose was the same as her own. Which, according to Rita, was some weak shit to begin with. So, how did Corey end up dead?"

"Back it up. Who handled the junk you gave her?"

"Okay, start with Alfie. He bought a few grams of dope and a gram of coke for the girls who like coke. From our guy, right? He bought it from the guy we got working the bar trade at the Paradise. Alfie then passed it to Gene and Gene passed the hits to me and I passed 'em out."

"So, Solly broke them down? The heroin and the coke? He parceled them out?"

"I guess."

"Guess?"

"I wasn't there, boss, so I can't be sure. But we've been doin' it this way for months now. And it's dealin', right? We show a profit on what we charge the girls. And you know Solly. He's not a fuckup."

I raise a hand. A problem's a problem, even though I don't give a shit about Corey. The women at the Paradise aren't kids. If they decide to walk, there's gonna be serious trouble. Not that I couldn't replace them. But debts have to be paid and some of these girls owe us money for room and board, for clothes, drinks at the bar, cosmetics, dope. And some of 'em had debts we paid off before they came here.

Bruce stops for just a second, staring up at me as he gauges my attitude. "So whatta ya want me to do?"

"First thing, Bruce, you explain the facts of life. Anybody leaves owin' us money, I'm gonna sell her debt to a shylock who'll break her elbows if she doesn't pay the vig. As for Corey, maybe one of the johns tossed her a bonus. A tip, right, but in powder instead of money."

I lean back when Dominick injects his two cents, remembering how he prayed over Corey's body. "Then where is it? The vial, the envelope, whatever it came in? The only thing in the room when Rita found her was identical to the envelope Bruce handed out."

"Rita had plenty of time to clean the room." I'm fed up now. "The whores work for us, not the other way around.

If they don't like the way I handled Corey, let 'em pay up and find another line of work."

"You should pardon my sayin' this, boss," Dominick says. "But that ain't gonna make things better. The girls aren't complaining about the work. They're sayin' Corey was pregnant."

"Pregnant?"

"Yeah, they're sayin' she was pregnant and that she was murdered."

It jumps into my head, but for once I manage to keep my big mouth shut. I'm not thinking Corey was murdered. It's like, too off-the-wall. But if she was, only the man sitting in front of me could have done it. He passed out the goodies and he controlled who got which envelope, a fact that he's already admitted.

CHAPTER ELEVEN

CHARLIE

"**S**o, I'm not gettin' it, Charlie," Bruce says. "You want us to just leave the assholes sittin' there? Because if we do, the guy and his people are gonna come back on us. It's not like we're exactly disguised."

"Nobody hurt unless I say so."

I'm sayin' this to impress the fourth member of our party, who we just picked up. His name is Stitch Kreuter. In return for a piece of the action, Stitch is gonna get us through the door of a drug dealer named Heyman Weymouth. Heyman's not a street guy peddling ten-dollar bags. He's sells high-grade coke by the ounce, which means he buys pounds, at the least, maybe even kilos. According to Stitch, who isn't stupid enough to lie to us, Weymouth just re-upped.

"I still don't get it," Bruce complains.

"You don't need to get it." It's Dominick who speaks up this time. "What you need to do is shut your big fuckin' mouth because what's comin' out of it's aggravatin' my ulcer."

Bruce and Dominick both worked for Ricky Ricci in New York, so they know each other from way back when. I don't think Bruce is intimidated, but he's just smart enough to acknowledge his place on Ricky's totem pole. Dominick could kill Bruce and have Ricky look the other way is what it boils down to. Not so for Bruce. Ricky and Dominick were already best buddies at St. Peter's Grade School in Staten Island.

I turn left on Rose Lane, then right onto an unmarked street. We're back in Oakland Gardens, hard on the border of a neighborhood called Mount Jackson. As before, when we visited Titus Klint, I drive past Weymouth's home, half expecting a well-guarded fortress. But there's only a chopped Harley parked a yard or two from the front door. Like it's some kind of talisman, a string of garlic maybe, or a vial of holy water. Swear, there's no end to the arrogance when it comes to these bikers. You can see it in their colors, an eagle in flight, its talons piercing the side of a rabbit, a little rainstorm of blood running between those talons. Enough to strike terror in the hearts of little children everywhere.

◆

Weymouth opens the door when Stitch, his biggest customer, knocks. We're to either side of the door and we kick our way inside, guns drawn, a second after it opens. Heyman's a big guy, real big, and he'd most likely put up a fight if he wasn't stoned. As it is he stumbles backward, revealing two people on the couch, a girl and an older man. To my surprise, the girl's dressed and the guy's naked except for his socks. I nod to Dominick, who cracks Weymouth across the side of the head with the muzzle of the .44 revolver in his right hand. Weymouth drops to his knees and lays his hand against the side of his head.

I bring my gun to bear on the girl. Her jaw trembles and she seems about to cry, but she answers when I ask, "Anybody else in the house?"

"No, I swear." She's young, maybe still in high school, and the situation here is way above her pay grade. "Don't kill me," she adds.

I nod to Dominick, who goes off to check the other rooms. The room we're in, the living room, desperately needs painting and there are motorcycle parts, including a motor, scattered about. A nice contrast to a brown leather couch and two armchairs new enough to still be in a showroom.

"You got a weapon in your pants?" I point to the man's clothes lying alongside the couch.

"Uh-uh." He's got to be closing in on fifty and flabby too. Maybe a john out for an evening of humiliation? He jumps to it when I tell him to get dressed.

"Okay, down to business." I face Weymouth directly. "If you don't tell me where it is, I'll kill you and your honored guests. Then I'll find it on my own."

Weymouth takes his hand from the side of his head and stares for a moment at the blood on his fingers and palm. "In the first bedroom," he mutters, "under the fucking bed."

I nod again to Dominick, who ambles off, taking his time, a calculated insult that I doubt escapes Weymouth. He returns a few minutes later, hauling a battered suitcase and a pair of semiautomatic handguns.

"How much, Dominick?"

"Coupla kilos, maybe a little more."

"Of what?"

"Coke."

I give it a minute, like I'm thinkin' it over, which I'm not. Business first, that's the motto, but there are times I gotta mix business with pleasure. I know what the two men and the woman are thinking. They're thinking I'm going to kill them because I don't want to be identified by goons bent on recovering the gang's stolen property. The girl is shaking and her eyes are as round and shiny as headlights. The man next to her sits open mouthed, jaw dangling as though unhinged. Weymouth does a bit better. His tight lips show defiance, just as if he hadn't caved on the location of the coke. Meanwhile, he's not making a move. He's waiting for me.

I'm a god here.

"Okay, Heyman, this is how it's gonna go down. You're gonna go back to Zak or Zeb or whatever you're callin' him these days. You're gonna go back and tell him this. If he thinks, between the tats and the beards and the stinking armpits, the whole world's afraid of him, he need to revise his opinion. But if he's not willin' to make the jump, if he wants war, he can have it. On the other hand, if he wants his coke back, or the equivalent in cash, he should contact the bartender at La Mina de Oro to set up a meet."

I can almost read Weymouth's mind, almost watch his thoughts as they crawl through his brain, slow as slugs in a garden. "One more thing." I point to little Stitch, the dealer who got us through the door. "As a gesture of goodwill, I'm gonna leave Stitch for you to handle. We don't like double-crossers any more than you do. And just in case he invents some bullshit story about how we forced him, he's in it for a four-ounce cut of the coke."

Which, of course, he'll never get.

We're driving toward Boomtown, taking our time, what with the cops busy on the other end of town. Bruce and Dominick are bragging away, congratulating each other on a job well done. I'm not really interested. No, right this minute, I'm after a little more action once I deal with this last chore. I punch in a number on my cell and call Adelyn.

Adelyn runs our jewelry store in Baxter. I plucked her out of the Paradise because she studied accounting in college, dropping out in her senior year when the dope world became her only world. I don't know if she likes me, or if she believes this is the price she has to pay for a job where she remains vertical for the most part. I only know that when I call, she never begs off. Plus, she knows how to keep a set of books, straight or cooked.

La Mina de Oro in Boomtown has become an informal meeting place. No whores and no gambling, it's a straight-up bar where drugs are sold discreetly. No lines of blow on the bar. Keep it to yourself. I'm headed there to reward a lowlife triple-crosser named Stanton Jarret. He set the cops on the smash-and-grab bandits who provided cover for tonight's operation.

Stanton figured it out right away, who was gonna be who in Boomtown. And he was smart enough to position himself under our umbrella before it started raining on his head. Unlike Titus Klint. Jarret's been dealing in and around Baxter for a decade. He's never been to prison, but he's done county time twice. He didn't hesitate when he got busted at Randy's. And he didn't give up anyone who counted either. The cops were under heavy pressure. They jumped when Jarret offered the Barrow brothers up. Even the dyke, Mariola. Ms. Supercop.

◆

I meet Jarret in a small office I keep in the back of the bar. I don't want us to be seen together. The world, including little Baxter, is full of informants. If Mariola suspects Jarret's playing a double game? The consequences are obvious enough. Jarret would switch sides in a heartbeat. He'd set us up, just like he set up the smash-and-grab junkies.

This is a complication I'll have to handle somewhere down the line. The scary part is I think Jarret knows that too. The man's smart, maybe too smart for his own good.

"How'd it go, Charlie?" Muscular once upon a time, Jarret's way past working out. He's carrying a modest spare tire around his middle, along with the start of an impressive double chin. Reasonably well-dressed in designer slacks and a leather jacket soft enough to pass for silk, he claims to be college-educated as well.

I don't answer. There's no point. I open a kilo of coke and cut about a half ounce. Jarret will step on the powder before he sells it, even though it's already been cut. A good deal, for the both of us, and he doesn't complain when I hand him the bag.

"Stay in touch," I tell him as I open a door leading to the lot in back.

CHAPTER TWELVE

DELIA

The perp walk, as perp walks go, is as pathetic as it is popular. The local press attends, of course, with representatives from every TV station, two weekly newspapers and the *Baxter Bugle*, the city's lone daily. More than a hundred good citizens show up as well. They come to see four dastardly criminals led from police headquarters to a van that will carry them exactly one block to the county jail. Already seventy degrees at ten o'clock in the morning, the temperature's expected to close in on eighty before nightfall. This winter's been long and cold, but now you can almost taste the seasonal uplift as the prairie springs back to life. You can smell it, even above the acrid stink generated by trucks servicing the Nissan worksite.

My son and my closest friends have come too. They're standing at the back of the crowd. Lillian Taney in the center, with little Cora tucked into a sling that crosses Lillian's chest. Then Mike standing to one side of his mom, next to Danny. On the other side, Emmaline holds Lillian's and Zoe's hands. They've been drawn by a press conference to be held after the suspects are safely transferred.

◆

I don't ordinarily resent the politics of policing. Politics and policing have always gone hand in hand, especially true because the mayor usually appoints the police commissioner. But I'm having a hard time in this case and I've foregone the honor of holding one of our suspects by the elbow as they're led through the door. The oldest is twenty, the youngest barely eighteen. Their crimes were nonviolent and none were armed when we brought them down. Nor do they have extensive criminal records. They have to be punished, no doubt, but I can't make them celebrity criminals. There are no serial killers among them.

Three of the four have pulled their hoodies up to cover their faces. The fourth, the youngest, stares straight ahead, an act of defiance I find pathetic. The kid's dope-sick, like the other three, and if they can't make bail, they'll go through withdrawal in a cell.

I find Danny's eyes and throw him a little shrug. We spoke about it this morning before I left. I'd made a really stupid vow to myself. I'd promised to reform Baxter, to drive the dealers out of town, but it was a fool's errand from the beginning. Many of the dealers on my list are moving to Boomtown, where they can operate with virtual impunity. Only the addicts are still with us, content to stroll over the top or along the bottom of the construction site to a wide-open drug market.

Leaving the Baxter Police Department to settle for a quartet of hapless fools.

◆

The crowd begins to wander off once the smash-and-grab bandits enter the van. Not the press though. With no real choice, they gather round a sidewalk podium to listen as Mayor Venn, then Commissioner Taney, followed by Maya Kingsley and Cade Barrow, tell the same tale. How the Baxter Police Department, through a fierce dedication to the welfare of Baxter's citizens and a relentless pursuit of the evidence, routed the social deviants who menaced our city. I'm standing well back, stone-faced, though I know the truth, as does everyone else, including the reporters.

Nevertheless, I'm fascinated by Vern's performance. Though he's in a uniform that sports a pasteboard of ribbons, his folksy charm is on full display. He doesn't blink when Katie Burke hits him with a surprise at the very end of the press conference.

"My sources, Commissioner, are telling me that the unidentified woman found in Oakland Gardens two weeks ago was pregnant. Is that correct? Was she pregnant?"

"Yes, she was in the early stages of pregnancy when she overdosed." Vern's expression doesn't change as he sweeps the crowd. As if he's been expecting the question all along. "Be assured, Katie, we haven't forgotten this woman. We're actively investigating her death and we will not stop until we're satisfied."

◆

The news conference ends at eleven with the day's main event several hours distant. The Goldman High Warriors, Danny and Mike's team, are playing their archrivals, the Baxter High Tigers. I'm sure Major League fans would be profoundly unimpressed, but the boys see it differently. For them it's do-or-die, the war to end all wars. Proving, I suppose, that they're still children, that the size of the world and its eight billion people has yet to make its mark.

Complicating the tension, Coach Harmon, manager of the Warriors, has decided to convert Danny into a pitcher and Danny's been working at it for the past couple weeks during the team's practice sessions.

"Coach thinks I throw harder than any pitcher on the team," he explained.

"Only there's a lot more to pitching than throwing hard?"

"Yeah, exactly, and I haven't learned any of the lessons."

"So what do you want to do?" The question was naïve and Danny brought me up short.

"Baseball isn't a democracy. If Coach says pitch, you pitch."

CHAPTER THIRTEEN

DELIA

S ex with a woman is a longer, slower process than with a man. That's according to Zoe, who can speak from experience. More touching, more kissing. A lot more kissing. After the press conference, Zoe and I head to my apartment so I can change out of my public-appearance costume, an off-white pantsuit over a blouse that's almost (but not quite) man-tailored. Zoe stands off to one side, watching for a moment. Then she begins to shed her own clothing. I have toys, of course, tucked beneath the sweaters on the lowest drawer in the bureau. We rarely use them and we don't use them today, the taste of Zoe's throat, hinting vaguely of salt, being arousal enough.

I can't say I'm in love with Zoe, but I'm not that far away. I want her in my life as she wants me in hers. We speak to each other every day, no matter how busy that day might be. On nights we can spend together, my thoughts at work continually flip back to her. There's a carnal aspect to those thoughts. Can't deny it. But there's affection, too, along with a dose of pure need. I've been alone for many years.

It's so far, so good, but there's a line we've yet to cross. We've not yet appeared in public as a couple.

Zoe and I have eaten lunch and occasional dinners in one or another of Baxter's restaurants. We sit across from each other, trying to ignore an intrusive tension that doesn't want to be ignored. Can I reach across the table to hold her hand, even for a brief moment? Can she put her arm around my waist as we leave, both a little high after finishing a bottle of wine? Neither has yet to happen, but there's an event coming up that will test those waters. Every year, on his birthday, Mayor Venn hosts an outdoor party at his Mount Jackson home. I've been invited, along with my son. Zoe's been invited as well. Independently invited. As have the entire Baxter City Council, our patrol chief, and a dozen prominent church leaders.

The party will take place three weeks from today, weather permitting. Zoe and I want to attend as a couple. That wouldn't be a problem if we were straight. As it is . . .

I think most of the people scheduled to attend have heard that Zoe and I are involved. As for my end of the deal, I know my orientation hasn't gone down well in Baxter's more conservative churches, where pastors routinely declare gay marriage to be an abomination.

Though unspoken, the message I intuit, from the mayor on down, is keep your love life in the closet. I've pretty much done that in the past, not a big deal because the romantic side of my life was limited to hookups as short-lived as they were impulsive.

◆

"I think we should go together," Zoe tells me as we begin to dress. "As a couple."

I don't respond immediately because Zoe's walking toward the bathroom and my attention is focused elsewhere.

"Nothing to say?"

"I still haven't talked it over with Danny."

"Well, time's a-wasting, lady." She pauses long enough to give her butt a shake. "But I'm willing. I want us to be seen together and anybody who doesn't like it can kiss my ass."

◆

I need this as much as I love it, this respite, the small-town normalcy, kids on the field, proud parents in the stands. No toothless tweakers, no cadaverous junkies, no lifeless bodies. Just this warm afternoon, sitting beneath a spring sun, good friends on either side, Danny and Mike in their white, home-team uniforms. But I'm not kidding myself. There's no cleavage here, no line with my cop life on one side and my off-duty life on the other. To some extent, you carry the carnage with you, like it or not. Vern proves that when he arrives and signals me to join him off to the side.

"I had it out with our esteemed coroner," he tells me.

"About Corey Miller?"

"Yeah, I wanted him to declare a manner of death." Vern shakes his head. This is not a job for a police commissioner, but Arshan Rishnavata, a cautious man by nature, has been unwilling to put his name to what I'm convinced was a murder. The level of fentanyl found in Corey Miller's body was high enough to make an accidental overdose very unlikely, and no fentanyl overdoses were reported in the days before and after the woman's overdose. The two facts shrink the likelihood that her fatal dose was accidental to the vanishing point. Her pregnancy has now become a possible motive.

"Did he finally show a little spine?"

"Yeah, he's calling it a homicide. A double homicide, considering the embryo. And by the way, it's probably better for us now that her pregnancy is on the table. Maybe it'll inspire somebody who knew her to come forward."

◆

Danny and Mike begin the game on the bench, as usual. I know their status frustrates the both of them because they've told me so. The kids truly believe they'd be as productive as the starters if given a chance. They also know they better keep their frustrations to themselves when they're with the team.

"We're paying our dues, Mom," Danny explained. "Besides, Harve McCallan's starting at short and he's a senior. He's not going to college, either, so it's his last season."

"Harve's a pretty good hitter too. In case you forgot."

"Yeah, he can hit, but he can't get out of his own way in the field."

Danny's judgment proves itself in the fifth inning as a hot ground ball takes an erratic bounce on Goldman's nubby infield and hits poor Harve McCallan square on the nose. The game stops right there as Coach Harmon rushes out. I quickly join him, but there's nothing I can do. Harve's nose is badly broken, a judgment confirmed by two paramedics who arrive a few minutes later in a volunteer ambulance. They lead Harve and his mom to the ambulance as I make my way back to my seat. Despite the bloody towel Harve presses to his nose, the boy proves himself adept at public relations. At the last moment, he turns and waves to the crowd, drawing an enthusiastic round of applause.

I'm smiling to myself as I head back to the stands. Not Emmaline. Her eyes wide, she wraps her fingers around mine and squeezes as hard as she can. I can almost taste her fear and I have to think she's flashing back to some unhappy episode from life with her meth-addicted father.

"It was an accident," I say, but her expression doesn't change. "That means it isn't anyone's fault. It just happened."

"Could it happen to Danny or Mike?"

"Yes, but look, the boy's gonna be okay. You can believe me because I'm a cop and I've dealt with plenty of injuries."

Emmaline's still apparently skeptical, but her attention shifts abruptly when Danny trots out to the shortstop position. "Danny's playing now," she explains.

One player's bad luck is another player's big chance according to Danny and Mike, a fact of baseball life that works at every level, right to the Major Leagues. I watch Danny pound his glove, realizing that he's among the taller players on the field. Is he confident? Or feigning confidence? Harve will miss several games, more if Danny proves himself on the field and at the plate. With the game scoreless, he'll bat second in the bottom of the inning.

CHAPTER FOURTEEN

DELIA

With two outs, the Baxter High batter, a lefty, swings late at an outside pitch and pops the ball high into the air. I watch Danny backpedal, muttering, "Please let him catch it. Please, please, please."

A few seconds later, the ball drops into Danny's glove. Without, I suspect, the intervention of whatever god I beseeched.

"Danny's a good catcher," Emmaline observes.

And a good hitter as well. The Tigers' pitcher, a gangly eighteen-year-old named Ethan Braddock, has to stand six-five. He's all arms and legs and he throws above ninety mph, at the upper range for high school pitchers. Ethan's been setting Goldman batters down all day, giving up only two hits, both of them dribblers that didn't leave the infield.

Now he blows away Goldman's first hitter, who slams his bat down as he heads back to the bench. I'm seated behind Danny as he strolls toward the plate, trying to divine his state of mind from his walk and his practice swings. But then he throws me a quick glance and winks.

Don't worry, Mom. I've got this.

And he does. Rather than swing for the fences, he chokes up on the bat, slaps the ball toward the third baseman and flies toward first base. Baxter's third baseman would be wise to hold on to the ball, but he charges in, grabs the ball with his bare hand and attempts one of those throws only the best Major League players can make. Unfortunately, his weight's going toward home as he throws across his body and the ball doesn't pass within ten feet of the first baseman. Danny, who never slows down, ends up on second.

The Goldman fans cheer wildly, especially Emmaline, but it comes to nothing as Ethan Braddock strikes out the next two batters. Braddock's an adrenaline-fueled pitcher. He pumps his fist after every strike and screams when the last hitter swings at strike three.

◆

Vern cheers when Mike heads out to left field. Mike's a talented kid, more graceful than Danny and a little faster. He carries Danny's glove and they exchange fist bumps as he passes it over. Both kids in the game? Exactly what I need, exactly what I've been looking forward to all afternoon.

Then my phone, stashed in my purse, begins to vibrate. For just a second, I pretend I can't feel it rattle against my keys, but there's no avoiding the call. As a supervisor, I'm never off duty.

I pull the phone, hoping the caller ID will read *Spam Likely*. No such luck. It's Marcus Goodman, the only Black detective on the squad. I let the phone ring out as I make my way down under the stands, then call back.

"Hey, boss."

"What's up, Marcus?"

"Got ourselves a body in Oakland Gardens. Man we know."

"Who would that be?"

"Stitch Kreuter."

I can't say I've memorized the names of every mutt in the city, but Stitch Kreuter makes the list of those I'd rather forget. A marvel of sheer persistence, the man's been arrested again and again. Shoplifting, kiting checks, small-time dealing, misdemeanor assault. Stitch can't stay out of trouble for more than a few weeks, but judges don't want to send him to one of our overcrowded prisons either. Sixty days, ninety days, thirty days. Stitch spends half his time as a guest in the county jail.

"An overdose?"

"Nope. Beaten to death is what it looks like. Maybe with a tire iron, but over his entire body without touching his head. He's still in rigor, boss, so I'm thinkin' he bought it late last night."

Marcus doesn't have to speculate. I get the message. Left where he was sure to be found and recognized, Stitch is meant as an object lesson. He crossed someone too powerful, reached up too far, and paid the ultimate price.

"Where are you at the moment?"

"The scene's been sealed and we're waitin' on a State Crime Scene Unit." Marcus hesitates for a moment. "One other thing. The body's only a block from Heyman Weymouth's place. You know him?"

"The name's vaguely familiar."

"Heyman's a dealer, works with the Horde. He's one of 'em, actually. Keeps his bike parked in front of his door when he's home. Anyway, after I secured the crime scene, I went to his house. Just thought I'd ask around. Only the man must've pulled up and left in a hurry. We found the door open, but the closets empty except for a few hangers. And get this, all the furniture was left behind, including a new couch and two matching chairs. Leather, boss, like they didn't come out of a thrift shop. Blood on the floor, too, lots of blood."

"You're not still inside, are you?"

"Uh-uh. Backed off right away and called you."

The initial entry without a warrant can be justified by the open door and the possibility that somebody was lying injured inside. But not a full-on search. I tell Marcus to put a watch on Weymouth's residence, then organize a close search of the Kreuter crime scene. "We'll need a warrant for

Heyman's residence. I want you to get it before the Crime Scene Unit finishes up with Stitch and returns to the state barracks. Just be sure no one goes in or out."

"Got it."

I head back to my place in the stands, but I can't evade a puzzle that's been working its way into my consciousness from time to time. After the Titus Klint murder, most of the squad, myself included, expected the Horde to retaliate, and the retaliation to be as crude as possible. Mindless violence is a Horde specialty. So far, though, nothing, and I have to wonder if Stitch, beaten over his entire body, doesn't fill that niche.

If Marcus Goodman's estimate of Stitch Kreuter's time of death is accurate, the homicide must have occurred while the Baxter Police Department's entire patrol force was busy apprehending the smash-and-grab bandits. Did Stitch's killer have advanced notice of our operation a couple miles to the south? If so, that notice almost surely came from the mouth of Stanton Jarret.

◆

When I return to my seat, I find the game still scoreless, but a Baxter High player is standing on second base. There's one out and Coach Harmon has come to speak with his pitcher. I can't hear what's being said, but my heart rate kicks up when Harmon looks over at Danny. I'm thinking, *Not now, not with the game on the line,* but my prayer goes unheard.

Harmon motions Danny over as he takes the ball from Goldman's pitcher, a kid named Paul Santini.

A few seconds later, Danny's standing in the middle of a small crowd. His catcher's out there, along with the first and third basemen. They talk for a minute or so, then Coach walks away, followed by the infielders and Danny's catcher, Kyle Loughlin, who claps him on the shoulder. Kyle's back is to me, but I see Danny nod at something he says. Then, his shields gone, Danny stands atop the mound, the ball cradled between the fingers of his right hand.

The sixty feet, six inches between the pitching rubber and home plate seems to me the approximate width of the Grand Canyon. The plate itself, by contrast, a mere sliver. And my anxiety isn't relieved when Emmaline takes my hand and squeezes.

"Danny's throwing," she explains.

"Yes, honey. Danny's throwing."

Danny's lucky that the runner on second is Baxter's catcher, a chubby kid with wide shoulders and a broad back. I watched him lumber to first on a pair of ground balls in the early innings. Fast he's not.

Just as well, because the hitter at the plate lines the ball to left field on the first pitch, a fastball over the heart of the plate. Already playing shallow, Mike charges in to glove it on one hop with his throw going toward home plate. The tendency here is for high school outfielders to throw as hard as they can, but Mike doesn't fall into that trap. Mike releases the ball as Baxter's catcher rounds third base.

He should stop right there and he knows it, hesitating for a second before charging toward home as the Baxter coach waves him forward. The game is scoreless. This is Baxter's golden opportunity.

Danny keeps his cool, coming from the mound to back up our catcher. He needn't have bothered. The ball comes to Kyle Loughlin on a single hop and he fields it cleanly with the runner a good thirty feet up the line. I'm expecting a collision at the plate, an attempt to knock the ball out of Kyle's hand, but the oncoming runner settles for a weak slide that doesn't carry him within a yard of home plate.

So far, so good, but the batter took second on the throw and Danny still has to pitch with a runner in scoring position. I watch him walk back to the mound, watch him turn and look into his glove as though realizing for the first time that his catcher still has the ball. Then he grins as he glances at me.

I don't know the batter's name, but he's small and slender, and obviously nervous. He holds off on the first four pitches, probably hoping for a walk. Instead, he watches the count reach two balls and two strikes. Nervous or not, he can't allow himself to strike out looking. He's got to swing the bat, which he does on the next pitch, tapping the ball to Danny who flips it to first base. Side retired.

The Goldman fans sitting on the third base side of the field leap to their feet, hands slapping together, mouths open as they lift a cheer. Without thinking, I put my arm around Zoe's shoulder and pull her toward me. I don't kiss her. I'm not that far gone, but I don't pull my hand away as we jump up and down like twelve-year-old cheerleaders at their first Little League game. Beside us, Vern swings Emmaline in a circle. The girl's wearing a red sweatshirt with a grinning kitten on the front, red jeans, and pink sneakers. Her delighted laughter, as bright as her clothing, is living proof that at least some wrongs can be righted.

CHAPTER FIFTEEN

MAGGIE MILLER

It took us a fair bit of time to get settled in Boomtown. First off, we headed home. Not to Grissom, but to the homeland. That would be in Kentucky, near the eastern border where Kentucky, Virginia, and West Virginia close on each other. I'm speakin' about mountain country with mountain ways of thinking that have nothing to do with the police.

There are people in this country who brag about tracing their families all the way to George Washington. I can trace my line back to ancestors brewing whiskey when George Washington was still havin' his diapers changed. Fought in his war, too, but revolution for the Miller family didn't end with a peace treaty.

You might say we took the revolution back into the mountains and made it permanent. There was law, yes. In the form of county sheriffs wholly owned by the timber barons who came first, or the coal barons who came later, and even the casino owners who came last. And, yes, we worked in the forests or in the mines or at the blackjack tables. Didn't have any choice because farming and hunting couldn't be stretched far enough to get families through the mountain winters.

But we held ourselves apart, always apart, and we didn't go runnin' to the sheriff if we had troubles with other families. No, what it boiled down to was this: Don't leave any offense unaddressed. Step back once, you'll be steppin' back forever. Consequences be damned.

◆

Me and Corey grew up in Redmond Lake, in the heart of Appalachia, and I lived there from birth through high school, where I did better than most. Which left me with two choices, the casino or the military. This was an easy decision and I didn't think twice when I made it. I joined the Air Force two weeks after Principal Flowers put a diploma in my hand because I wanted to see the world. What I saw, for the first three years before they posted me stateside, was Al Asad Air Base in Iraq and Bagram in Afghanistan. I accepted the deployments, including the rocket attacks, with Corey my only regret. I texted her for about a year, and spoke to her on occasion, even after she left Redmond Lake. Then she stopped responding. Then she vanished.

Maybe I left home because I was tired of ATVs traveling at high speed along trails that didn't appear on any map, tired of poaching deer on property owned by families too rich to visit more than once or twice a year. I think my own extended family, the Miller-McKibbin clan, truly believed that pulling out-of-season trout and largemouth bass from the creeks and lakes made them authentic rebels.

I'm goin' on and on for no good reason. But what isn't speculation, what's pure fact, is that my sister lost her way after I left. My father was no help, at work six days a week, married to his beer and his ball games when he come home. Or out huntin' with his friends, or in a tavern Jim McKibbin runs out of his barn. Some of the aunts tried to get Corey under control, but what she needed, and what I took away, was an older sister with a steady hand.

◆

All the time since I left, and all the time with Corey gone, don't amount to a hill of beans. Not even the hard as-rock beans my daddy tried to grow in a garden he never tended. If Corey died from an overdose, or even suicide, that's on her. But my conference with Captain Mariola and Baxter's coroner left me with suspicions that won't go away. Cause of death? They were quick to put cause of death on the table. An overdose, simple as that. But manner of death? That was a different story. That line was left blank, meaning they were considering the possibility that she was murdered.

I explained myself at a family meeting in Jim McKibbin's tavern. Now, once upon a time, the tavern was a barn, with boards laid on oil drums for a bar top. The casino changed that because it brought tourists into the county, which the timber and coal industries never did. The tourists came to gamble, of course, and for extras like the hookers who worked the floors or the drug dealers who worked the lounges. But there was an appetite among some few tourists for the countryside, for the mountains and lakes and streams. Folk who liked to hunt and fish, or hike an unmapped trail to ridges with fifty-mile views. Those views are hard to come by. The Appalachian Mountains are forested to the top, with trees so closely packed you can be within thirty feet of a cliff without knowin' it. You have to locate a rocky ledge to find a view, and while the most prominent are found in tourist guides, others are known only to locals.

Me and Corey had our own special place, courtesy of a dog named Hannibal, who took after a deer and didn't come back. Too stupid to hunt and too friendly to kill, he was the family pet and there was no choice but to go after him and bring him home.

We found Hannibal with his nose in the leaf litter, a few yards from a ledge that snaked out between the trees; we named it the Castle.

Flanked by oak and hickory on three sides, the Castle became our special place. As kids, we treated ourselves to cookies snuck out of Gramma's cookie jar, then Daddy's cigarettes, then an occasional joint. The view took your breath away, especially in fall. The mountains in the east don't have peaks like the Rockies. Instead, running north–south in long ridges, they appear as waves in a fairy-tale sea, retreating to some far-off paradise that teased our imaginations.

Did Corey seek out the Castle after I left? Did she sit up there by herself, wondering how to conduct her life without a guide? Or did she shun the Castle as a reminder of my betrayal? I wish I knew. I wish I could one more time hold her close. I wish all her dreams had come true. And if I get the chance, if I get to her killer before the cops, I'm gonna put him in ground.

I'd held to a heap of childish fantasies when I enlisted. Saw myself flyin' jets or helicopters, guns blazing, the speed of sound left far behind. Instead, I was assigned to the Security Police and charged with investigating crimes committed by on-base personnel. Kind of a joke, really, in light of my family's anti-police principles. But the military doesn't explain itself. You go where you're told to go and you do what you're told to do. In my case, doin' the man's work meant investigating assaults of all kinds, including sexual assaults, drug and alcohol smuggling, and even murder. And I'd still be at it if Daddy hadn't gotten sick. Not with Alzheimer's, but kidney failure related to Covid.

I left the Air Force to care for my father, but not at home, where health care was limited to an underfunded regional hospital. I took him to Indianapolis where I had friends to guide me. I would have given him one of my kidneys, too, but I wasn't a match. That left me to make sure Daddy took his meds and got to his dialysis appointments while the rest of the family were tested. One at a time, as it turned out, with many not all that eager to volunteer. That last category, the reluctant, included a third cousin who won the prize. A near-perfect match is what the docs called her.

Arrangements were being made for Joanna Miller to fly to Indiana when Daddy's kidneys began to work. Doctor Felicia Howard, a wide grin pushing aside her generally grim expression, explained it to Daddy.

"Long-term Covid is a lottery, Mr. Miller. Especially when it comes to virus-related organ damage. Some people improve, most don't. Your blood work clearly indicates that you are among the first group. Congratulations."

◆

Daddy and I needed financial backing if the pair of us were to remain in Baxter, and we got it after hours of debate. The commitment won't allow us to live in luxury, but luxury isn't called for. We need to dwell among the people.

Among the people is where we finally land after our return to Baxter. The battered trailer we rent in Boomtown, located between Main Street and the Paradise Inn, cost more than a house back home. By contrast, the dilapidated house we lease in Oakland Gardens comes a good deal cheaper, but it's just as important. We need a hideout close by, a retreat if things get too rough, which is not only possible, but likely. That's because the news became official on the day we returned. First, there was nothing accidental about Corey's overdose. Second, she was pregnant when she was murdered.

The final piece of the family's commitment came in the form of Jimmy-Jack Haas, twenty-eight years old. Called Jay-Jay, Jimmy's married to Felice McGibbon's oldest daughter. An orphan, he'd welcomed the chance to be part of our family and didn't raise a fuss when his father-in-law asked him to join me and Daddy in Baxter. Jay-Jay brings a pair of virtues with him. He knows how to keep his mouth shut, and he worked on the construction of the casino for two years. That last gave him a good reason to live in Baxter. The boy knows rebar, which has to be laid and tied before concrete is poured. He won't have trouble finding work. Meantime, he'll lay low until the day comes when he's needed.

◆

It's eight o'clock in Baxter and the sun's been up for two hours. Me and Daddy are sitting in lawn chairs outside our trailer, soaking up some rays. The feeling of spring, but there's nothing growing around us, no trees, no flowers, no grass. The whole of Boomtown was cleared by bulldozer and nothing planted to replace whatever crop was growing at the time. If it wasn't for a sprinkling of gravel over the bare earth, every yard in Boomtown would be a mud field whenever it rained.

Daddy wears a light jacket, while I've donned a red sweatshirt with the Georgia bulldog on the front. Beside us, two frying pans sit on top of a propane grill. I've got eggs frying on one, bacon in the other. A two-quart thermos of coffee spiked with cream and sugar sits on the ground between us. Myself, I prefer tea, a habit I picked up in Iraq, but our image must be preserved. If necessary, I'm ready to sing, "Okie From Muskogee."

The Paradise Inn's quiet, the last customer emerged an hour ago, but the rest of the street is busy with people, mostly men, heading off to work or coming home. I wave to them, sometimes follow with, "Mornin'." Daddy joins me in the waving sometimes, and sometimes not, but I know he's takin' a hard look. I feel him tap my knee as a car pulls up to the Paradise and a man gets out. The man's big across the back, and has to stand a couple inches above six feet. Wearing a leather jacket that falls to narrow hips, he moves with a confidence that isn't quite a swagger, shoulders squared, chin up.

I dealt with all kinds in the Air Force, from milquetoast civilians who found ingenious ways to divert government matériel, to bullies who got what they wanted by inspiring fear. The man entering the Paradise better fits that last category, though something in his graceful stride hints at a more casual attitude. He turns at the last moment and I register his face, storing it in the back of my brain. I won't forget him.

◆

Daddy and I have just finished our breakfast, piling the dishes on a slim coffee table that came with the trailer, when a woman exits an Airstream parked across the street. A well-behaved German Shepherd walks beside her, timing its walk to hers. The dog's head swivels right and left as she approaches, its ears up, nose twitching, reminding me of the dogs I'd worked in Iraq. Always alert.

"Howdy," the woman calls as she starts toward us.

"Hello."

She comes to within ten feet, then stops, her eyes fixed on the dent in Daddy's forehead. The dog immediately sits beside her. I'm guessing that she's in her fifties, in good shape except for a small roll at her waist. A gold cross rests in the hollow of her throat and her sweatshirt proclaims her beliefs, no inquiries necessary.

SAVE

THE

BABIES

We have churches aplenty back home and we, Daddy and myself, attend on most Sundays. Like everybody else in the clan. But I don't wear my beliefs on my sleeves, or on my chest. Daddy neither.

"Name's Bertha Framm."

"Maggie Miller. And this is my daddy. He's . . . confused."

"Well, I guess I know what that means. My uncle had Alzheimer's. Lingered on for near five years." She stops for a moment, but I have no comment to make. "Y'all here for the construction? Good pay out here. My husband, Bill, is workin' a shift right now."

"No, ma'am, we—"

Daddy speaks up, interrupting me. "Wilma?" he says to Bertha Framm. "I thought you was dead."

"She ain't Aunt Wilma, Daddy. Her name's Bertha."

Daddy's head swivels side to side for a moment, as if he's lookin' at someone nobody else can see. Then he settles back.

"He don't wander. That's the only good thing come out of this." I tap my forehead. "Say, would you like a cup of coffee?"

She looks down at the Shepherd and shakes her head. "Stonewall needs to get to his business. So, how do you like Boomtown?"

Is she serious? There's not a tree in sight, nor a bird singing, and the land's flat as a table. "Didn't come for the scenery," I tell her. "For the work, neither. You hear about that pregnant woman in the morgue? One they say was murdered? That'd be Corey Miller. She's my sister, and what me and Daddy are doin' here in Baxter is waitin' on justice. Waitin' for her body, too, which the city don't wanna release. We're waitin' on my sister's remains."

Bertha can't help herself. She tosses a rapid glance at the Paradise Inn, then covers by scratching the dog's head. "That's terrible," she declares.

"Yes, ma'am, it is. And Corey? I know she didn't walk a righteous path, but that's no good reason to slack off. We mean to see that whoever killed her is brought to justice and we don't plan to let up till it happens."

CHAPTER SIXTEEN

MAGGIE MILLER

Mariola's office looks as if it was furnished by the same designer who furnished the squad room. Nothing matches, from the shelves on the wall, to the chairs in front of her desk. And while the ergonomic chair behind her desk looks expensive, the puke-green file cabinets against the wall are scratched and dented. Maybe the coming of Nissan promises a better future, but the present is all about a decaying city. I should know because we've got decayin' towns and cities by the score in my part of Kentucky.

"Please, sit down."

"Yes'm."

"Your father isn't with you?"

"Daddy's not havin' a good day. I left him back in the trailer we're rentin'. It's okay, though. Some folk in his condition like to wander, but long as there's a TV goin', Daddy stays put."

The door opens and a woman steps inside. Maybe thirty, she's wearing a short-sleeved blouse that reveals toned forearms and biceps. Her red hair, which I make as enhanced, not dyed, hangs to her shoulders and works nicely with a pair of sharp green eyes. If not for a badge clipped to the belt of her off-white slacks, I might take her for Mariola's girlfriend.

"This is Detective Weber," Mariola says. "She's going to be the primary investigator now that your sister's death has been declared a homicide."

I barely glance at Detective Weber. "When you say 'your sister,' does that mean the DNA tests came back?"

"Ms. Miller . . ."

"Maggie'll do."

"Maggie, then. Please sit down. And no, the tests haven't been processed. But we don't doubt that . . ." She hesitates and I suspect she's determining whether to give the body a name. "We believe that our victim is your sister, but we have to be sure. Please, sit down."

I take a seat in one of the chairs before Mariola's desk. Detective Weber takes the other, while Mariola drops into her ergonomic chair. I cross my legs, but say nothing. Who will speak first, Weber or Mariola? Who's really running the case? I know that me and Daddy are inconvenient. It's a lot easier to give up on an investigation if there's no relative demanding justice.

"Maggie, let me brief you." Weber gets the prize. She's got the faintly hoarse voice of a smoker. "Most people think you can recover forensic evidence at every crime scene. That's not true, especially if the victim's body was moved away from the original crime scene. In your sister's case, though our coroner is convinced that she'd recently engaged in consensual intercourse, no seminal fluid was recovered. We did identify chemical traces consistent with an over-the-counter douche, but it's also possible a condom was used." A pause, maybe waiting for me to get upset about her characterizing that recent sex as consensual. When I don't, she takes up the thread. "Although it remains to be determined, we believe her body was sanitized, postmortem. If that's the case, her killer did a good job. We didn't find a single pubic hair on her body. Her own pubic area had been shaved a day or two before she died."

I raise a hand. "Can we cut to the chase? You haven't arrested anybody. That much I can figure out for myself. But are you at least lookin' at someone? And if Corey overdosed on heroin, what makes you think it was murder?"

Detective Weber isn't about to answer either of these questions. Mariola neither. I watch the redhead fold her arms across her chest before she leads with the expected cliché: "I can only tell you that we're investigating."

The woman's chin is a square block, which she gradually lifts, a gesture I determine to mean get the fuck out of my office. Or, my boss's office. I'm not impressed because I commonly employed the same tactic when I had nothing to offer victims of vicious sexual assaults. Yes, you were dragged behind the barracks and raped, but your assailant wore a mask. You couldn't identify him immediately afterward and you won't be able to identify him in the future, even if we find him. So, hello . . . and goodbye.

"There was another killing," I say. "On the day Corey was killed. Pimp name of Titus Klint, accordin' to the *Baxter Bugle*, which I been readin' every day. Happened close to where Cory's body was found. You see any connection?"

"Again, Maggie, we can't comment at this stage of our investigation." Detective Weber has a ring with a small pearl at the center on her right hand, but no wedding ring. She twists this ring as she continues. "But we'll certainly update you as the investigation progresses."

I ignore the reassuring smile and stand. "Where I come from, we have a reputation for bein' blunt, so let me say this at the outset. I'm not satisfied, and neither is my family back home. Right now, me and my daddy are rentin' a trailer in Boomtown a few doors from a whorehouse called the Paradise Inn. That's a place where you can't go, accordin' to Mr. Basil Ulrich. Is he right?"

Detective Weber pushes her jaw even further out. She doesn't care for my aggressive tone. Mariola, on the other hand, seems almost amused, and I know I'm not fooling her. I know, too, that if I'm determined to put myself out there as bait, it's perfectly fine with her.

"Let's stay in touch," she tells me.

◆

Main Street in Boomtown is ongoing at six o'clock when me and Daddy take a drive over its roller-coaster surface. The joint is jumpin', as they say, with bars and restaurants alternating with convenience stores sellin' more than chips and soda, judgin' from how many customers emerge without packages. No pharmacies, though, or supermarkets, or even well-stocked grocery stores. Instead, food trucks sell tacos, burgers, mac and cheese, guacamole, and fries, while hookers parade from one end of Main Street to the other.

"Time for dinner, Daddy. You sufficiently confused?"

"Is it Christmas yet?"

The restaurant we've chosen is housed in a large tent, with the kitchen in a shed out back. The larger sign reads, BOOMTOWN EATS. The smaller sign below, JUST LIKE MAMA MADE.

My mama couldn't cook to save her life, and there are halfway decent restaurants in Baxter, with more opening every week. But we're eating with the working folk because we're not about stayin' private. Just now, I'd bet a sizable chunk of my pitiful savings that Bertha Framm's already spreading word of our appearance. But I want more and a youngish, reasonably attractive woman with her addled daddy in tow is sure to attract attention.

Boomtown Eats is heavy on meat and potatoes, with tossed salad the only plant matter on the menu. There are no tables for two, or four, or even six. Instead, the working men, along with a sprinkling of working women, sit at twenty-foot display tables, the arrangement haphazard. No waitstaff, either, only a long buffet line with servers behind it. Pork chops, anybody? Barbecued ribs? Fried chicken? The restaurant's crowded with workers let loose after a long hard day. But they're friendly enough and the hum of conversation forces me to raise my voice when I drag Daddy along the buffet line.

We find seats next to an older man wearing a Desert Storm cap. He watches me struggle to set down the tray and get Daddy seated for a few seconds, then gallantly assists, taking the tray from my hands and laying it on the table.

"Name's Yank Framm," he tells me.

"Maggie Miller, and this is my daddy, Aaron." Daddy's already attacking his beef stew, chowing down like he's alone in his kitchen. I explain the situation with a smile and a pair of raised eyebrows. "You a vet, Yank?"

"Sure am. And you?"

"Air Force. Served at Bagram and Al Asad."

Yank's twenty years older than I am, but I note that gleam in his eye. As I already said, I'm no raving beauty, but I never had trouble attracting male attention. Truth told,

I could have done with less. But Yank isn't offensive and neither are the other men and one woman who introduce themselves. In fact, I'm reminded of the mess halls where I ate most of my meals in Iraq and Afghanistan, the shared experience of men and women far from home.

"So," Yank Framm asks, "what brings you to Baxter? You lookin' for work?"

"I'm here about my sister, the girl lyin' in the morgue." The conversations around me stop dead. "The cops are now sayin' she was murdered. Me, I'm not big on trusting cops. I need to find things out for myself. And I don't plan to leave this city until I do."

◆

"You did just about perfect," Daddy tells me once we're back in the car. "Didn't ask for pity. Just spoke out with your chin raised. You had 'em eatin' out of your hand."

"We need 'em on our side. Way I'm thinking, somebody who knows somethin' is gonna come forward now that Corrie's death's been ruled a murder. If I want the somebody to come to us instead of the cops, we need to make our existence known."

We're cruising on Main Street, heading toward the southern end of Boomtown. It's dark now, but the road is brightly lit on the construction side as well as the Boomtown side. There are hookers working in clusters, calling out to the off-duty workers as they come in and out of the bars. We're on the prowl for an aging hooker, someone reasonably isolated, and we find her down near First Street. The woman is leaning against a light stanchion that would fit nicely into a hastily erected military base. Older than most of the other hookers we passed, probably in her early forties, she's the kind of unhealthy thin I associate with meth addicts approaching the dead end of that particular street.

The woman looks up when I pull over, then sneers when she discovers that I'm a woman. I don't know what she's thinking and I don't care. I put my left hand in the window. The hundred-dollar bill it's holding produces an instantaneous change of attitude. Her eyes widen, her jaw drops, her tongue takes a quick swipe at her lips. This is not a woman who commands escort prices.

"What do you want?" she asks.

"Honest talk, no bullshit. Give me a half hour and you can walk away with this C-note in your bra." I lean back to give her a look at Daddy.

"Wait a—"

"No waitin', lady. Get in or I'll find someone else."

She gets in.

◆

"Give me a name," I tell her. "Something to call you. Don't give a damn if it's real or not. This isn't about you."

"Lily."

"All right, Lily. My name is Maggie Miller and this here is my daddy. You know that woman they found a couple weeks ago? The one they're sayin' was murdered?"

"Sure."

"Her name's Corey Miller. My sister, my daddy's daughter."

Far from concerned, Daddy's staring out through the windshield like there's something out in the distance that needs close inspection.

"Sorry to hear that," Lily says, her tone making it apparent that she couldn't care less. Meanwhile, her eyes never leave the C-note in my hand. She can buy enough meth with a hundred dollars to stay high for days. "But if you're askin' me who did it, I gotta disappoint ya. I don't know and I don't wanna know."

"I'm not thinkin' you do. But I'm tryin' to uncover what happened and I have good reason to believe that Corey was active in the trade. Plus, you have the look of a woman who's been around a while. Excuse me for statin' the obvious."

"No apology necessary." Lily's shoulders drop as she relaxes. "Just tell me what you want. And I'm not particular about gender if that's—"

I interrupt her with a laugh. A few seconds later, she joins in. Daddy turns to us for the first time, drawn by our laughter. "Say, Maggie, you ain't heard from Corey, have ya?"

I draw a deep breath, then shrug. "Why don't you start with the hooker scene in Baxter. Before Boomtown."

Lily doesn't hesitate. As a general rule, meth addicts can't stop talking if they've indulged recently. Which Lily apparently has.

"Okay, so before the construction started, there wasn't no street action to speak of. The cops were aggressive up and down Baxter Boulevard. And the Yards, which was what they called the section where the plant's being constructed, was like the end of the world. No girl in her right mind would walk those streets, and no john wanted to drive them. Place was jam-packed with addicts and homeless crazies. The rats outnumbered the people, like ten to one."

"Point made, Lily, but there must have been workin' girls in Baxter."

"Yeah, usually workin' in a house, maybe up in Oakland Gardens. In fact, that man who was killed, Titus something? Found him shot in his house the same morning your sister's . . ." Lily stops on a dime. She doesn't want to upset me by mentioning that my sister was dumped naked in the dirt. There's still that hundred in my hand. "Some of the pimps, like Titus and my own, did outcalls. They'd send a girl to your room, or your house if you lived by yourself. Cops didn't care much if we kept our business on the down-low."

"Tell me about the outcalls. Did you take outcalls?"

"I did, once upon a time." Lily runs the tips of her fingers through her thinning blond hair, exposing a wave of dark root. "You know, when I was younger and still pretty? But I turned that corner some time ago."

I'm not finding a hint of regret, or self-pity, in Lily's tone. Only resignation. She'll take from each day whatever pleasure the day brings. And whatever pain. "Tell me about Boomtown. How did Boomtown change things?"

"No cops, okay. Boomtown's outside the Baxter city limits, so the Baxter cops have no authority. And the Sprague County sheriff? He hasn't got enough deputies to police Boomtown, even if he wanted to, which he definitely does not. First off it went fine. I mean everybody got along. A few bars opened. Me and the girls did what we do. Dealers started dealing to those who wanted, and there wasn't as many as you'd think. The workers who come here? They come here to work, not party. So, while they didn't mind a few drinks after they washed up, and maybe got laid every so often, they weren't crazy wild. Everybody got along, from the dealers to the carpenters, live and let live. Then they showed up. Out of nowhere."

I wasn't buying Lily's thug-paradise description, but I wasn't about to slow her down. "They?"

"From New York, the mob, or that's what I'm guessing. The mob part I mean. They're definitely from New York and it's not like they're lyin' low." She hunched forward, dropping her elbows to her thighs. "Now, I'm not in their heads, and I've never spoken directly to any of them, but I believe they came here planning to take over. Tell you this, Titus had words with one of them. I don't know his name, but he threatened Titus in public. Next thing you know, the cops find Titus with a bullet in his head. Now the . . ." She hesitates for just a moment, though her mouth continues to work. I think she's searching for a neutral term, but can't find it. "The pimps are payin' up."

"Including yours?"

"Yeah, I'd be too scared to work if he didn't and I told him so. These guys, the ones from New York, they don't fuck around. They run a whorehouse called the Paradise Inn. A couple doors down, they have a bar, the Lucky Tavern, with a casino in back. Also, they have dealers, bookies, and loan sharks in just about every bar in Boomtown. Believe me, I'm not giving away any secrets. Everybody on my side of the law knows. They want us to know."

I glance at Daddy. He's tryin' to look like he's not payin' attention, but I can almost hear the wheels turning. Daddy's never been all that honest, and I believe he got himself involved in some scheme for drainin' the casino back home. It fell through when one of his buddies, an uncle of mine, got himself shot by a casino security guard.

"My sister, did you know her?"

"Nope, but I seen her around."

"Did she work the street?"

"Uh-uh, times I saw her she was shopping for necessaries. In Baxter. You know how they say that gay men have gaydar? How they can tell if someone's gay, even if they're tryin' to pass for straight? Well, I got whore-dar. I can spot a working girl from ten blocks distant. Your sister worked at the Paradise."

That's enough. I hand over the C-note and Lily reaches for the door handle, but stops as a buzz in the distance quickly grows into the full-throated roar of a motorcycle. And not just one. They come by us, bikers on chopped Harleys, every shape and size, from a fat guy whose gut hangs over the gas tank to an emaciated scarecrow who has to stand close to seven feet tall. Knowing they're not on a beer run, I count them automatically, reaching forty-two before the last chopper passes my car. All wear cutaway vests with an eagle on the back. The eagle holds some small animal in its talons, though I can't tell exactly what it is.

"That would be the Horde," Lily explains after the last bike passes. "The Horde controls most of the drugs coming into Baxter. Titus? He was one of them. Killing him was like spitting in the gang's face. Looks to me like they've come to spit back."

That's enough for Lily. She opens the door and gets out. Daddy and I watch her cross the street. She's wearing a blue print dress that barely covers her butt, which she is not shaking. No, Lily's stride is rapid and purposeful. She's headed for whatever happy house supplies her drug of choice. Or maybe drugs of choice, one to get up, one to come down.

"Maggie, you thinkin' what I'm thinkin'?" Daddy asks.

"Don't know what you're thinkin', Daddy, but I'm thinkin' about the money."

"That's my girl."

I don't doubt Lily's tale of New York gangsters come to exploit the situation in Boomtown. Dope, whores, gambling? Lots and lots of cash money piling up. Money that somehow, some way, has to move from little Baxter to New York City, more than a thousand miles away. Somehow. Some way.

CHAPTER SEVENTEEN

CHARLIE

I'm in the Laundromat, which is the name I've given to Stardust Jewelers, our store on Baxter Boulevard. The Stardust will never compete with Tiffany's or Graff. True, we display a two-carat engagement ring in the window. J color and heavily included, the diamond is better suited for industrial use. Still, it's a precious stone, like the small assortment of tinier diamonds, rubies, sapphires, and an emerald so dark the green part is only visible in direct sunlight.

While most of our low-end rings and pendants are legit, a smaller number are hot, but too generic to be identified. Precious stones, though, form only a small part of our stock. The rest is artisan jewelry, which basically translates into silver or base metal, and no precious stones unless you include turquoise that's not only been dyed, but created from bits and pieces joined with resin. Gem dealer ethics require that both these treatments be revealed to customers, but they rarely are.

The Stardust has remained economically viable since we opened the doors, its main clientele being ordinary workers buying gifts for their families. Gold-plated hearts on gold-plated chains for the dearly beloved. Amber pendants on silver chains for the daughters. But jewelry sales are beside the point. The store could lose money hand over fist as far as I'm concerned. For us, meaning Ricky Ricci's operation, the Stardust serves two purposes. First, it launders enough cash from our various Boomtown enterprises to pay the rent on the Lucky Tavern and Paradise Inn. Second, because the Stardust is an obvious target of thieves, it has a one-ton safe in back. Our gem inventory goes in the safe right after the store closes, as do the proceeds from our Boomtown operations.

Cash money, of course, and lots of it. Even at this early stage, business is booming.

◆

I roll into the Stardust through the back entrance two hours before the store's ten o'clock opening. Adelyn is already there. She's a good-looking woman in her midthirties, with alert blue eyes that miss nothing. Her dress is conservative, an off-white skirt that falls below her knees, topped by a violet jacket. She wears a string of lustrous pearls, with earrings to match, and a gold bracelet of linked butterflies.

"Where'd you spend the night?" she asks.

"In my own bed."

"What, mine wasn't good enough?"

There are times when I almost believe that Adelyn really wants me in her bed. But either way, whether she wants me or tolerates me, our relationship simplifies both our lives. We're work oriented, the two of us, especially Adelyn, who hopes to keep the store open after the construction finishes. Adelyn's on the pudgy side, with sharp blue eyes and a full mouth that opens to an infectious smile. A welcoming smile that's perfect for retailers hawking a product that nobody actually needs.

◆

Adelyn and I head into the back room where a five-foot safe rests against the far wall. I watch her open the safe, revealing jewelry display cases on narrow shelves fronting a solid steel divider. I wait for Adelyn to move the display cases onto a desk, then come forward to punch six numbers into a digital keypad. The steel divider pulls away to reveal a second set of shelves, the shelves holding my boss's money. I carry the money to a table as Adelyn joins me. The bills, fifties and hundreds mostly, represent a week's proceeds, less expenses, from our various hustles. Altogether, I'm lookin at $42,850 on the table. I know this because I've already counted it.

I intend to recount it, bill by bill, this time with Adelyn watching. I want her initials on a slip that'll travel, along with the money, to Ricky Ricci in New York.

There was a time, and not that long ago, when I would have skimmed a few percent off the top before I put the money in the safe. Never mind if Ricky found out. Never mind the near certainty that I'd take one to the back of the head if he did, that I'd be left on the street as a warning to others. I'd have done it anyway, no consequence severe enough to deter.

◆

I learned the Lesson, which is what I call my life-altering experience, at the Beacon Correctional Facility. Beacon's a true country-club prison, designed to provide white-collar criminals with a safe environment. Truth be told, the only white part of my white-collar crime was the color of my skin. But I didn't object. I settled right in, secure in the knowledge that I wouldn't have to fight off prison-hard perverts bent on turning me out. Young and fit, I spent most of my time at the weight benches and the kitchen, where my rehab included training as a cook. Not in any four-star restaurant, of course. More like grilling and gravy.

It was easy time, as easy as it gets, but no day passed without me thinking about running away. I won't call it escape because there were no fences, only a threat to ship me off to a maximum-security prison like Attica, where I'd have to fight every day.

I met Jerome Clark two months into my bid. He came up on me at breakfast one morning, laid his tray on my table, and plopped himself down.

"You related to the jewelry setters?" he asked. No preamble, mind you. Just the question from a man who had to be in his fifties. And thirty pounds overweight to boot.

"Who's askin'?"

"Jerome Clark, also in the jewelry business."

He held out his hand, and though I was tempted to spit on it, there was something about his confidence that penetrated an ego big enough to fill an amphitheater. I shook his hand and said, "My *family's* in the jewelry business. I'm in prison."

Clark had a high forehead, a tiny nose, and a tinier mouth. His ears more than made up for both. Altogether, he was the kind of guy you wouldn't notice twice on the street, a total nothing. I watched him pinch his nose, a habit I'd see repeated many times.

"On the outside, I was a jewelry fence," he told me. "High-end only."

◆

Over the next few weeks, we spent more and more of our time in each other's company. The midsummer sun was hot enough to keep many of our fellow prisoners inside, but we usually found shade under a tree. Naïvely, I thought he was recruiting me. In fact, he was testing me.

The game had changed, as he explained it. In the past, you'd buy up the stolen goods at twenty cents on a dollar and sell it to an unscrupulous jeweler at thirty to forty cents on the dollar. The internet had opened new possibilities. You'd still pay twenty percent of the auction value for a piece, but now you'd employ VPNs to sell it on pop-up websites that could only be traced back to you after a long search. The strategy was unvarying. Open the site, sell off a limited inventory, vanish before the cops started an investigation.

"Most important, Charlie—Jerry had a habit of double-pointing with the index fingers of both hands when he said something you needed to hear—you can buy lists of consumers who've purchased jewelry online. They're not that expensive either. Plus, you have your own list of customers who bought from you previously. You invite them to visit the site with, say, a tease offer of some gemstone at a super-low price. Half what they'd pay a retail jeweler. A quarter what they'd pay at Tiffany's. That brings them to your site, where they find seriously good stones at the right price."

"You're tellin' me they don't know what they're getting?"

"You're veering off course." His tone sharpened and he pointed again. "Who cares what they know? Or what they think they know. You gotta focus on the goal. Sell the inventory, shut down, count the profits, open another site."

Jerry didn't hint around. He wanted to expand his business and he needed a co-conspirator who could tell a Burma ruby from fissure-filled junk. I couldn't do the sort of microscopic analysis employed by gem labs, of course, but I could sort gemstones based on color, clarity, and saturation. A 10X loupe was all I'd need. I'd been raised to the task and I could describe a stone's qualities precisely. Certain gemstones, for example, are expected to be eye-clean. Think aquamarine. Others, emeralds, for example, are classified as Type 3 and heavily included. Jerry hoped that I'd not only have the skill to evaluate the hot stones, but the ability to describe a stone's virtues precisely.

◆

As I've already said, Beacon was designed to protect white-collar white men who'd committed crimes like tax evasion or embezzlement. But at any given moment, its population also included twenty or thirty paroled convicts transitioning from a maximum-security prison to the outside world. A test, really. With only a few months left on their sentences, would they tough it out or run? I don't know of any who ran, but they were far from model prisoners, and some dealt in smuggled drugs.

I desperately wanted to get stoned, cocaine being my drug of choice, but had no money. As my parents were my only hope, I wrote to them asking for a donation. A prudent man would have awaited their reply. An asshole would jump in with both feet, which is what I did, securing the coke with a promise to pay within a week.

My parents didn't respond to my letter, no surprise, and I caught a serious beating that put me in the prison hospital. A beating and a warning. If I didn't pay up, next time I'd be shanked.

Jerry visited me in the hospital a few days after the attack. I hurt just about everywhere, but I finally had my drugs. Painkillers (how I love that euphemism) in the form of morphine.

"I'm not gonna ask you how you're feeling because I don't give a shit," Jerry told me. "Here's what you need to know. I squared the debt. You're clean. I didn't want to, Charlie. I wanted to give up on you, but my boss in New York, I'm not gonna name his name, told me to give you another shot. So, here it is, the test. Myself, I can use someone who knows his way around gemstones. But what I can't use is an out-of-control jerk who'd risk his life for a few grams of cocaine. So, pull yourself together, Charlie. You won't get another chance."

Without dragging this out, I did pull myself together. I grew up.

CHAPTER EIGHTEEN

CHARLIE

The count finished, I put the money into a small suitcase and lock it up. Ten minutes later, our mules come through the back door. They would be Joe and Edith Pinella. Seventy-five and seventy years old respectively, they're wouldn't-hurt-a-fly types out of Edison, New Jersey. Joe's wearing a short-sleeved Hawaiian shirt. Edith's wearing a pink pantsuit. Together, they'll drive the money over a thousand miles to New York. The route is simple as simple can be. They'll pick up Interstate 80 north of Baxter and follow it east to the George Washington Bridge and the island of Manhattan. Along the way, they'll stop for one night at a Holiday Inn, their room already reserved.

Joe's younger sister is married to Ricky Ricci's Uncle Frank, so it's all in the family. In return for services rendered, Ricky will hand the pair fifteen hundred in cash, a needed supplement because the Pinellas can't survive on Joe's Social Security check and small pension. As it is, they'll make the trip in their 2020 Camry at least twice a month.

"I love to travel," Edith Pinella tells me as she follows her husband out the door. "Don't you?"

◆

Adelyn's assistant, a twenty-year-old local named Josie, arrives a few minutes later. Her gem-related skills are limited to reading numbers from a sales tag, but she's full of energy and eager to please.

"Mornin', Adelyn. Morning, Mr. Setter."

"Good morning, Josie," Adelyn returns. "Why don't you fill the cases while Mr. Setter and I run out for a quick coffee."

We buy coffee at the only Starbucks in Baxter, an espresso for me and a cappuccino for Adelyn. It's too nice to linger inside and we carry our drinks a couple blocks to City Hall Green. Still a bit raw after a massive rehab, the grass is nevertheless thick beneath my feet, a shag carpet, and the yellow-green leaves on the newly planted saplings flutter in a slight breeze. We find a bench and I set my espresso down for a moment while I fire off a text to an unknown recipient: RACE DAY. Just the two words to let folks know the loot is on the move.

"You hear about the woman?" Adelyn asks. "Corey's sister?"

"She's not exactly makin' herself invisible. Living a few doors away from the Paradise. Plopping herself and her dent-head father in lawn chairs every morning."

"What do you think she's up to?"

"Don't know, Adelyn." I sip at my espresso and smile. "Maybe she's appealin' to my conscience."

I'm expecting Adelyn to drop the subject, but she keeps on. "I guess she's all fired up now that it's being called a murder."

"That don't mean it was actually a murder. Unless you wanna tell me with a straight face that you trust cops. Because I'm thinkin' the Baxter cops are lookin' for an excuse to operate in Boomtown and this could be it."

"Having the sister run around demanding justice? Hell, Charlie, she's been on the news three times already. Talk about stirrin' the pot."

"And exactly what do you expect me to do about it? Maybe shoot her?"

I'm trying not to get worked up, but talkin' about the sister leads me to naturally think of Bruce. I'd like to believe some john treated Corey to a little package. Or maybe paid for some extra service with a bag of dope. But where's the bag or vial it came in? And Rita swears up and down that if Corey had a little extra, they would have shared it between them.

The dope and coke Bruce passed to the girls the night Corey died was secured by one of our guys, Alfie Corso. He personally handed the two packages, of coke and heroin, to another of our guys, Solly Tarentini. Solly broke the packages into smaller packages, one for each of the girls, then passed the goodies to Bruce, who distributed them. I spoke to Solly at length and he insisted that his end of the operation was routine.

So, what am I gonna do about it? Bruce is a good manager and the Paradise is turning a very nice profit, so I'm tempted to do exactly nothing. On the other hand, in this state, whoever handed the drugs to an overdose victim is on the hook for a manslaughter charge, at the least. The cops wouldn't have to work very hard to find Bruce. He's been dispensing the goodies ever since we got here, as every girl working at the Paradise knows.

◆

"Hey, Charlie, where are you?"

I raise my eyes to meet Adelyn's, but say nothing. This afternoon I'll be meeting with a biker named Zeb, no last name provided. The stakes are high and I've no idea what Zeb will do when I demand that he turn over retail drug distribution to me. I don't have a fallback position here. Or, I do, but the fallback is all-out war with the Horde. I made that clear enough when I robbed Heyman Weymouth.

I lean back as I relax just a bit, enjoying the hopeful bustle, when my phone beeps at me. It's an encrypted WhatsApp text message. Very simple: *Saturday, 5:00.*

It's Tuesday, four days until I report to Ricky Ricci in New York. He'll have his money by then, which should make him happy. As for the rest? That remains to be seen.

"Bad news?" Adelyn asks.

"Routine, and not your business anyway."

Adelyn lays a hand on my forearm, a gentle hand a hair's breadth short of erotic. "Everybody needs someone to talk to, someone they trust."

"And that would be you?"

"I'm on your side, Charlie. I want this to work as much as you do."

Except she doesn't have to answer to Ricky if things go bad. "Okay, let me hear your wise counsel. About Corey. What needs to happen?"

"That's easy. First and best choice, kill Bruce and disappear his body. Second choice, send him back to Ricky. Because all the girls liked Corey. Dumping her body in a lot was bad enough. Now they're thinkin' maybe the overdose wasn't accidental." She waves a finger in my direction. "Take that back. There's no maybe to it. They believe that Bruce murdered Corey."

"When did that start?"

"After they found out she was pregnant."

I take a moment to consider what I'm going to say next. I don't want to leave any room for misinterpretation. "The girls, they drop into the store once in a while?"

"Yeah, some of them. The ones who like jewelry."

"Tell 'em this, Adelyn. If the cops come around, they need to keep their mouths shut. There's no law forcing them to cooperate. If necessary, if the cops harass them, I'll supply the lawyers. But know this. If any one of them does any fucking thing to jeopardize . . ." I'm about say, Ricky's operation, but catch myself at the last second. "Anything to jeopardize our thing, I'll put her in the fucking ground. And if it comes to some kind of open rebellion, I sell them off and start over."

CHAPTER NINETEEN

CHARLIE

'm in one of our bars, La Mina de Oro, the Gold Mine. Or
so I hope. The bar was delivered in pieces on a flatbed
trailer, then bolted together in less than two days. The outer
shell of the flat-roofed structure is corrugated metal, but
the inside is finished with Sheetrock. There's even a half
bath and a second room I use for private conversations.
Still in New York when the bar went up, I played no part
in its decor. But I don't believe I would've chosen posters
depicting the joys of the Sicilian countryside. Or painted
the walls mustard yellow.

I'm waiting for Zeb, fabled chief of the Aryan Horde.
He'd ridden at the head of the column when the gang
ripped through town last night. Most likely, he believed the
show of force would cow us. Maybe we'd see ourselves as

the rabbits in all those talons and drop to our knees. What I saw was a thug mentality that assumed any challenge can be met with brute force.

Zeb's late, though he was the one to specify the time. No surprise, really, but I'm annoyed because I've closed the bar. Normally, we'd be going strong by now because the day shift has just come off the construction site. I don't reveal my inner state to Dominick or Bruce, who I've recruited for the occasion. Neither is armed, though we've stashed three shotguns behind the bar. By agreement, neither Zeb nor the pair of men who'll accompany him will be armed. In case they are, I've got other men lying up in buildings on either side of the bar, and across the street. That wouldn't help me, of course. If Zeb comes in shooting, I'm sure to be the first one he shoots at.

◆

He's not that stupid, as it turns out when he enters the bar five minutes later. Zeb's a good six inches shorter than either of his bodyguards, but whatever he lacks in height, he makes up for in width. His shoulders are humped with thick muscle and about as wide as he is tall. As expected, he's wearing the gang's colors over a T-shirt that was probably white on the day he pulled it off a shelf.

Zeb comes to within six feet and stops. His brown eyes lock on mine, another attempt to intimidate, but I like what I'm seeing. Or what I'm not seeing. The man's not crazy and he's not wasted. Yeah, he wants to scare me, what with the dagger tattoo climbing the side of his neck, and a trio of prison-ink tears at the corner of his left eye. So what?

I signal to Dominick and he opens the office door. Two objects rest on a table in the center of the small room. The bag we took from Heyman Weymouth and a small gym bag. The gym bag's unzipped, but its contents aren't visible.

Zeb's eyes move from the table to me. The look is one I haven't seen before, an intelligent reptile, a snake ready for an IQ test. But I don't do fear, as I've already mentioned. My own expression remains stubbornly neutral as I gesture toward the room.

Zeb heads inside. His minders start to follow, but he waves them off without speaking. I trail behind, alone, and close the door.

"That mine?" Zeb points to the bag containing his two-and-a-half kilos of cocaine. His voice is surprisingly high-pitched, like he's been punched in the throat too many times.

"It could be."

He doesn't rise to the bait, pointing to the gym bag instead. "What's in there?"

"Thirty thousand dollars."

"Thirty? For exactly what?"

"For two-point-five kilos of heavily cut cocaine."

"And I'm supposed to take that? Because Heyman—"

"Look, Zeb, let's not bullshit each other. I know that Heyman mostly sold eight balls, maybe an occasional quarter ounce. He was a retailer and retailers always cut their product. I could smell the mannitol from across the room when the bag was opened." I give it a beat, expecting Zeb to react poorly to my snotty tone, but his expression doesn't change. "You bring me kilos worth twenty large, I'll pay you twenty large. Not for this."

"I'll take the cocaine then. You keep your money."

"Uh-uh. I stole that coke fair and square. You want it back, or the money, you have to meet my terms."

Still no reaction. "And what exactly would those terms be? If I'm allowed to ask."

"I become your only customer in Baxter and Boomtown."

Even if my negotiating tactics are crude, the deal's solid. True, the Horde's bottom line will be sharply reduced, but their risk will also be reduced. They'll be dealing with me instead of mid-level dealers, most of whom are druggies and likely to flip if arrested.

"What about price?"

"A fair price for whatever product you offer. Meth, dope, coke, pills. Whatever."

Zeb has a big problem. The gear, the attitude, the chopped Harleys, substance abuse on a grand scale? They're meant to intimidate, and I'm sure they mostly do. But they're also conspicuous and I don't believe they can just cut their greasy hair and pass unnoticed in Boomtown, or even Baxter. Not after all the shit they put up their noses or pour down their throats.

"You don't mind, I'm just gonna turn this conversation," Zeb says. "Heyman? He took a few stitches, but he'll be okay. Titus Klint? His life was taken with the boy still in his prime. That's a hard thing to swallow. Real hard."

If there's any skill I possess in such abundance that I can truly count myself among the super-talented, it's lying. "I know who you're talking about, Zeb. His name was all over the news. But I had nothing to do with killing him."

"You and him had words."

"We did. Only, if I killed everyone I ever had words with . . ." I shrug my shoulders. "I'm a sane man, believe it or not. And what we're here to talk about is business. You control the supply, but not demand. And the point I'm tryin' to make is that me and my people, we're your demand. No fronting, no collecting from the deadbeats, just cash on delivery. You won't get a better deal."

I think I've gone too far. Zeb's mustache starts at his nose and reaches over his slash of a mouth to graze the top of a beard that starts below his lower lip. Both now move as he forms unspoken words driven by what I assume to be rage. Nobody talks to him like that.

"See, you got what belongs to me." He points to the bag on the table. "And now you're tellin' me if I don't jump through that hoop you're holdin' up, I won't get it back. Me, I ain't a dog."

"I'm not taking you for a dog. I'm taking you for a bottom-line oriented businessman. There a lot of money to be made in Baxter and Boomtown. That money flies out the window if there's a war." I raise my hands and smile. "Forget about what I said. Take the money. A gesture of goodwill, right? Like turning the snitch over to Heyman? So, take the money, go home, and think it over."

Two hours later, the bikers roar out of town. I'd been wondering if they'd leave a few behind. To maybe throw it in my face. Zeb wasn't that stupid.

CHAPTER TWENTY

DELIA

D anny's full of questions as I drive toward his school. It's still early, not even eight o'clock, but Coach Harmon wants him in before class to work on a changeup. I expected Danny to be upset, even rebel, when I heard the news. That's not the case because Coach Harmon has promised to play Danny in the field on days he doesn't pitch. Now he imagines himself the next Shohei Ohtani.

As a topic of conversation, baseball's off the table this morning, for which I'm grateful. Competitive sports are not on my entertainment-of-choice list. Not unless Danny's the entertainer. But I'm not thrilled with the alternative either. Late last night, Katie Burke interviewed Maggie Miller at length. Folksy as ever, Maggie piously described her mission. Justice must be served, and she intended to stick around until the killer's head was served up on a platter. Damn the consequences, Maggie won't allow her sister to be forgotten.

"Isn't she taking a big chance?" Danny asks. "Living in Boomtown. That's where her sister lived, right? The killer might be living next door."

"I think that's the point." I don't add that Maggie's chosen to locate herself fifty feet from the most notorious brothel in Boomtown, the Paradise Inn. Or that our snitches insist that Corey Miller plied her trade in that very same brothel.

◆

The whole Maggie Miller deal stinks to high heaven, but there's not much I can do about it. Boomtown is still off-limits. I'm hoping that's about to change. Vern Taney and I have an eight-thirty appointment with Mayor Venn to discuss an "exploding" crime rate. Three dead in the past week? The Horde riding through Boomtown? Rumors of a New York crime family operating close at hand? The mayor won a very close election this past November. He can't ignore the impending storm.

◆

We're four months into Mayor Venn's third go-round, long enough for him to have created an office that reflects his position. Hardwood floors are topped by a delicate

Aubusson carpet woven in muted shades of blue and gold. Fluted columns mark the corners of a desk surrounded by a frieze of identical columns. As though pointing to the frieze, a hardwood grain rises from the bottom rail in narrow, honey-yellow flames.

The wall to the left as Vern and I enter is given over to a pair of built-in bookcases holding his law library. To the right, the wall is divided in two. Closer to the desk, photos of Venn with three different governors, both our senators, and President Bush. Toward the door, cowboys driving herds of cattle line the borders of an 1881 city map.

A coffee table almost as ornate as the desk is flanked by an early American love seat and a pair of upholstered chairs. The chairs are occupied by Gloria Meacham, City Council President, and Mayor Venn. That leaves Vern and me to squeeze onto the love seat. Vern is a very large man, while svelte plays no part in my own profile.

We exchange polite greetings, then Gloria makes a show of folding her hands and dropping them to her lap. "I'm not trying to interfere," she claims, "but it appears things are getting out of hand. Three murders?" She shakes her head. "Why don't we begin with an update. Where are you?"

I'm listening to Gloria's tone as I recall our heroic status only four days ago when the smash-and-grab bandits were brought to justice. That status has endured for about as long as the news cycle. Now it's cover-your-ass time for the two politicians on the other side of the coffee table. For politicians, deflection is a vital skill. Like deflecting blame from the administration to the Baxter Police Department.

"We believe all three homicides can be traced to competing organizations," Vern begins. "Our information at this point is limited and very general, but it appears that some element of the New York mob has taken advantage of the chaos in Boomtown. They've come with a plan of action and they've come in force. Prostitution, gambling, hard drugs, loan-sharking. You name a racket, they're workin' it. At this point, however, they're not totally dominant, which we believe to be their objective." Vern makes brief eye contact with Gloria and Mayor Venn. Both respond with a simple nod. "You're familiar with the Horde, so I won't drag this out. The Horde and this New York crew work the same rackets, only the bikers have been here a lot longer. They won't go down without a fight. When they rode through Boomtown yesterday, they made their intentions plain. And with Boomtown currently off-limits, our own options are also limited." Then he looks at me and nods. My turn.

◆

Over breakfast this morning, I vowed to control my temper. I intend to honor that pledge. Without holding back.

"A year ago, we began a long-term effort to reduce the flow of drugs into Baxter. We made dozens of arrests and decimated three separate drug rings. That effort, not to mention the cost of sustaining it, flew out the window when Boomtown popped up. It doesn't matter how many dealers we arrest in the city proper. You can get anything you want in Boomtown, including women like Corey Miller. We believe she worked at the Paradise Inn, a notorious Boomtown brothel, but . . ."

I don't have to complete the sentence. With our ability to investigate limited, we'll have to wait until someone, maybe a friend, grows a conscience and comes forward. We're passive where we should be active.

"Corey Miller was almost surely a prostitute. Titus Klint was a pimp. Stitch Kreuter was a low-level drug dealer. Heyman Weymouth, who rented the house where Kreuter was killed, is a mid-level drug dealer. One thing our snitches agree on, the mobsters in Boomtown are highly organized. If I had to guess, I'd predict they'll disappear when the plant's completed. In the meantime, they intend to run the show. Even if that means going to war."

"And you see no solution?"

"Not as long as Boomtown remains off-limits."

◆

We observe a moment of silence as images of open gun battles, maybe on the streets of Baxter, but surely in Boomtown, dance through our heads. For me, it's innocent victims, passersby, who wander into the line of fire. In truth, I don't think these New York gangsters operate that way. But the Horde surely does. With no presence in Baxter outside of the occasional pimp or dealer, they have no choice.

"What do you suggest, Vern?" Gloria Meacham asks.

Gloria's family arrived in Baxter about the time the map on the wall was printed. As a young mother, she worked the family farm while her husband drove an eighteen-wheeler from city to city. Often gone for weeks, he nevertheless managed to father six children. Her own rise was station to station, beginning with election to her local schoolboard.

"Patrol Boomtown. Drive the prostitutes off the streets. Arrest the drunk and disorderly. Every bar has its own dealer, its own bookie, its own loan shark. Drive them underground. Primary responsibility belongs to Sheriff Fletcher. But if he won't or can't handle that responsibility, let the Sprague County Board of Supervisors hand authority to us. If they refuse, turn to the governor and the state police." Vern brings his hands together. "Without order, there's no hope. Even if we close all three murder investigations by arrest, the crime rate will continue to explode. In Baxter and in Boomtown."

Mayor Venn looks down before shaking his head. A great little speech, yes, and obviously true, but it won't fly.

"If the City of Baxter were to somehow gain jurisdiction over that strip of land in Sprague County," our mayor explains, "we'd have to enforce city building codes. In which case, not a single existing structure could remain occupied. I don't exaggerate, Vern." Always heavy, our mayor has grown more and more portly over the years. Now he fills his chair, virtually immobile except for his mouth. "From basic electricity, to buildings foundations that don't exist, to the unlicensed stores and bars, to third-world sewage systems. If we accept responsibility, it has to go, all of it. Displacing several thousand workers in the process. Vital workers, Vern. As in, we gotta have 'em. And face it, there's not enough housing in Baxter to shelter half of them."

I'm not surprised when Gloria Meacham turns to me. We're both women, right? Just like several billion other human beings. I try for a look that demonstrates independence, yet still encourages.

"As Chairwoman of the Construction Committee, I meet regularly with Nissan representatives. They bring three concerns to every discussion. Is the construction on schedule? Are to-date costs in line with the projected budget? Will the walls be up and the roof installed before it gets too cold to work outside? As to Boomtown and the crime, even the murders? Not one word. Not one." She rubs her hands together. "The fate of this city depends on getting the factory up and running. The fate, Delia. Baxter's very existence. I think your personal involvement in the homicide cases would be appropriate. A quick arrest will buy us time."

◆

This is the moment when I'm supposed to climb onto my white horse, don my white hat, toss my badge onto the coffee table, and ride into the sunset. Even though it's eight o'clock in the morning. Instead, I nod dutifully.

"If I'm going to run Baxter's police department," Vern says, "I need to know the rules. And without disrespecting you, Mayor, let me repeat myself. If Boomtown is left to itself, the homicide rate won't be dropping anytime soon."

"I understand your dilemma, Vern, and I'm sympathetic, but Gloria's right. The plant must be built. Bear in mind, these workers have come a long way and they're going to find . . . find distractions no matter what we do. Now, I've straightened things out with Sherriff Fletcher. No more restrictions on your investigations. Go where you want, speak to anyone you want. Follow the evidence. Patrolling, on the other hand, is simply not our problem."

Gloria Meacham lifts her chin. Her face is heavily weathered, her cheeks lined with parallel rows of very fine wrinkles. They make her appear older and wiser. Me, on the other hand, I look into her pale eyes and see only cunning.

"I don't know if you'll find this useful, and I admit that it's mainly based on rumor," she tells me. "The strip of land called Boomtown is owned by the Shearson Investment Group, an LLC with headquarters in Panama. I've been told by a man I dearly trust that the majority shareholder in this LLC is known to both of us. That would be Zack Butler."

CHAPTER TWENTY-ONE

DELIA

As per my instructions, Stanton Jarret has been located and detained. By Cade Barrow, as it turned out. Jarret was first arrested almost a year ago when a search warrant turned up enough coke, two ounces, to send him up for the next six to eight years. No fan of prison, Jarret agreed to inform on a regular basis, to become a kind of undercover cop. And he came through, pinpointing the smash-and-grab bandits most recent project. At the same time, he set us up. Us being the Baxter Police Department. Busy apprehending the bandits, most of the city was unpatrolled for several hours, during which a drug dealer named Stitch Kreuter was beaten to death in the home of another dealer named Heyman Weymouth.

Not that I can prove it. Not yet, anyway.

Jarret's seated when I come into the box, one wrist hand-cuffed to a metal ring bolted to the table. He starts to rise, his customary shit-eating grin on display, but resumes his seat when I smack him on the top of the head.

"Given your rap sheet," I tell him, "you'd be lookin' at six to eight years for the coke found in your home. And while I admit that your double cross can't be used against you at trial, it can and will be included in the probation report sent to the judge before sentencing. How do you think a sentencing judge will react to your treachery resulting in a murder? Remember, I don't have to prove anything, not in a probation report. Remember this, too: you could receive up to ten years." I give it a moment to sink in before continuing. "There's somewhere I have to be and I'm already late. That'll give you plenty of time to think about what you're gonna say next."

◆

The place I need to be is at Stitch Kreuter's autopsy. Gloria Meacham made the administration's wishes clear. There were three murders to be investigated and she wanted me personally involved. Danny will not be happy.

When I enter Baxter Medical Center's autopsy room, Arshan Rishnavata's bundling into a hospital gown that's much too big for his frame. Short and slim, he owns a quick smile that somehow amplifies a basic insecurity. He wants cops to respect him, even like him, and they do. But it's not enough.

"Captain Delia," he calls out as I cross the room. "I'm honored."

"You were expecting who?"

"A minion." He slides a mask over his nose and mouth, then pulls down a face shield that's been sitting on top of his head. "I don't believe you will find here anything useful, but we shall see."

Stitch Kreuter's lying on an autopsy table at the other end of the room. He's naked except for two clear plastic bags that enclose his hands. I had high hopes as I made my way to the autopsy room. Hope that Stitch had fought back, that he'd drawn blood, or scraped his attacker with his nails. That seems unlikely. Both of Stitch's hands are broken, his fingers as well, bent back or to the side. One finger is dislocated so badly it lies against the back of his wrist.

I'm looking at defensive wounds. The man saw it coming, but could do nothing about it beyond raising his hands. Average in height and weight, Stitch Kreuter would have had no chance against Heyman Weymouth. According to an extensive rap sheet, Weymouth, at six-three, weighs two hundred and sixty pounds.

The front of Kreuter's body is covered with bruises, from his shins to his throat. The savagery of the attack indicates a mindless rage that I associate with biker culture. So what? The blood found in Weymouth's home has already been typed. It matches Kreuter's blood type. But the rest of the trace evidence recovered in the house, everything from hair and fibers to saliva on the rim of a glass, awaits analysis in the state's lab.

◆

I'm not squeamish, but there's something about witnessing a human being reduced to a simple machine that makes my skin crawl. And that's what Stitch Kreuter becomes on Arshan's autopsy table. Find the loose gear, the broken connection, the burnt transistor. Remove all the parts that make the machine run. Brain, heart, lungs, spleen, on and on. Examine, measure, weigh. There seems no point, the cause of death here obvious, but Arshan observes the protocol. I have to wonder what he's searching for? Pancreatic cancer? Inflammatory bowel disease? COPD?

I'm glad when it's finally over, but still defeated. Arshan's found nothing to link Kreuter's death to his killer.

◆

Like I said, I'm not squeamish. I head directly for Lena's Luncheonette. Jarret's been stewing for several hours and it won't hurt to let him stew for a while longer. Lena's kept a promise made to me last fall. She's gone upscale, her restaurant now dominated by gleaming chrome fixtures and startlingly detailed photos of various dishes. I find a seat beneath a celadon platter holding a selection of Thai spices. At least that's what the legend on the frame declares. I have no reason to doubt the claim, but Lena, for all the upscaling, has stayed with the basics. She's still closing the restaurant at four in the afternoon, still in the kitchen at four o'clock in the morning. Frying the doughnuts that made her restaurant profitable from the day she opened the door.

"I'm waitin' on a liquor license," she tells me as she takes my order. "Then I'm gonna find me a chef. I'm thinkin' Tex-Mex-Asian. Fusion's the big thing now. Globalization for the taste buds."

I don't know if she's disappointed when I order a burger with a small garden salad and a side of onion rings. The diet will have to wait another day. Or week, or month.

Lena slides a mug of coffee in front of me a moment later and I take a few minutes to text Danny, who's in class. The message is simple. I'll probably be late getting home, in which case I'll miss Danny's game this afternoon. For now, though, Heyman Weymouth is priority number one. He's probably in the wind, returned to his biker pals, but if he's still in Baxter, or Boomtown, I intend to run him down. If he didn't kill Stitch Kreuter, he surely knows who did.

◆

I'm not at all surprised when Vern walks into the restaurant as I'm about to start on my lunch. We're in this together. It's our job, which seems nearly impossible at the moment, to guide Baxter through the construction period. Mayor Venn and Councilwoman Meacham made that much clear, as they also made clear that any failure to accomplish that end would fall back on the Baxter PD and its leadership.

"I don't have a lot of time." Vern waves Lena away and I can see he's pissed off. For all his easy charm, Vern's a law-and-order type. Looking the other way has never been part of his game plan. "I have to give a speech to the Baxter Better Business Commission in a half hour, but I want to make something clear. Let's say we isolate major criminal activity in Boomtown, say a high-end dealer. If I can't convince Sheriff Fletcher to act, we're gonna close it down ourselves. Our beloved mayor and the City Council can scream bloody murder, but the people of this city will back us if we put on a show. You understand what I'm saying?"

"A press conference with the confiscated goodies displayed on a table?" I can easily visualize the scene, having participated in similar scenes many times in the past. Kilos of drugs. Pistols, rifles, shotguns lined up. The optics are way too good for the press to ignore and they scream victory.

"Exactly. But know this, if we charge into Boomtown and there's nothing to find, we'll be hung out to dry. Now, I'll leave you to your lunch."

I lift my burger and take a bite. I appreciate Vern's attitude. What cop wouldn't? But Gloria Meacham and the mayor weren't wrong either. The Nissan plant must be finished and the workers in Boomtown are the ones who have to finish it.

CHAPTER TWENTY-TWO

DELIA

S tanton Jarret's where I left him, sitting behind a small table, his right wrist cuffed to an iron ring bolted to the tabletop. He seems relieved, but apprehensive as well. I smacked him once. Maybe I'll smack him again.

"You been thinking about what I said, Stanton? About spending the next ten years in a cage?"

Jarret's a soft man functioning in a might-makes-right world. Credit where it's due, he's dipped and dodged his way through that world with a degree of success. But there's no dipping and dodging in prison. The cons will eat him for breakfast.

"There's nothing else to think about," he admits.

"Except how to talk your way out of it."

"Yeah, except that."

I sit down at the other side of the table. "You understand, everything we do and say here is being recorded. Video and audio. You won't be able to deny anything later. I'm gonna read your rights to you now." I run them off quickly, assuming he already knows them word for word.

"Okay, I got it."

"Great. Now, do you need to use the bathroom? Are you comfortable?"

"I went a half hour ago. Had something to eat too. I'm okay."

He offers a forced smile and raises his eyebrows expectantly. Ready for question number one, but I'm not gonna help him out. I lean back and wait for him to speak first.

"Look, Captain, you asked me, and directly, to identify the smash-and-grab crew. You asked me to pinpoint their next operation. And that's what I did."

He again stops, and this time I ask a question. "We're you there when Stitch Kreuter was murdered?"

"No, I swear."

"Then you've got nothing to tell me." I rise to my feet, pleased to note Jarret's stricken expression. I'm the top of the food chain. If I walk out, he's finished. He's already copped to ownership of the cocaine found in his house.

"Okay, okay, I get it." He waits for me to sit, then opens up. "Boomtown came out of nowhere, Captain, and likewise for these New York mob guys. I been livin' in Baxter my whole life and I didn't see it comin'. Nobody I know did. But you gotta adjust. You gotta be flexible." Jarret spreads his hands, palms up, as if we're buddies sharing a basic truth. But I already know that he's an opportunistic type. Whatever he stumbles into. Weed, meth, dope, coke, even the odd burglary.

"I'm sayin' it all happened fast, especially with the New York crew. They've got their fingers into everything that happens in Boomtown and they've only been here for a few months. So, you gotta ask yourself. How could they pull it off this fast unless they planned it out before they arrived? Like carefully. I mean, think about it. A double wide showed up almost as soon as there was room for it. Two days later, there's maybe nine or ten girls at work. That's the Paradise Inn. And think about the Lucky Tavern. How'd the craps tables and the roulette wheels get in there so fast? These ain't things you buy at your local Walmart."

I wave him to a halt. I'm not here for a history lesson, but Jarret raises some interesting questions and they all point to Zack Butler.

"Fast-forward, Jarret. To how and when you set us up. No bullshit, now."

"Hey, you asked me specifically about the smash-and-grab crew. And if you remember, I offered to give you names, but you said that wasn't enough. You wanted to know where and when they'd hit next. That info I got from the man runnin' the show for the mob. Guy named Charlie, and don't ask me for his last name because I don't know and I wasn't about to ask. See, Charlie had a project he wanted to pull off, only it was in Baxter proper and he was nervous about random patrols because he was gonna be personally involved. Now everybody knows how much you wanted the smash-and-grab burglars, including Charlie. But Charlie? He also knew the crew was about to pull off a job because they were into him for a few hundred dollars of fronted dope. See, when they asked for the front, they promised to pay him back when they sold whatever they managed to steal."

I chime in with the obvious. "So, Charlie put two and two together. If we knew where the bandits would strike, we'd pull units from every corner of the city. And there wouldn't be all that many if the burglary took place late at night. So, how to convey the info to the Baxter police? That's where you came in."

"Yeah, I volunteered to play the snitch."

Play the snitch? There's no playing in Jarret's survival strategy. "In return for what, Jarret?"

Jarret's eyes widen. This is not where he wanted to go, but he can't just clam up. Not now. "A piece of whatever they took off Heyman," he finally admits.

"And what would that be?"

"Whatever he was holdin'. Coke, in this case."

"Where does Stitch Kreuter fit into the picture?"

"Stitch was one of Heyman's customers. He was gonna get them through the door."

"Who is them?"

"Charlie, Dominick, and Bruce. Dominick's muscle, and believe me, this is a man you don't wanna fuck with. Bruce manages the Paradise Inn. You know, the whorehouse."

"I wanna make sure I have this right. Charlie's running the whole operation, but he personally took part in this robbery?"

"Crazy, right? But that's Charlie. He loves the action. He didn't kill Stitch, though, and I don't think he expected Heyman to kill him. The way I heard it, Charlie didn't give a damn about the coke. He only wanted to get the Horde's attention. So, yeah, he ripped Heyman off, but he left Stitch."

"Why?"

"As a gesture of goodwill. Kind of like, we can do business together, only . . . It kinda goes blank from there, but what I'm thinkin' is that the New York crew wants to control distribution in Baxter and Boomtown. They'll buy from the Horde, or anyone else dealin' weight, but in Boomtown they run the show. No exceptions."

Jarret tries to bring his hands together, only remembering that his right hand is cuffed at the last minute. "Another reason I'm sure Charlie didn't kill Stitch is because I was there when Charlie, Dominick, and Bruce returned with the coke."

"To make sure your piece came off the top? Like before they could step on it?"

Jarret waggles his head. He's feeling good now that he's into his spiel. The man who can talk his way out of any jam. "Something like that," he admits. "But I'm just gettin' to the good part. See, Heyman wasn't alone when Charlie showed up. There was a girl there, maybe underage, and an older guy. And check this out, the girl's dressed, but the guy's stark naked. Dominick, he's a cigar store Indian. One expression, right. Grim. But even he's laughin' this time. And that's how I know Charlie didn't kill Stitch. They wouldn't be jokin' around if they just committed a murder. See, you can't touch 'em for rippin' off Heyman because Heyman can't report the robbery. But a murder that maybe Dominick committed and I know about? I never would've left the bar alive. Personally, I think Charlie thought Stitch would only catch a beatdown."

"So far, you've given me exactly nothing," I tell Jarret. "A robbery that can't be prosecuted. A murder with no identifiable witnesses. A suspect who could be in Canada by now. If this is all you got, say hello to the bologna sandwich you're gonna eat for dinner."

Jarret's still smiling, but his blue eyes narrow as he considers his prospects. "Look, I gave you the snatch-and-grab crew. That's what you wanted."

"You're repeating yourself." I fold my arms across my chest while Jarret weighs his fate. I watch him nibble at his lower lip for a moment, then his eyes widen. Did he just remember? Or was he holding back, a card up his sleeve?

"Remember I told you that there were three people in the room when Charlie showed up? And one of them was a middle-aged guy."

"Yeah, the only naked body in the room."

"Right, naked except for one item. That would be a class ring with a green stone that Charlie claims is an emerald and which he took. The guys laughed when Charlie put the ring on his finger. It only fit his pinkie, and Charlie, he barely made it through high school."

My brain is already protesting, but I have to ask the question. "Do you remember the name of the college?"

"Yeah, Stanford University."

◆

For Mayor Venn, it's shaping up to be a me-and-my-big-mouth kind of day. The mayor gave us carte blanche to work Boomtown if the original crime was committed in Baxter. And that's exactly what we're doing. That would be Cade Barrow, Blanche Weber, and myself. Blanche is behind the wheel. I'm riding shotgun. Cade is in the back, sitting next to Jarret Stanton. We're investigating the crime of robbery, specifically the robbery of a class ring by a New York wise guy named Charlie. Jarret's task is simple enough. He's going to identify our suspect, after which he'll be driven to the Greyhound Depot in Baxter. We won't force him onto a bus. No, if he wants to hang around and take his chances, he's free to do so.

We're parked a few doors away from a bar named La Oro de Mina, the Gold Mine. According to Jarret, Charlie usually spends the early evening in a back office where he meets with his crew. It's four o'clock, but there's no sign of him. I'd send Jarret inside to see if he's already here, but I'm afraid Jarret will run out the back door and keep on running until he reaches the Gulf of Mexico. It's a chance I'm not willing to take.

The clear blue skies of the last couple days are rapidly disappearing. A watery sun, strained through thickening clouds, spreads evenly over the chaos around us. Small trailers dominate the unnamed street, but there's the bar and a BBQ joint with a smoker out front. I'm thinking the food must be good—it certainly smells good, even from fifty yards away—because a steady stream of workers make their way inside, only to emerge a few minutes later carrying their dinners home.

"Hey, Jarret," Blanche asks, "you think the BBQ joint pays for protection?"

"Not yet."

"Not yet?"

"All I can say for sure is that Charlie plans to run Boomtown as if he owns it. Just now, he's focused on the Horde. Me, I think he pulled the trigger on Titus Klint."

"Did you hear that from him?"

"No, but . . . wait, there he is."

I turn my attention to the man walking along the uneven sidewalk. Over six feet tall, he's well-built, wearing an untucked white shirt with a gold pattern running up the left side. He's good-looking, too, despite an arrogant mouth that turns slightly down at the corners. He has to see me when I open the door and step out of the car, along with Cade, but he continues on his way until I step in front of him.

"Hello, Charlie," I say, laying a hand on his chest, a deliberate violation of his personal space that I'm hoping he'll take personally. His eyes do narrow, but only for a moment.

"And you would be?"

"Ah, never ask a question unless you know the answer. You must've studied law. You know, before you became a gangster."

Charlie doesn't so much as glance at Cade Barrow. "Speaking of lawyers, Captain, I'm thinkin' you might wanna talk to mine."

"About what, Charlie?"

"You tell me."

"Okay, let's talk about the ring on your pinkie. I was told you were an arrogant jerk, but this is really stupid. See, I know that ring was stolen a few nights ago. The value of the emerald, by the way, elevates the offense to a Class One felony."

He hesitates for just an instant, his eyes again narrowing, but finally smiles, revealing teeth so white they have to be porcelain caps. "You're talking about this?" He yanks the ring off his finger. "I found this ring an hour ago. Kinda nice, don't you think? But if it's stolen, why don't you take it? The ring doesn't fit me anyway." Another grin. "Are we done here?"

"One more thing, Charlie. Your last name."

"Setter. Charles V. Setter."

◆

Stanford University has its place on everybody's list of the top ten universities in the country, along with schools like Princeton, Harvard, and Yale. People who graduate from these schools don't keep their achievements a secret. That's probably true even in big cities like New York or Chicago. In failing Baxter, a city in sharp decline before Nissan came along, Stanford graduates are about as rare as Martians. They don't hide their pedigree. No, they wear thick gold rings, class rings in this case, with an emerald in the center.

I know of only one Stanford graduate in Baxter, a man named Landon Gauss. Gauss Packing was the second plant to open in Baxter and the first to close. The family fortune, by that time, had shrunk to a house in the Mount Jackson neighborhood. But the Gauss family name still has clout in Baxter, and Landon Gauss makes a decent living as an accountant and financial advisor. He's also Baxter's comptroller, with a second office inside City Hall, and the authority to review every dime of spending.

I drop Cade and Blanche off at the station before heading up to Mount Jackson in the northwest corner of the city. On the way, I pass the Gauss mansion, a Victorian extravaganza awaiting demolition as soon as a buyer can be found for its six-acre lot. The mansion's wraparound porch has fallen away from the body of the house and one of its turrets has collapsed. Every window is broken.

Needless to say, Landon Gauss has made no effort to restore the family seat. His aspirations are more modest, yet his sprawling ranch house at the foot of the hill impresses. Landon's done a lot better than most Baxterites and his home is a long way from Heyman Weymouth's home in Oakland Gardens.

Landon's married, with two children, a boy in his midteens and a girl about nine or ten. They appear with him at every city function and there's always a photo of them together, the kids in front, the proud parents behind them. His presence at Weymouth's when Stitch Kreuter was killed will destroy that image, genuine or cultivated. Me, I'm going to help the man if I can, but murder is murder. I set my phone to record as I leave the car.

CHAPTER TWENTY-THREE

DELIA

The door opens before I reach it and Landon Gauss steps out, closing the door behind him. I'm wondering what he told his family, but I'm not about to ask. There's a chance, if I move fast, I can watch the last innings of Danny's game.

"Don't mean to be rude, Delia, but my mother-in-law's visiting." Landon shrugs as if that explains it all. He's a pudgy man with a habitually worried expression that can't be hidden by a politician's mechanical grin. "So, what's up?"

I show him the ring and his breath rushes out of him as though he's been punched in his soft gut. With relief? Fear? Some combination of the two? He reaches out, but my hand closes before he can get to his property.

"You should have come forward," I tell him. "We're talking about murder, a human life taken. I understand that you're afraid, but you shouldn't have been in Weymouth's house in the first place."

Gauss draws back, his small mouth pursing. He's an aristocrat, after all, the direct descendant of a Baxter founding family. Dyke cops from Minnesota can't speak to him this way. Then he glances behind him as if he expects his mother-in-law, wife, and children to appear at his back.

"All right, Delia, I'll keep it simple. There's a knock on the door and Heyman goes to answer it. He asks who it is and I hear someone say, 'Stitch.' I don't recognize the name, but Heyman opens the door and four men push their way inside, three of them holding guns. Swear on my life, Delia, they looked like cannons." Landon's talking fast, but he can't get it out in one breath and he's forced to pause. "The first man inside pistol-whips Heyman, one time really hard, and Heyman falls to the floor. Heyman's a big man, as big as the man who hit him, but he doesn't try to get up. He rolls onto his back and says, 'Whatta ya want, Charlie?'"

"Heyman called him by name?"

"Yeah. Charlie." Landon raises a hand, revealing perfectly manicured fingernails. "I'm telling you, Delia, if Charlie didn't mean every word, he's a great actor. And the men with him, one of them anyway, had the coldest eyes I've ever seen."

Again, Gauss pauses, his expression inquisitive, as though he's expecting me to supply a detail I can't possibly know. I have nothing to say and I wave him on.

"When Heyman tells him the drugs are under the bed, I feel a little better, but not all that much. That's because I'm looking at Charlie and it's obvious how much he's enjoying his power play. So, maybe he'll take Heyman's stash and shoot all three of us. Then he tells me . . ." He has the decency to look away. "Charlie tells me to get dressed. He wouldn't do that if he intended to kill me. Then he took the ring, the one in your hand. Even that felt good. If he expected to kill me, he'd wait until I was dead, right?"

"As it turned out, yeah. So, what next?"

"Charlie told Heyman—and I'm telling you, I was amazed—that if the Horde wanted their coke back, they should contact him at some bar. The bar had a funny name . . ."

"La Mina de Oro?"

"Yeah, that's it."

"Did Heyman respond at any point?"

"Outside of telling Charlie the drugs were under the bed, he kept his mouth shut."

"What about names? Say the girl in the room. Did you get her name?"

"Sarah-Lee, no last name. One other name too. When Charlie first came in, he sent one of his men, the one with the eyes, to check if there was anyone else in the house. He called him Dominick." Gauss clenches his fist and lets his breath out. The next part will take him back to a place he'd rather not revisit. "The fourth man? The one called Stitch? I guess Charlie didn't need him anymore, because he left Stitch there. Charlie called it a gesture of goodwill."

"Do yourself a favor, Landon. Don't censor what you're about to tell me."

Landon nods, closing his eyes for just a moment. "Heyman's home was about what you'd expect from a biker. Bits and pieces scattered all over the room. I remember a motor on a table and several bike frames, cans of oil and grease, and tools. Lots of tools, including an enormous pipe wrench that Heyman picked up and swung at Stitch's head. Stitch got his arm up, and the wrench hit him near the elbow. Then he dropped to the floor and curled up, but Heyman just kept hitting him. His chest, his shoulders, his back, his legs. Like again and again, beating Stitch while Stitch was on the floor. I knew he wouldn't stop and I didn't have . . ."

"The balls?"

"Yeah, I didn't have the balls to stop him. No, I ran out of the house, Sarah-Lee right behind me."

"You're saying Stitch was alive when you left?"

"I'm not a doctor. All I can say for sure is that he wasn't moving. It looked like Heyman was beating a sack of rice." Landon runs the fingers of his right hand over his chin as he collects himself. "There's one thing you might use to find Sarah-Lee. A tattoo of a dragon, a purple dragon with green eyes. I don't know how far down it went, but the head and part of the neck extended above her collar."

"I gave the ring back," I tell Vern. I've stopped by on the way home. Danny's game is long over.

"What'd you tell our esteemed comptroller?"

"That tomorrow morning, I'll draw up an arrest warrant for Heyman Weymouth based on the statement of a confidential informant who witnessed the attack. That'll keep Landon Gauss's name out of it, at least until Heyman's apprehended. After that, we'll see how it goes."

"No protection if it means a killer goes free?"

"None at all."

We're standing on the porch, me feeling guilty. If I come inside, I'll have to spend time with Emmaline and I just don't have the energy. I want home, Danny, Zoe, and a glass of wine. Not to mention dinner and a late-night backrub.

"Landon took it well," I add.

"He was grateful?"

"We could've made him a scapegoat, but this way is better. Three murders in the last week? Bad. Already solving one? Good. And if the media decides we've got the crime wave under control, even better."

"For how long?"

"With Boomtown unpoliced? Until the next atrocity."

"Like a war between Charlie's crew and the bikers?"

"Yeah, like that."

CHAPTER TWENTY-FOUR

MAGGIE MILLER

"It's all over the news, Daddy. They've got the man who killed that dealer, Stitch Kreuter. Well, not exactly got him, but they know who he is and they'll have a warrant for his arrest by noon."

"Wouldn't be this fella named Charlie, would it?"

"'Fraid not. Somebody the name of Heyman Weymouth. Biker, according to that Katie Burke at WBAX."

The weather's turned gray, like it's April again. The May flowers will just have to wait. The clouds overhead are the color of sheet metal and dense enough to appear solid. Meanwhile, the work goes on. Beams and girders have been arriving all night. Precut in Ohio to fit together like parts of an erector set, the beams and girders vary in length and weight. Each is designed to be installed in one place and one place only. A mistake, the wrong girder in the wrong spot, can delay a project for weeks.

I learned this from Cousin Jay-Jay last night. Me and Daddy had dinner at Jay-Jay's little house in Oakland Gardens. The man's been fascinated with construction since he was a boy and the work he's doin' now has him all fired up. The money, most of which he claims to be sending home, doesn't hurt either.

We weren't at Jay-Jay's, me and Daddy, for a lecture on industrial worksites. My cousin's been employed steadily and he's a friendly type. The men he's workin' with are also friendly for the most part, like the men I met at the restaurant. They let their mouths run at coffee break and lunch, Boomtown's various pleasures and distractions being a favored topic.

The New York crew running most of those distractions has also drawn attention. Like all red-blooded Americans, when they don't actually hate New Yorkers, these workers mistrust them. But respect is a different matter, the consensus being that these are serious gangsters and it wouldn't pay to get on their bad side.

"The leader," Jay-Jay told us over an under-spiced curry, "is named Charlie. Big guy. Drives a used Honda with a SUPPORT YOUR LOCAL POLICE bumper sticker on the back. Maybe so he won't be noticed."

Daddy and I laughed at the little joke, but we'd already identified Charlie, who appears at the Paradise every morning. More than likely, he's collecting the night's take, a job he might have left to a subordinate. But as I learn more about Charlie, I get the feeling that he likes people knowin' he's a badass. He gets off on it.

There was no talk of a dead whore named Corey Miller, according to Jay-Jay. Most of his worker companions failed even to recognize her name. Those that did merely shrugged. Another whore gone to her maker.

◆

I assigned a job to Jay-Jay last night. I wanted him to drive through Boomtown in the hope of finding Charlie's car. I didn't expect much to come of the effort, but we got lucky twice. First, Charlie left his car unattended a hundred yards from his bar, La Mina de Oro. Again, that arrogance. Nobody's gonna mess with my car because I'm so big and powerrrrrrful. Second piece of luck, a steady midnight drizzle turned into a sudden deluge a moment before Jay-Jay happened by and the sidewalks emptied. It took him all of twenty seconds to attach a GPS locator to the underside of Charlie's Honda. Professional grade, the locator's protected from water and pebbles by a hard case, while its magnets will hold it securely to the gas tank.

At Bagram, every transportation vehicle was equipped with a GPS locator. Factory-installed, of course. But locators small enough to hold in the palm of your hand can be legally purchased from hundreds of websites. The one on

Charlie's car is functioning perfectly. I'm following it on a laptop, the beep-beep-beep steady. Until a few minutes ago, the Honda was parked in front of a house in a neighborhood called Norwood. I used Google Maps to locate the home. Small, but well-maintained, like others on the block, a white picket fence at the edge of the front lawn projects an image familiar to rural Kentuckians. We ain't rich, but we ain't shootin' dope either.

Charlie's moving east now along Maple Street. Headed right here, most likely, for his morning visit to the Paradise Inn. The many pleasures offered by the Paradise are not on Charlie's agenda. Not unless Charlie's the fastest gun in the Midwest. He doesn't stay inside more than ten minutes. Me, I'm assuming he's there to pick up the prior night's take, so it's where he goes next that matters. I don't think he's keeping the loot from the Paradise and his other enterprises under a mattress. He'll take it to a location where he believes it'll be safe.

Daddy's sitting next to me. He gets cold easily these days and he's bundled up in a heavy woolen blanket. There's coffee, as usual, and corn muffins. I bought the corn muffins late yesterday afternoon at a bakery-diner called Lena's Luncheonette. The luncheonette is a cop hangout, always a good sign, and their doughnuts and muffins are off the charts.

"Say, look here, Maggie," Daddy says. He's watching the local news on my cell phone. "They've found the murder weapon. The one killed that biker, Stitch Kreuter. Probably, anyway."

"How so?"

"Sayin' a jogger found it by the side of the road. Lyin' in the grass. Hang on a sec."

Daddy focuses on the phone's screen as Bertha Framm comes out of her house. On his leash, Stonewall keeps pace, his head at her knee. She's wearing a Christian sweatshirt, a hoodie this time:

FAITH

OVER

FEAR

"Well, good morning," Bertha says as she comes up to us.

"Good morning," Daddy returns. "Name's Aaron Miller."

I register Bertha's confusion and jump right in. "Daddy's havin' one of his good days," I explain. "Daddy, this is our neighbor across the way, Bertha Framm. And that beautiful dog by her side is named Stonewall."

"Had a cousin named Stonewall," Daddy says. "Named after the general. Stonewall Garcia."

"How do, Mr. Miller."

I don't know what Daddy plans to say next, because a car, a brown Honda, turns onto the block, interrupting the conversation. I know who the car belongs to, and so does Bertha. She stares at the driver as she draws a deep breath.

"Ain't no place," she says, "the devil don't visit."

I'm thinking the Paradise Inn is just the place the devil might visit, along with a few dozen fallen angels. But it's just more of the same. If Bertha recognizes Charlie, the man's surely made no effort to move in the shadows. He makes no effort now, stepping out of the little car and walking right at us. Bertha's eyes widen and her head swivels left and right, a prey animal looking for escape.

"Believe I'll skedaddle," she announces. "Let Stonewall do his thing."

Charlie gives Stonewall a wide berth as he approaches, something else I register. The man's nervous around dogs. But if he's nervous around humans like me and Daddy, he doesn't show it.

"Well, good mornin' to you, Mr. Charlie." I get my two cents in before he can speak. Daddy follows up quickly.

"Do we know this man, honey?"

"Not as such, Daddy, but I believe he knew Corey."

"Corey's dead, Maggie."

"Which is how come I used the past tense." I wink at Charlie. "Daddy's havin' one of his good days."

Charlie's a large man and he's lookin' like he wants to shut my fresh mouth. As Daddy has a .45 caliber pistol beneath the blanket folded over his lap, that would be a big mistake. Then he surprises me.

"You date?" Charlie asks.

"No sir, not at the moment. I'm occupied these days by more serious matters."

"And they would be?"

"And they would be my sister, name of Corey Miller. As I said, I believe you knew her."

Charlie squats, so that our faces are on the same level. "Not personally, although I've seen her around. As have many."

I'm not prepared to escalate the banter. It's very familiar, though, as it would be for any investigator. Charlie's testing me. Can I be intimidated? Can I be provoked? Either would be viewed as an advantage. Only problem for Mr. Charlie, I'm not showin' fear and I'm not angry. I'm studying him as he studies me.

"Tell me what you hope to accomplish, camped here, stirring my pot like you were a chef."

"I want justice for my sister. As you know well."

"You do, huh? So, where were you while she was still alive?" When I don't respond, he continues. "How about money, instead? Reparations for the unfortunate accident that befell your sister. Would that work? Because I need you to go away and patience ain't my strong point. Never was."

"What's he talkin' about?" Daddy asks.

"I believe he's issuin' a threat, Daddy."

"Why is that? We ain't done nothin' to nobody."

"Mr. Charlie finds us inconvenient." I nod to Charlie. "Sorry, but money will not do the trick. My sister, dumped like a rotting corpse of a dog . . ."

"I did not kill your sister."

"No, you didn't. But someone did. Her death's been declared a homicide."

I don't know what Charlie intends to say, but he's about to say something because his mouth opens, then snaps shut as a car rounds the corner. The car's black with a light bar across the top; bound by a gold line, the words *Baxter Police Department* are arranged in a circle on the door. The driver, Captain Mariola, waves as she comes up the street. There's someone beside her, another woman.

"I did not arrange this, Mr. Charlie. Did you?"

Charlie stares at the cruiser until it rolls to a stop and both cops get out. He doesn't seem upset, only thoughtful. "You think about what I said. Compensation for the accident that killed your sister. And don't be listening to the bullshit comin' from the cops. They got their own motives here. Your sister liked her goodies. Every night, Maggie. She loved a taste, expected it. The possibility of an overdose comes with the territory. No one killed your sister. She killed herself."

◆

Charlie walks past Captain Mariola and her companion, Detective Weber. I hear Mariola call out, "Hello, Charlie." Charlie doesn't answer. He heads for the Paradise, or struts, really, his walk halfway to a snarl. Leaving me to consider the question he'd posed. *Where were you while she was still alive?* But it wasn't me who up and disappeared. And there wasn't ever a time when my sister couldn't reach me, even when I was deployed. And I did try to contact her, many, many times until she changed her phone number and email address. That should let me off the hook. Right?

"Say, I remember you," Daddy says. "You're the chief."

"Captain Mariola," Mariola responds. "How are you, sir?"

Daddy looks over at me. "Am I sick?"

The corners of Mariola's mouth rise a few millimeters as she smothers the beginnings of a smile. "Glad to see your father's feeling better," she says.

"Yes, ma'am, he's havin' a good day."

"I can see that. Say, Charlie there, he didn't threaten you, did he?"

"No, Captain. Only stopped by to offer his condolences." I nod to Detective Weber. "Good morning to you, Detective. What can we do for y'all?"

Weber speaks first, actually stepping toward us while Mariola fades into the background. Not her eyes, though. Mariola's eyes are front and center.

"We stopped by to let you know the DNA results are back," Weber says. "Confirming that the victim in this case is your sister, Corey Miller. You can have her transported to a funeral home at any time. Just have the funeral director call the pathology department at Baxter Medical."

I think I'm supposed to be grateful, to offer thanks, but it's almost like I'm hearin' that Corey's dead for the first time, like there's no bringin' her back, like it's finished, final, over and out. I hear my daddy sob and I know it's for real, not pretendin' now, no game to play.

I put my arm around Daddy's bony shoulders. Growin' up, he seemed a god to me and Corey, but he failed the both of us and maybe one of us makin' her escape is all that could be hoped for.

CHAPTER TWENTY-FIVE

MAGGIE MILLER

D etective Weber and her boss mutter their condolences, then head for the hills. Or they would if there were any hills within miles. Around us, the Boomtown symphony continues, diesel motors pulling trucks under heavy load, a pile driver slammin' away, workers comin' and goin'. They glance our way as they pass. A few wave. They've seen me with the cops, and with Charlie, who leaves the Paradise and returns to his car without glancing our way.

"C'mon, Daddy, there's work to get done." I flip open my laptop and monitor the tracking app. Beep-beep, beep. Charlie hasn't traveled any great distance. His car's parked close to Baxter Boulevard, probably in an alleyway behind the stores.

Daddy and I head off a moment later, after I switch the tracking app to my phone. We find Charlie's empty Honda behind a still-closed hardware store. I drive past, hook a U-turn, and park across the street, keeping the Honda in view. Fifteen minutes later, a rear door opens and Charlie emerges, followed by a woman who pauses long enough to lock the door behind her. We're too far away to make much of anything besides her blond hair and a lavender business suit that flatters her soft figure. But we don't miss Charlie's arm as it slides around her waist.

"You think we're lookin' at Charlie's girlfriend?" Daddy asks.

"Can't say for sure." I watch Charlie and his companion get into Charlie's car, watch Charlie drive to the far end of the alley. When he turns right, then disappears, I put my car in gear and pull into the alley, stopping by the door used by Charlie and his companion. A small sign above the narrow door reads: STARDUST JEWELERS.

"You figure that's where the money goes?" Daddy asks as the Honda heads for the opposite end of the alley.

With his fingers in all those pies, in prostitution and gambling and shylocking and drugs, profits inevitably flow from many locations. Those revenues must be gathered first, then safeguarded until they can be shipped east. I suppose Charlie could appoint someone to stand guard 24/7, a strategy sure to draw unwanted attention. But jewelry stores have safes, usually safes too big to carry away. Otherwise, there'd be burglars climbin' through the windows every night.

"Let's not jump to conclusions, Daddy. Let's see if he returns tomorrow morning."

"Got a better idea. Let's have Jay-Jay install a camera." He points to a chain-link fence overgrown with a climbing weed. "Do that, we can enjoy our mornin' coffee in peace."

◆

With time to kill and nothin' substantial in our bellies, we head for Boomtown Eats. The tent's crowded with workers coming off the night shift, the buffet line dominated by stainless steel tubs filled with scrambled eggs, bacon, more bacon, ham steaks, sausages, home fries, and more bacon. Single-serving boxes of cereal sit on a display case, along with bananas, oranges, and plastic containers of fruit salad, with no takers as far as I can tell.

Daddy and I, our trays loaded, look over the crowded room in search of seats, only to find Yank Framm pointing to a pair of empty chairs beside him. Perfect. I lay my tray on the table as we exchange good mornin's.

"Question I've been meanin' to ask you," I say. "Are you Bertha Framm's husband?"

"Yes, I am."

"Guess that makes us neighbors."

"Rightly so."

The gleam in Yank's eye leads me to conclude that he may not be as committed to the Lord as his wife, but I'm not here to judge. I recognize several of the other men from our last visit and renew acquaintances. Keeping it low-key until I'm asked the question I'm waiting for.

"Have you heard anything about your sister?"

"Yes, sir. Captain Mariola stopped by my house this morning. Told me that Corey's body will be released soon as I pay a funeral home to take it. I plan to have a viewin' tomorrow and I'm hopin' folks'll turn out. Corey deserves to be recognized. A life's a life, the way I been taught."

I leave off at that point, concentrating on my breakfast, as delicious as it is unhealthy. The men and women around are hungry after a night of calorie-burning work. I have no excuse, Daddy either. He's not sayin' much, but he's shovelin' biscuits and gravy into his mouth, regular as a factory robot.

I'm content because the conversation first turns to a general discussion of Charlie and his mob, then to possible suspects in Corey's murder.

◆

Fifteen minutes later, a boy-man follows me and Daddy as we leave the restaurant. The boy-man's name is Eliot. He's tall and strong across the shoulders and chest, with the last traces of adolescence visible in the acne running across his left cheekbone.

"Speak to you for a minute?"

"Sure."

"About the Paradise? I've been there."

"Go ahead, Eliot. We ain't squeamish."

"Okay, well, the Paradise is managed by two men. There's women, of course, but they're not in control. No, it's Bruce and a younger man named Gene." Eliot hesitates for a moment, then plunges forward. "I been seein' one of the girls, name of Stephanie. I mean outside the house, just the two of us."

"Your business, Eliot. Strictly."

"Okay, Maggie. Lillian claims Bruce or Gene hand out drugs after the doors close. Like every night. A reward, right? And that includes the night your sister overdosed."

"Will Lillian talk to me?"

"No, ma'am. Too scared. These guys, they got big ambitions and they'll whack anyone who gets in their way. Fact, Lillian's thinkin' they . . ." He waits for me to nod before continuing. "She believes they whacked Titus Klint the same night they left your sister in that lot. So, I'm just sayin', you oughta be watchin' your backs. Like every minute."

◆

The Fulton Funeral Home is exactly as advertised. It's homey. A large white colonial with navy shutters and a gray roof, with an American flag out front and an appropriate black double door. An oversized sitting room with comfy couches and armchairs in muted shades of gray and green and blue greets me and Daddy when we come through the door. As does John Fulton himself, a tall, solid man in a gray suit, blue tie, and a starched shirt so white I'm reaching for my sunglasses.

"Good afternoon," he announces, his tone somber. "What can I do for you?"

"We'd like to make arrangements for a funeral service."

John Fulton leads us to an office just off the sitting room. He gestures to armchairs set before a highly polished wooden desk.

"You'll please excuse my daddy," I explain as I take a seat. "He's not himself these days. But I'm hopin' we can make arrangements for my sister. That would be Corey Miller."

John Fulton's good. I catch only a glimmer of surprise when he realizes who we are. Then the dollar signs return, as does his solicitous manner.

"Corey's body is at Baxter Medical Center," I explain, "in the pathology department. She needs to be . . ."

"That won't be a problem, but what have you planned for her funeral?"

"We mean to have a proper viewing tomorrow afternoon."

"Will you need a gravesite?"

"No, sir. As I believe you know, my sister was murdered. Plain as that. And what we're fearin', me and my daddy, is she'll be forgotten if we leave Baxter. Lackin' that consideration, we'd take Corey back to where she came from and bury her with her relations."

Fulton nods. "If you plan to stay in Baxter, can I assume you want your sister cremated?"

"That's exactly right, but first there needs be a viewing. I won't just put her in a fire like I was tryin' to see her gone for good. No, sir, I want a proper viewing and a preacher to send her off."

◆

Back in the car, I place a call to Mr. Basil Ulrich at the *Baxter Bugle*. He approached me one afternoon, complaining about Katie Burke gettin' all the good interviews. I'd been interviewed by Katie exactly twice, and neither could be termed extensive. But I took the reporter's card, thinkin' there might come a time when I'd need him. Which is now.

"Have you heard about my sister?" I ask once I get through. "Her body's been released."

"First I've learned of it, Ms. Miller.

"I'd appreciate you callin' me Maggie."

"Well, sure, Maggie."

"Can I speak frankly here?"

"Speak away."

"I'm afraid the police are hopin' this whole thing, my sister bein' murdered, will just up and fly away. Like back where we come from. But I don't plan on goin' anywhere till I see justice done. No, Basil, I'm gonna have my sister cremated and keep her close. Before that happens, though, I've authorized a public viewing tomorrow from one o'clock to seven o'clock with a service at six. Anybody interested in justice for Corey Miller is welcome."

Twenty minutes after I hang up, Katie Burke calls. She's in a bar with Basil Ulrich, an accidental meeting, and will I please, please, please give her an interview.

Yes, I will.

◆

I can't say I'm feeling bad as Daddy and I drive on back to our little trailer. Events are unfolding as I hoped they would. Only, I was a cop long enough to sympathize with other cops and I've been trashing Baxter's cops for the last few days. I've been implying that their efforts lack urgency. And why? Because dead whores don't count. What we call this, where I hail from, is bullshit. Mariola and her squad are competent and dedicated. They proved that when Corey's death was declared a homicide. It would have been so, so easy to rule it accidental and walk away.

Detectives can't control the hands they're dealt. Some hands are good and some are bad. This one, the murder of Corey Miller, falls on the bad side. Without forensic evidence, you have to put together a circumstantial case. That requires witnesses. Mariola's visit this morning leads me to believe she knows that Corey worked at the Paradise. And given the time of death, it's almost certain that Corey died inside the trailer. That's where her witnesses, if there are any, can be found. Effectively controlled by Charlie and his thugs.

"What you thinkin' about, baby girl?" Daddy asks.

"I'm thinkin' about Mariola and that we're doin' her wrong."

"How's that?"

"She ain't neglectin' us, Daddy. And come tomorrow, we're gonna put the heat on when she in no way deserves it."

Daddy laughs that mean laugh I remember from when me and Corey were growin' up. "It ain't that she don't deserve the heat. It's just we're puttin' the heat on for the wrong reason."

"And what's the right reason?"

"She's usin' us as bait."

CHAPTER TWENTY-SIX

CHARLIE

I shouldn't be here. I don't know if you can call it conscience, but some part of my brain I can't shut up keeps nagging me. You're the smarts of the organization, the peak and the base of the pyramid. If you go down, the operation goes down. And Ricky Ricci? Being who he is? Failure is not an option.

That's what I keep tellin' myself, only I'm not listening. No, what I'm hearin' is that some opportunities come along only once. Like creeping through what passes for a forest toward what passes for a canyon in this tabletop of a state. We're not talking about a Rocky Mountain canyon deepened a few millimeters a year over millions of years. We're talkin' about a depression, a gully, hollowed out by dynamite and steam shovel, a limestone quarry with sheer cliffs on both sides of a little creek. The cliff on my side is about sixty feet from the stream, leaving plenty of room along its banks for amateur naturalists or drug-addled bikers.

In this case, the bikers have won the competition. The Horde has been using this spot for years. As a hangout, a rallying point, a home for homeless bikers. Just now, they have a big decision to make. I gave them an ultimatum, underlined by the death of Titus Klint, and they have to decide what to do next. And whatever that something might be, it'll have to be done as a group. One on one, they can't survive. Not on our turf. Not in Boomtown.

We can hear them, me and Dominick, as we creep forward, keeping inside the shadows thrown by the stringy trees between us and the edge of the cliff. Two hundred yards behind us, parked on a hiking trail, a pair of our associates sit in a Jeep Wrangler with a beefed-up suspension. They'll back us if we stumble into lookouts. Not likely, though.

First thing, according to several Baxter locals, one an ex-member, the gang's been using this spot for years. Second, it's three o'clock in the morning and I can hear some crazy amalgamation of country and rap bouncing between the cliffs on either side of the stream. I don't know what sound system they're using, powered by a vehicle obviously, but it's playing at a volume that speaks to the condition of the bikers close by. Stoned, is what I'm thinking, stoned and tired and feeling a hundred percent safe on their home turf.

Overhead, the moon is a pale blur behind thin clouds, the stars completely obscured. My only fear at this point is that I'll stumble over the edge of the cliff, but the trees give way about thirty feet from the rim. I stop and kneel, Dominick beside me, and look around for anybody or anything that might prevent us from completing the mission. I find only an owl sitting on a branch, staring straight at us. I understand its point of view. The owl is a pure predator. It would carry us back to its nest and feed us to its young if it was big enough. Survival of the fittest. Or the biggest, or the smartest.

Dominick crawls to the edge of the cliff and peers down for a moment before moving away. "To ya left, about fifty feet."

I follow directions. This is Dominick's world, after all, the whole plan his idea. New men have been trickling in for the past week. There's almost forty of us now, scattered throughout Boomtown. In the bars, in the Paradise, in the new stores we control. Dominick is their commanding officer, my Secretary of Defense, a man with long experience. We're prepared for an attack.

That's exactly what I don't want. Boomtown is a gold mine. The money's pouring in and it'll keep pouring in unless . . . Unless there's a gun battle involving seventy or eighty combatants firing off a thousand rounds of ammo inside three minutes. Do the math. A thousand rounds, eighty shooters, hundreds of innocent bystanders.

The politicians would have to act. Cops would pour in, be they Baxter cops, deputy sheriffs, or state troopers. And my boss? His heart would surely break if his little gold mine had to shut down. Even temporarily.

◆

"Okay, boss, here we go. Take a quick look."

I come forward on my belly until my head clears the edge. Only then do I open my eyes. I'm not big on heights, but there's no getting out of it this time. I'm dizzy for just a second, then pick out what I need to see.

The creek is flanked by sandbars that give way to dirt and rocks, the dirt and rocks to a flat sheet of limestone where the quarrymen cut and leveled the stone. The Horde has taken advantage of this table, and for a good reason. Leave a four-hundred-pound Harley Davidson motorcycle parked on dirt? If it rains and that dirt gets muddy, bikes are gonna fall over. Better to park your bikes safe and sound on a limestone platform. Even if you have to park them almost on top of one another.

I rise to my knees as Dominick slides out of his backpack and reaches inside. He comes up with two M67 hand grenades, recovered from our storage locker sixty miles north of Baxter. My heart's racing now and I can't slow it down. I don't tell myself to cool off, because I know from experience my adrenals won't listen. I need to go with the flow, the flow of adrenaline. Channel the energy. Focus, focus, focus.

Neither of us, me and Dominick, are familiar with hand grenades. We're not military types, not about to risk our lives for a flag. Money, yes. Flag, no. But we do have a man in town, Marty Marillo, who made it to Ranger training school before he was dishonorably discharged after an affair with the colonel's wife.

Marty's instructions were simple. If you fire a gun by accident, at least the barrel's not pointed at your head. You fuck up with a hand grenade, they'll have to find your head. The M67's called a pineapple by soldiers, but it's shaped more like a Christmas tree bulb, the body rounded to make it easier to grip. It has two parts that command attention, the pin and the handle. The way it works, if you squeeze the handle when you pull out the pin, the grenade doesn't arm itself. It won't until you let go of the handle, called the spoon, which breaks off. From that point, you have six seconds to throw the grenade before it goes boom. Marty's instructions in this regard were real simple. Don't let go of that spoon until the last second, an instant before the grenade leaves your hand.

Dominick and I are now about ten feet apart, with the mass of parked motorcycles directly below. The bikers themselves are about fifty yards to our right. The blast and flame of an M67 has a kill radius of about fifteen feet. The shrapnel generated from the casing travels much further, but killing bikers isn't our goal tonight. We're more into killing their bikes. On foot, they pose no threat.

Dominick signals me to kneel a foot or so from the edge, then motions me to toss the grenade underhand. Me, I have a death grip on that spoon as I pull the pin. I'm half expecting the grenade to blow there and then, but it lies quietly in my hand. Reassuring? My heart's beating so fast it's about to explode.

Dominick raises his left hand. "One, two, three."

I flinch when I let go of the grenade and the handle flies off, only to have my fear give way to a stupendous sense of exhilaration as both grenades disappear on their way to the bottom of the cliff.

"C'mon, boss, let's get the fuck outta here."

But I don't move, not until the grenades explode, almost simultaneously, followed by a burst of flame that lights the rock face on the other side of the creek. Only then do I rise and fall back a few feet as the gas tanks on the bikes, torn apart by the blast and the shrapnel, blow off like a string of firecrackers, scattering still more flame and shrapnel. Then I'm finally running for the Jeep, outpacing Dominick, who grunts with every step.

◆

I can barely stop myself. I wanna whoop it up. I wanna let go of the exhilaration that replaced the fear I felt when I yanked the pin out of that grenade. We've pulled it off. We've struck a blow the Horde will never forget. Their bikes are their pride. Their bikes are who they are. Their very expensive, customized choppers. And how many dead? How many wounded?

Like I said at the beginning, I shouldn't be here. I should be planning, not executing, but I live for this. I live for the risk and the reward, even knowing that if I keep taking risks, it'll go bad sooner or later. Long shots win races too.

This time, though, I'm not afraid of pursuit. Certainly not by the Horde, and not by the cops either. Knob Canyon is fairly remote and the first responders will come in through a road that leads to the bottom, to the wounded and the dead. With no idea, at that point, what happened, they'll stay put until they have answers. Meanwhile, we're running over back roads, another hats off to Dominick, who mapped the route. Ten minutes from now, we'll enter an interstate. Just another SUV rollin' down the highway.

◆

Adelyn's still up when I walk into her house, sitting in a chair, sipping at a glass of wine. She doesn't know what or where, only that something was up, something big. A woman of long experience, she's wearing a white negligee and a knowing smile enhanced by lipstick the color of a high-end ruby. She rises, slowly, as if we had all the time in the world, then leads me into the bedroom.

We don't speak as she undresses me and lays me on the bed, as she tucks a pillow under my head. I close my eyes as her hands slide over my body, my throat, my chest. Bright as an exploding star, I see that first flash again, the flames reflected in the cliff face on the far side of the creek, the rock itself on fire. I feel Dominick's hand on my shoulder, urging me to leave. Instead, I watch those gas tanks explode, even though I'd already turned away. I see slices of hot metal ripping through the air, bikers too stunned to get out of the way. I hear their screams, though I couldn't possibly have heard them.

I like what I see, what I hear. As I like what Adelyn does to me. This moment is what I have and it's enough. Fuck the future.

CHAPTER TWENTY-SEVEN

CHARLIE

U p in the morning and back to work. Or I will be after I finish the breakfast Adelyn's prepared. Adelyn's going on about the Stardust and what she could do with the store if given the opportunity.

"I had two men come in yesterday, one in the morning, one in the afternoon. They wanted to look at engagement rings. Five minutes later, they walked out the door. That's because the rings in our display cases are such crap even the yokels aren't fooled." She sits down on the far side of the table. "Before they walked out, I asked them how much they were lookin' to spend. Six thousand dollars, Charlie. And I'm sure I could've convinced them to spring for eight if I had something decent to sell."

"Selling jewelry's not the point, Adelyn. Not sellin' jewelry and makin' it appear that we're sellin' jewelry is what the game's all about."

At this point, I could give Adelyn a lecture about the retail jewelry business. About a high-dollar inventory that moves very slowly. About reliance on Christmas and June weddings to stay afloat. You compensate with a three hundred percent markup, followed by a twenty-five-percent-off sale. And whenever the economy takes a nosedive, you hang on by your fingernails.

I'm not gonna deliver the lecture, not now, because the only thing I really want to do at this point is turn on the local news. Yeah, the explosions and the fires were impressive, but how much damage did they do? And how many casualties were there, dead and wounded? Still, I don't even suggest turning on the TV. Adelyn knows something was up last night, she's not an idiot, but I don't intend to even hint at what it was. Let her draw her own conclusions. As long as she can't quote me.

We have an understanding, Adelyn and I. It's more than don't ask, don't tell. Sooner or later, what with the store and her house inside Baxter, the cops are gonna knock on her door. My instructions are simple: Ask for a lawyer. If they say you're not a suspect and not entitled to a lawyer, walk away. You're not obliged to cooperate. And that's true even if you're an eyewitness to murder.

"This thing with the store?" Adelyn says. "It's a chance, right? For a woman who's spent most of her life in the game? I can't go back to hooking."

"I don't want you to," I say, surprising myself. "And I'll try to set you up with the store after we leave. Hear me? After we pull out, which is at least eighteen months from now, I'll try to leave you with the store. Until then, profit just ain't the point."

I stand up. Collections need to be made and I don't want to deviate from my normal routine. Just in case someone's watching. Adelyn follows me to the door. She kisses me on the cheek and says, "Thank you, Charlie." For just an instant, I think I'm feeling an emotion, but then she ruins the moment by adding, "But we can still go upscale, right?"

◆

I flip on the radio as I drive toward Boomtown. Three dead, sixteen wounded, extensive property damage. A reporter named Jack Catton's at the scene, but the cops won't let him close enough to describe the carnage. Catton does manage to interview the Leland County sheriff, Elvin Morrow. There were a series of explosions, Morrow confirms, origin unknown. Drugs were also found on scene, though not in the possession of any individual. Is it possible, Catton wants to know, that the bikers set off the initial explosion themselves? Perhaps accidentally?

"I won't speculate, Jack. We're just beginning what promises to be a long investigation. At this point, we can't rule anything out."

Music to this gangster's ears. I feel that same rush, though not as strong as last night, and I quickly stifle the exhilaration. Boomtown will belong to us exclusively. No competition. But not Baxter. First, Baxter's under the control of the Baxter PD and there's a minor bust every few days. Better it be some local and not one of my people. As long as the Baxter dealers buy from us, they're free to service their customers as they see fit. Knowing, of course, that if they get busted and snitch, they'll go the way of Titus Klint.

I've calmed by the time I reach the Paradise and not even the presence of Maggie Miller and her cuckoo father upsets me. Maggie's laptop is open and it's likely she's aware of what happened to the Horde in Leland County. Hopefully, she'll think twice before she runs her mouth at her sister's viewing. Hopefully, she'll reconsider my generous offer. I'm willing to go five grand if she'll leave town with her sister's ashes.

◆

The Paradise Inn's interior is about what you'd expect. Patterned red wallpaper with a velvety feel, black leather couches and chairs arranged on a blood-red carpet, a plain wooden bar with shelves behind it, a condom dispenser in a corner. Numerous paintings imitate the more lurid offerings of the baroque era and the space reeks of cheap room deodorizer.

Bruce greets me when I come through the door, but he doesn't tell me what I want to hear. "Some of the girls wanna go to Corey's viewing," he says. "Pay their respects." Then he shrugs, setting his jowls in motion. "They're, like, pretty determined."

I walk to the bar and pull a Coke from the soft-drink chest. As I pop the cap, I make a decision I don't really wanna make. My whores have to go, replaced with hookers who never heard of Maggie Miller. There's another decision I have to make, but I don't have to make it now. Bruce has to go too. Because the more I think about it, the more I'm coming to believe that Bruce murdered Corey Miller by feeding her a dose of fentanyl he knew she couldn't survive.

Bad Bruce. Maybe dead Bruce.

◆

Later is later, and now is now. I've kept my hands off the Paradise, left it to Bruce. No more. I head for the rooms in the back, opening doors, yanking whores out of bed.

"In the front, right the fuck now."

One girl resists, shooting off her big mouth about how she's not a dog and she won't be treated like a dog. A backhand across the mouth adjusts her attitude. I'm not playin' here. Five minutes later, they're assembled, eight girls in various states of undress, one completely naked.

"Get a robe, for Christ's sake." I'm standing in the middle of the room, staring at each of the girls in turn, wondering if any will meet my gaze. None do. Meantime, I'm not angry, just annoyed at having to deal with this Maggie Miller bullshit. I'm doin' what Bruce, if he was a decent manager, would already have done.

"I don't know what you're thinkin, maybe that you're livin' legit, that you're good citizens, you can go where you want, do what you want. Well, you can stick that bullshit up your asses. You're whores, engaged in criminal activities for which you can be arrested. If that should happen, it'll come back on my operation, which is a development I'm gonna prevent. Any way I have to."

The women are pulling back. I can see it in their eyes. They're not gonna challenge me, not to my face. No, they'll watch and wait and eventually do whatever they want. That's what I'm reading and I need to make myself clear.

"You're not goin' to that viewing, or whatever Maggie Miller wants to call it. Not one of you. You're gonna stay right here and you're gonna do your jobs. You don't like that? Then pay your fucking debts and move on. Like far away, like to another state, like to another country."

Rita Lafayette, Corey's roommate, suddenly finds the courage to speak. Thin, with a sharp nose and a tight body, she raises her dark eyes to meet mine. "What about Corey?" she asks. "Murdered and dumped. That ain't right."

"Corey overdosed. That's all. And nobody forced her to put that shit up her nose. Just like nobody forces you to put shit up your nose, or down your throat, or wherever you put it. You can just say no." I step toward Rita, moving close enough to tower above the small woman. "But if you don't, if you don't say no? Do I need to explain the risks? As for where Corey's body was found, sometimes events pile up and you have no choice. But it doesn't matter. None of it. Not whether she overdosed or whether she was murdered. You're gonna keep your noses out of my business. If you don't, I'll make you *wish* you died from an overdose."

I stop for a moment, letting my eyes move from one whore to another. "Anybody think I'm bluffing? Anyone volunteering to prove it one way or the other? How 'bout you, Virginia?" Virginia's sitting on the floor, her hand covering an eye already blackening.

"No," she says.

"No what?"

"No, I don't think you're bluffing."

◆

I head out to complete the morning's collections, ignoring Maggie Miller's wave as I drive off. Forty minutes later, I'm en route to the Stardust when I receive a text message from Ricky Ricci: *Morning Bird Eleven.* Ricky loves his little codes, simplistic as they are. He wants me to call him on my satellite phone at eleven this morning. I don't know what he wants, but at least I won't have to call him again tomorrow. Probably.

I come into the Stardust's office through the back door. First thing, I count the take, more than twenty fat ones. One day, right? And now I'm smiling. Twenty-plus thousand dollars, with the drug business still in its infancy. A month from now, the take will triple.

Business, business, business. When I walk into La Mina, Sal, our bartender, is busy stocking shelves. "You hear?" he asks.

"Hear what?"

"They arrested Heyman Weymouth. Found him in the canyon after the explosions. Wounded."

"But not dead?"

"Stable condition."

I'd prefer him dead, but does it really matter? To Mariola, definitely. A killer arrested, a murder cleared. No bad news in that. Weymouth can testify to the robbery, but not without admitting what was stolen. Besides, I left Weymouth's two guests alive, though I don't expect they'll be anxious to cooperate.

I head into the office and call Ricky on the satellite phone. Me, I'm a technological moron. A hundred years ago, I would've been neutered by the eugenics movement. But I'm told the conversations are heavily encrypted on both ends. Even if the signal's intercepted, it would take one of the spy agencies, NSA or CIA, to unscramble the conversation.

"Heard about the incident last night with the bikers," Ricky says after we exchange good mornings. "Nice work, very nice. See, I been reaching out through a friend of ours for the past couple weeks. Tryin' to shore up our supply. So, the friend calls me back this morning. The bikers are yesterday's news and their source, some bullshit cartel or other, wants to make nice with the winners. That's how the beaners work. Loyalty don't count for shit. It's a dog-eat-dog world and they'll deal with the dog who takes the last bite."

"Which is us."

"Exactly. We get an exclusive in Baxter and Boomtown, exactly what we wanted. Tonight, you'll be contacted by a beaner named Chaco. Be in your office. And one thing, Charlie. You don't fuck with these guys. I know you like to play games, but this time you gotta keep your dick in your pants. Hear me, Charlie? You can negotiate price. Fine. But if they even think that you're fuckin' with 'em, pieces of your body are gonna be found in cornfields."

In fact, I plan to bring order to Boomtown. Between Titus Klint and the Horde, we've made all the points we need to make. It's zero tolerance from here on. No robberies, muggings, burglaries, assaults, rapes. Just now, the cops are standing off. The Baxter cops, the county sheriff and his deputies, the state troopers. The best way to maintain the status quo? Peace in the valley.

CHAPTER TWENTY-EIGHT

DELIA

Word first reached me at four o'clock, long before sunrise, but I'm only now getting the details. Heyman Weymouth's been formally arrested by the Leland County sheriff, Elvin Morrow. His numerous cuts have been stitched up and he presently occupies a hospital bed, to which he's cuffed. I've already dispatched two patrol cops to Mercy Hospital. They'll carry a formal warrant and escort him to our jail when he's cleared to travel, in a couple days at most.

I'm in the kitchen, slicing and dicing strawberries, bananas, and papaya. It's wholesome day in the Mariola house. The dawn of a new health-conscious era that might, if I employ all the willpower at my command, last a week. My phone's propped up on the counter and I'm talking to Leila Dox, Leland County deputy sheriff.

"The bikes are gone, Delia," she tells me. "Melted almost. There can't be more than two in working condition and even those are scorched."

"Any thoughts on the cause?"

"Yeah, a hand grenade. Or more than one."

"Seriously?"

"We found the pins on top of the bluff." She laughs. "Once the explosions stopped, bikers scattered in all directions. The ones not wounded or dead. But there's nowhere to go, really, and we've been picking them up all night. Nobody saw anything. That's the party line, which you'd expect. But my instinct? They're telling the truth for once in their miserable lives. Somebody snuck up to the edge of the cliff and dropped those grenades. Not on the bikers, but on the motorcycles. I think the bikes were the target."

Danny takes that moment to wander into the kitchen. He's rubbing his eyes, still groggy as he heads for the coffeepot, another sign that he's growing up. And if that isn't enough, Fetchin' Gretchen, Danny's first girlfriend, is coming for dinner tonight. Fetchin' Gretchen's the name I've chosen for the girl, who I've never actually met, but already hate for taking Danny away from me. Which she hasn't done, but that's all right. I'd hate her anyway because she's a cheerleader.

"What's the count?" I ask the deputy.

"Three dead on scene. One died on the way to the hospital. Two in critical condition. Eight more wounded, but stable. The dead, I should mention, include a fifteen-year-old girl, a runaway from Minnesota."

◆

I'm as relieved as I am enraged. I've no doubt the attack on the Horde came from Charlie, whether or not he was present when the grenades were thrown. Maybe he was more interested in destroying property then pure carnage. I'll concede that much. But he surely gave no thought to the lives of whoever happened to be camping in Knob Canyon. On the other hand, for the past couple days, I've been imagining an all-out war in Boomtown and the effect the battles might have on the construction site. No more. Individual bikers may well come to Boomtown looking for revenge. But without their bikes, the damage will be limited.

"Did you hear?" Danny asks.

"About Leland County?"

"Yeah, the Horde."

I pull a tub of vanilla yogurt out of the refrigerator as Zoe walks into the room. She kisses me on the cheek, gives Danny a little hug. Ever the optimist, I thought I'd be the recipient of double the affection when Zoe moved in. Now I'm wondering if Zoe will replace me as Danny's confidant.

"Did you hear about the Horde?" Zoe asks.

There's no avoiding the topic and I briefly highlight my conversation with Deputy Miranda Dox. "Assuming the damage was caused by hand grenades, and that's not proven, I have to ask myself if the assailants deliberately targeted the motorcycles, or if they miscalculated. And before you jump to conclusions, no evidence ties the attack to the crew in Boomtown."

"C'mon, who else?" Danny wants to know. "What I heard, they were at each other's throats. Charlie and that biker, Zeb."

"Heard from who?"

"Whom," Zoe corrects.

Zoe's turning the temperature down and she's right. My tone is growing sharper, an indication of how frustrated I am. Me and all my detectives. The restrictions on our activities in Boomtown are grating, what with crimes being openly committed. But that's about to change. The mayor's given us broad latitude to investigate any crime that occurred in Baxter and that's what we intend to do. This afternoon.

"Sorry, Zoe, but there's something my son needs to understand. First, motive isn't evidence, no matter how often prosecutors use motive to influence juries. Motive can be used to isolate suspects, but until you find evidence, motive proves exactly nothing."

I lay bowls of yogurt and fruit in front of Danny and Zoe. My son doesn't exactly recoil, but he doesn't attack the food the way he attacks bacon, eggs, and toast. Danny's learning that his athletic ambitions come with sacrifice. Athlete's bodies are all they have to sell. You perform on the field or you don't perform on the field. That means caring for the only tool in the toolbox. Injury-prone can be a career-ending judgment.

"The way it works," I say, "motive points you toward suspects. So, yeah, Charlie and his people. They're obvious suspects and if it was our case, I'd start with Charlie. But I'd also want to know who else had a motive. Remember, we're talking about a biker gang heavy into drug dealing. They sell in Baxter, true, but also in at least four surrounding counties. One reason I'm glad the investigation is falling on the Leland County sheriff and not on the Baxter PD? Most likely, the Horde has enough enemies keep a detective squad busy for the next year."

"If these New York gangsters are responsible, they kept the attack away from their home base," Zoe observes. "I mean, it's brilliant, really. You look outside, it's just a normal day in Baxter. People going about their business, the factory going up, good jobs at decent wages. What's not to like?"

"Maybe that's the message," Danny says. "Leave Boomtown to us. We'll keep the peace."

"And before you know it," I say, "the factory will be completed. These temporary workers, here without their families, will be replaced by permanent workers. Boomtown will close down because it will no longer serve a purpose. So, relax. Don't rock the boat."

The conversation drifts at that point. Danny first, describing Emmaline's decision to become a ball player like Danny and Mike, her brother.

"She's not even five years old," Danny explains. "The glove is bigger than her head, but, like, she's determined."

"And Emmaline always gets her way?"

"Yeah, always. Only this time she's maybe wishing she didn't." Danny lowers his spoon to the bowl and glances up at me. "I was tossing the ball underhand. Like, I wanted it to plop into the glove without her moving. Just land there. And she did catch a couple balls. But then she started swiping at the ball. I tried to tell her not to move the glove, but . . ."

"But she moved it?"

"Yeah, moved the glove and herself. The ball landed on top of her head. I thought she was gonna break down, or at least cry."

"She didn't, though," Zoe says. "I'd bet my next paycheck on it."

"No, she laughed and rubbed her scalp. Then she said, 'Uh-oh.'"

We eat on, just another family starting its day. Wondering about the weather, organizing our activities, no hurry, nothing out there to fear. Baxter's crime rate has slowed and that's good news for the pols and the cops. As for the murdered fifteen-year-old runaway, what happens in Leland County stays in Leland County. You can say the same of Boomtown.

The boat didn't need rocking, but I couldn't stop thinking about Charlie. The Horde probably have other enemies, or at least rivals with an eye on the Horde's drug operation, and I can imagine an ambush, or even a direct attack. But targeting the motorcycles, leaving the Horde unable to counterattack? Too subtle for another outlaw gang. Not for Charlie, though. Smart and bold are the adjectives I'd apply to Charlie. Maybe too smart, maybe too bold. At this point, I'm only sure that I want to wipe the smirk off his face. I want to watch him endure the booking process, watch him cringe when a cell door closes behind him. I'll need a conviction as well. I ran Charlie Setter's name through NCIC late yesterday afternoon. He's been to prison. The booking process won't throw him. It'll take a judge's gavel banging down at sentencing time to slice away the man's arrogance. That or a bullet.

CHAPTER TWENTY-NINE

DELIA

Work, work, work. Heyman Weymouth's been arrested, but he won't be able to travel for a few days. No perp walk today. We have to settle for a press release and phone interviews with Katie Burke, Basil Ulrich, and a newcomer, Slate Harmon from WKRA, a local radio station. Slate's proud to be a "hardass conservative" and I'd ordinarily ignore him. Especially when the news is bad. Not this morning, not when we've nailed down a murder investigation.

Slate's not all that interested in the good news. He demands to know when the department plans to address the evildoers in Boomtown. Slate knows that Boomtown is out of our jurisdiction, but he's not big on facts. Nor is he anxious to give the Baxter PD credit for a quick investigation. He's more a doom and gloom reporter. I respond with the party line. Boomtown is in Sprague County and we lack jurisdiction. Slate needs to contact Sheriff Pickford Fletcher and ask the same question.

By ten o'clock, I'm on my way to the Mount Jackson home of Zack Butler. There are true mansions in Mount Jackson, enormous houses with dozens of rooms. Long abandoned, two are well into the demolition process, another completely gone. The mansions stood on several acres of land, room enough for the many homes destined to supplant the rose gardens and the towering oaks. The reinvention of Baxter is in full swing.

The din is unrelenting, with construction in progress on every block. Hammers, pile drivers, wood saws, trucks delivering every sort of construction material, from kitchen cabinets to concrete. Call it contractor heaven. Ditto for suppliers of construction material. Gregman Drywall comes to mind. The business opened within weeks of the Nissan deal's completion, along with another business, Tomas Cement. Were the investors connected in the capitol? Was Zack Butler? The sale of the Boomtown strip was finalized before the City of Baxter knew it was happening. Charlie and his crew arrived only a few weeks later.

❖

Zack Butler's home, a two-story brick colonial, impresses. The brick has been painted white, and black shutters frame the windows. Tapered pillars support a small porch that shields the front door, while a spacious lawn is so perfectly smooth it has me thinking Zack's gardener trimmed it with a pair of scissors. A freestanding lilac bush to the left of the porch is in full bloom, its fragrance drifting to the edge of the driveway as I step out of my car.

The door opens on my second knock to reveal a Latina woman. She hesitates for just a moment, until I display my badge, then steps aside. I cross a short foyer to enter Zack Butler's living room. Zack's sitting in a chair next to an oxygen concentrator. A clear plastic tube runs from the concentrator, over each ear, and into his nostrils. Still, he rises to his feet, somewhat unsteady, and smiles. We know each other, Zack and I, having met at fundraisers for Mayor Venn. I remember him as utterly charming, and very sure of himself.

"Captain Mariola, what a pleasant surprise." He gestures to an overstuffed chair. "Please, sit down. Miranda, the croissants, would you bring out a plate, and coffee? Please."

I think I'm supposed to refuse the refreshments, but I don't. This conversation is off the record, a polite exchange of views.

"I spoke to Git the other day," Zack continues. Bridget O'Rourke, universally called Git, figured prominently in a murder investigation two years ago. At one point, she became the perp's target, a problem solved when her mother killed him.

"If I remember, Git was your nurse for a time."

"Yes, I need a ventilator when I'm sleeping and Git made sure it operated properly. Saved my life one time when it broke down. She's in New Jersey, with her mom and her daughter."

"Doing well?"

"Better than well. She's completed her second year of nursing school and she's considering a program to become a nurse practitioner."

I maintain a neutral expression, but I liked Git. Tough as nails, she'd come up hard. One of those women who refuse to give up on life, for herself and especially her child.

Miranda returns from the kitchen, bearing a tray that she sets on the coffee table. Piled on a small platter, a dozen croissants, plain and chocolate, beckon. As does the coffee. In a cup, not a mug.

"From a French bakery," Zack explains. "Can you believe it? A French bakery in Baxter? Please, help yourself."

I add cream from a little pitcher to the coffee and take a sip. French roast for the French croissants. Nice.

"So, Captain, I'm delighted to see you, but I don't suppose you've come to comfort a sick, old man . . ."

He leaves it there, a smart move. I'll have to show my cards first, and I don't have any cards to play. Only rumors and Gloria Meacham's offhand comment.

"Boomtown, Zack, and please call me Delia. A little bird . . . no, make that a large bird. A large bird insists that you're a major shareholder in the holding company that owns all the land in Boomtown."

"Ah, I figured that's why you came, but I'm not prepared to discuss my investment portfolio. Except to assure you that my investments are all legal. Scrupulously legal."

"Even Charlie and his boys? You do know who I'm talking about?"

"I hear the rumors, Delia, but I've never met the man."

"Still, you must find it curious. Charlie arrived within weeks of Boomtown opening to development. He and his cohort." Over the past week, my detectives have been working their snitches, collecting information about Boomtown. Normally, I'd have to use my imagination to fill in the criminal blanks. Not this time. Charlie and his men fill each and every one.

"Perhaps he heard opportunity knocking."

"It must've knocked real loud to be heard in New York, fifteen hundred miles away. The brothel and the casino? Charlie's running both, with no opposition. Even the hookers on the street pay off. He's positioned loan sharks and dealers in every bar. Bookies too. Top to bottom, Zack, he means to run the criminal show in Boomtown, and he's already killed, here and in Leland County. Not that he's finished. No, Charlie means to control the flow of drugs, from cocaine to meth, in Boomtown and Baxter. You buy from Charlie's crew and nobody else. Me, I have to ask myself how that could happen. How could a mob family in New

York suddenly turn up in our little part of the world? And so fast, Zack. So, so fast."

I grind to a halt. Zack Butler's maintained a neutral expression throughout my little rant. Not a twitch, but no denial either. I turn to the croissants piled on a porcelain platter with a pale-blue windmill in the center. The plain croissants are so flaky they appear about to levitate. The chocolate croissants, by comparison, are a lot heavier. My wholesome resolution conveniently forgotten, I use a small pair of tongs to load one of the chocolate croissants on a plate bearing the same windmill in the same shade of blue. When I take a bite, I have to repress a shiver. I need to find out the name of this bakery.

"I don't dispute anything you told me," Zack says. "But wasn't it inevitable? Isn't . . . criminality? Isn't criminality true of Boomtowns since time immemorial? Economics 101, Delia. If a demand exists, a supply will arise to meet it. This is what the politicians never understood about drugs. Hammering at the supply end of the equation hasn't worked and never will. On the other hand, the futility puts lots and lots of money in the hands of the criminal justice system. More cops, more judges, more courtrooms, more prisons. Money, money, money."

"Thanks for the lecture. But tell me what happens when untreated well water results in an outbreak of dysentery? Or even cholera? Or what a trial lawyer will do after an outbreak?"

"How is that your problem? Boomtown's in Sprague County and Sprague County has its own building codes. Let Sheriff Fletcher worry about Boomtown."

I pass a moment luxuriating in my croissant. Zack's comment is nearly as appealing. Maybe I should do my Pontius Pilate impression. Maybe I should wash my hands. And I'd do just that if I wasn't a cop.

"Something else to consider," Zack says. "That land? Boomtown? Its value is rising and will continue to rise. Even if Boomtown is leveled. Perhaps especially if Boomtown is leveled. But all the workers here now, and all the workers to come before the plant's completed? Where will they go if you take a bulldozer to Boomtown?"

"And the bodies, Zack. Corey Miller, Titus Klint, the bikers in Leland County, a fifteen-year-old runaway? Any concerns there?"

Zack and his co-investors knew about the Nissan deal before the news was released to the public. That much is obvious. The Boomtown strip was sold three months before the demolition began. Sleazy, but par for the course, politics being politics. But inviting Charlie to the feast and maybe accepting a payoff crosses a major line.

"Tell me something, Zack. You're an old man in poor health. And you don't have children. So why get involved? What's in it for you?"

"It's about choice, Delia. How will I spend the rest of my life, short though it may be? As a player? Or watching *Family Feud* reruns?"

Corey Miller's body lies in an open coffin. The mortician's done a good job, adding subtle color to her cheeks and lips. Her hair's been neatly combed and brushed, perhaps even set. It flows to the top of a high-necked blue dress. Her hands are crossed and lie on her stomach, her only jewelry a gold cross at her throat.

It seems half the city's here. Corey Miller's the talk of talk radio, her fate, her abandonment. The more conservative hosts never fail to mention that she was a sinner, which Corey's sister openly acknowledges. But those same hosts are also law-and-order fanatics and they're using Corey to illustrate the depravity and utter lawlessness that's descended on the God-fearing citizens of little Baxter.

I wait in line to pay my respects, passing by Corey's coffin. Maggie Miller and her father sit on folding chairs and I nod to them as I pass. I'm surprised at the distress in Maggie's eyes, and by the dried tears that streak her makeup. Only a short time before leaving for the Fulton Funeral Home, Cade Barrow stopped by my office.

"I tapped into an old friend of mine, still in service. Maggie Miller? She's ex–Air Force, deployed to Afghanistan and Iraq. But she didn't see combat. She was a Security Forces cop. A detective, Captain."

I'm not seeing that now. Whatever game she's playing, Maggie Miller's heart is broken. Her father's too. Maybe he's having one of his convenient good days, but for now his head is bowed and it's all he can do not to cry.

Remorse. That's what I'm sensing. Remorse and a tightening resolve. The viewing room is crowded, like the waiting room outside. I know many of the people who showed up. They don't have the look of mourners, but I won't call them mere curiosity seekers, especially the working men and women from Boomtown. My hope is that a few of her friends will make an appearance, but if they're in attendance, I can't pick them out.

As I circulate, I'm approached again and again by people who recognize me, including two members of our City Council. Again and again, I recite the appropriate mantra: *The investigation is ongoing.* Curiously, I hear the name Bruce several times, always from men still in their soiled work clothes. Bruce runs the Paradise Inn. Talk to Bruce.

One man, who refuses to name names, not even his own, tells me, "Those girls, they all think it was Bruce who killed Corey."

◆

I'm about leave when I hear Maggie's voice. I move to the doorway and see her standing behind her sister's coffin. She's wearing a black dress, a bit too form-fitting to be a mourning garment. A cross that matches her sister's reflects enough light to be noticed.

"My name is Maggie Miller," she begins, "and this is my sister, Corey. Growin' up, me and Corey was tighter than tight. We was together more often than apart, sharin' a room in a small house. Now, I can't answer as to why, but after our mama passed, I just took to watchin' out for her. In school and at home. Neither was altogether safe, though I won't speak to the reasons.

"Maybe that was all wrong. Maybe standin' on her own at that young age was what she really needed, because when I joined the Air Force, when I abandoned her, Corey fell apart. Not fast enough to bring me runnin' home, which I couldn't do anyway. The military will grant leave for a funeral, but not for a sister who's travelin' with the wrong crowd.

"By the time Corey's life was out of control, I was stationed at Bagram, thousands of miles away. I tried to call her, but she didn't answer, tried texting, but she didn't reply. Then she was gone. And I wasn't by no means surprised when I saw her face on the TV with the host askin' if anyone could identify her. Overdose ain't nothin' new where I come from. I suspect it don't come as any big shock here in Baxter. Seems like drugs are everywhere, more and more every day and the bodies pilin' up. So, if Corey was took by her own hand, I'd mourn her proper and go on with my life. I could even live with her body left out in the cold, which is a common fate, nobody willin' to take responsibility. Yes, I could return home and try to measure my blame. I could visit all those places we went together. I could recall the stories my sister used to tell, the stories she made up on her own. I could open the picture album, relive the birthdays and our Christmas tree decorated with ornaments made of whatever came to hand."

Maggie stops for a moment, her head tilted forward as she stares into her sister's coffin. I watch her hands curl into fists, the tears begin to flow. Is she faking? Sincere? And which do I want to believe? I don't trust the woman. She's playing me and the obvious reason, to secure justice, doesn't sit right. Like a chair with one leg shorter than the others. I watch her chin rise until she's looking straight at her audience, the audience she worked so hard to get here.

"Corey didn't die by her own hand, another drug-addict casualty in a war there ain't no hope of winnin'. According to your own police department, my sister was murdered. And it wasn't only Corey who died that night, but the child forming in her womb."

Another pause, marked by gasps and nods. Maggie's raised the stakes and the gawkers are impressed. I feel a hand on my shoulders and turn to find Zoe standing alongside.

◆

"I've heard enough, Zoe. I've got a lot to do this afternoon and I need to prep my troops."

Zoe follows me through the crowded waiting room and into the street. The small parking lot is full and cars are parked and double-parked on the street. A dozen people, men and women, mingle on the lawn. At the curb, the reporters have formed a little posse. They seem upbeat, with good reason. Maggie Miller's unlikely to walk away from a chance to broadcast her message to the entire community.

"See if you can put off serving dinner until about seven," I tell Zoe. "I might be late."

"Yeah, no problem. What do you think of Maggie Miller's speech? You didn't stay for the grand finale."

"She's going to ask for someone to come forward. Plead for someone, actually. Well, you don't have to listen when you know the punch line."

Zoe smiles. A small smile that still projects amusement. "You think she'll succeed?"

"Corey Miller overdosed inside the Paradise. Given the time of death, that's nearly certain. So, if someone's gonna step out, it'll have to be a co-worker who's willing to buck Charlie. That's a big ask."

"You think Maggie's wasting her time?"

I shrug. "A small chance is better than no chance. But there's something else happening here. I only found out this morning, but Maggie Miller was with the Security Force in the Air Force. That the Air Force's equivalent of the Military Police. And get this, Zoe. She was a detective."

"You're saying she's not the grieving sister she seems to be? She's playing some kind of game?"

"Wrong about the first part. She's definitely grieving. Right about the second part. She wants justice for her sister, yeah. But she's got other things on her mind, too. I just don't know what they are."

CHAPTER THIRTY

DELIA

We hit the Paradise in a three-vehicle convoy. I'm in the first vehicle, a Chevrolet Impala, sitting alongside Blanche Weber. The two Ford Explorers behind me carry four cops in each. Cade Barrow is the only detective. The rest are in uniform.

The interior of the Paradise Inn is one giant cliché, from the crimson wallpaper to a hooker posse wearing leave-nothing-to-the-imagination lingerie. There are already a few customers, though it's barely four o'clock. They're nursing drinks while they peruse the merchandise. Two men, obviously management, stand at one end of the bar.

"You have a warrant?" This from the taller and older of the two. He appears soft, despite his broad shoulders.

Maybe it's the pudgy face or the protruding brown eyes or his thin red mouth, but I'm not confusing him with Charlie.

I signal to one of the uniforms, Sergeant Kolski, and he heads for the rooms in the back of the double wide. "I don't need a warrant to enter a place of business," I explain. "Let's see some identification."

"I don't have to show you anything. You got no fuckin' authority outside of Baxter."

"Cuff him, Cade, and dump him in the back of a car."

For just a second, he discovers his spine and straightens as Cade and two officers come toward him. Then reality sets in, or maybe he reverts to a core he's been hiding for almost as long as he's been alive. He snarls, but allows himself to be spun around and folded over the bar, to be cuffed, to be searched. I'm hoping he'll be found in possession of a gun or drugs. Not happening.

Escorted by my cops, three men and three women emerge from the back of the trailer. The men have at least pulled on their trousers, a small break from the law enforcement gods. The women wear robes, hastily donned I suspect. I look over the johns, then choose the youngest, a boy almost.

"Can I assume no money changed hands?" I ask.

"Not a penny, officer . . ."

"Captain."

"Not a penny," he repeats. "It was love all the way."

"Love for sale?"

"I didn't say that." His smile is genuine, but I can find no challenge in it. "Me and what's her name plan to marry."

"Should I send for a minister?"

"Nah, we're still saving for the honeymoon."

I can't help myself. I laugh out loud. The kid is good, but enough being enough, I point to each of the customers, dressed and undressed. "Get yourselves out of here before I decide to charge you. That doesn't include you," I tell the man at the bar as I wait for the johns to leave. "Tell me your name."

The man before me is tall and slender, with bright blue eyes that betray more curiosity than fear. He's given some thought to the situation and resigned himself to a basic understanding well known to cops and criminals. Might makes right. And we've got the might.

"Gene Casio."

"Are you armed, Mr. Casio?"

The question catches him off guard, but his hands remain where I can see them. "Yeah, I'm carryin' a gun. It's legal."

All around me, cop hands drop to their weapons. Casio responds to the obvious threat by raising his own hands, but his expression doesn't change. Cade Barrow steps forward and pulls a semiautomatic from a holster behind Casio's hip.

"It's legal," Casio repeats. "This is an open carry state."

"Correct, Mr. Casio. It is an *open* carry state. But your weapon was concealed and you need a license to carry a concealed weapon. Do you have a license, Mr. Casio?" Casio doesn't respond and I nod to Cade. "Search him, cuff him, put him in the car. And not with his buddy."

◆

Now it's just us and the girls, but I don't have a lot of time if I want to have dinner with Fetchin' Gretchen. The women appear to be in their late twenties and early thirties. Like any cop, I've had a good deal of contact with prostitutes. I've found many, especially streetwalkers, ravaged by time and drugs. These women have yet to reach that stage. They're hardened, but still defiant.

"Okay, here's what's going down. We're investigating the murder of Corey Miller. We know she worked here in the Paradise and we know she died here. So, if you claim you never heard of her when you're interviewed, I'll find some reason to bust you. I don't like wasting my time."

"We don't have to talk to you." This from one of the older women. In her early thirties, she's dyed her long hair electric blue. Maybe to match her eyes.

"You'll be interviewed one at a time, in private. We can do it here or at Baxter PD headquarters, in which case you'll be there all night."

If Corey was handed an overdose, it's only a matter of discovering who gave it to her. Whether sold or freely given or exchanged for a special favor is irrelevant. Even without intent, the giver would be up for a manslaughter charge.

I have an ace here, an ace in the hole I expect to play down the line. This morning, I learned that DNA was recovered from the embryo in Corey's womb. DNA that can be matched to a suspect.

◆

It nearly kills me, but I don't take part in the actual interviews. I let Blanche handle them. I do observe, sitting quietly in a small office at the rear of the trailer.

Though none of the women admit to knowing how the fatal dose found its way to Corey Miller, tidbits emerge. The jerk we put in the car is named Bruce Angoleri and he "manages" the Paradise. Corey was in the Paradise on the night she died, probably in her room. Most of the women use drugs in one form or another, generally after the Paradise closes.

The first women Blanche interviews draw the line at that point, and Blanche closes each interview with an appeal to conscience.

"Corey was murdered. Bad enough. But then her body was dumped like so much trash. Here, look at these." Blanche fans out three photos of Corey Miller's body. Two when she was first discovered. The last of her body as the paramedics folded it into a body bag. The photos produce a final tidbit. The women have to share rooms, a major grievance. They should be housed away from their workplace. Though promises have been made, they've yet to be kept. The girls are still doubled up. That includes Corey, who roomed with a woman named Rita Lafayette.

We've already interviewed Rita, but we bring her back for a second interview. Sharp-faced, Rita's dark eyes burn and she makes no attempt to disguise her dislike of cops, a common attitude among women who are arrested and rearrested while their customers go home to their families.

"Look, Rita," Blanche explains, "we know that you shared a room with Corey and we know that the two of you went back to that room after the Paradise closed on the night she was killed. Corey was alive at that point." Blanche points to the photo of Corey half-in and half-out of the body bag. "No more."

"You already showed me the picture." Rita's eyes are fixed on the ceiling. To show contempt? Or because she's afraid to take another look at her roommate's body? "Like it's somethin' I haven't figured out for myself. Like it's not somethin' I already know."

"Like you already know that your roommate was murdered? Like you already know she was pregnant?" Blanche waits for Rita to deny or confirm. She does neither and Blanche goes on. "Like you already know who gave her that overdose. Like you already know who impregnated the woman who shared your bedroom, night after night after night."

Rita takes her time, reaching for a pack of Newports lying on the only desk in the office. If I was doing the interview, I'd bring Rita up short. Who's in charge? That's the issue. Blanche has other ideas, something she senses in her subject. Hookers don't like pimps any more than they like cops.

"Funny thing," Rita finally says, "despite the sinful life, I still like breathing. In fact, you could say I'm addicted to suckin' down my next breath." She shakes her head. "Nothin' you can do will bring Corey back to life. Her baby, neither."

Blanche goes at it for another few minutes, until it's obvious that Rita's drawn a line in her personal sand. But lines drawn in sand can be washed away by the next tide. Without saying it out loud, Rita showed us that she cares, that Corey's death is not a big ho-hum. Given time, she may decide that she has to do something about it.

◆

Bruce will be released as soon as he formally identifies himself. Gene Casio will be charged with possession of an unregistered weapon, a misdemeanor in this state. Normally, we'd cut him loose on an OR, but I've decided to hold him until he's arraigned tomorrow morning. I've no doubt he'll make bail, if the judge even requires bail. That's okay. I want to rub it in. As for the women at the Paradise, there's no reason to suppose that Rita's the only one who can point that finger. With that in mind, Blanche offered her business card to each and no one threw it back in her face. Time will tell, but I'm feeling more positive than ever.

Taking and processing a DNA sample takes time. Comparing the results, when you have them at hand, can be done in minutes. Charlie Setter did time in a New York prison. Collected at the time of his arrest, his DNA profile is available to law enforcement on a federal database we readily accessed. Charlie Setter is not the father of Cory Miller's child and had no reason to kill her.

At the station, I wait until Cade escorts Bruce and Casio inside before speaking privately with Blanche. "Sorry," I tell my detective, "but I've got to get home. My son is bringing his girlfriend to dinner."

"Danny has a girlfriend?"

"Fetchin' Gretchen."

Blanche's laugh is genuine. "Do yourself a favor, boss," she says. "Soon as you walk through the door, lock your weapon in a gun safe. That way, I won't have to explain your Fifth Amendment right to avoid self-incrimination."

CHAPTER THIRTY-ONE

MAGGIE MILLER

I t's three days after Corey's viewing and I'm sitting outside the trailer alongside my daddy. My sister's already been cremated, her ashes at rest in a bronze urn. The urn's in the trailer close to the door, so it'll be handy in case we have to get out in a hurry.

Winter's made a comeback. Or not winter, really, more like a raw March day back in Redmond Lake. The air's wet-cold and the little beads of dew on Daddy's wool cap glisten. I've got one hand wrapped around a mug of hot coffee and the other stuck in my pocket.

"Been a long while, baby girl," Daddy says. "Can't help but conclude them ladies in the Paradise are more scared of Charlie than concerned with justice for Corey. Even if she was one of them."

"You could be right, but just maybe they picked the other horse in the race."

I don't have to fill in the blanks. The other horse is named Mariola. Her raid has made its mark on Boomtown and Baxter both. There's no denyin' the Paradise Inn's purpose, not by the good citizens of Baxter. Doesn't matter that none of the ladies workin' there has been charged with a crime. Probably won't be, either, because the bar's empty most nights.

Men and a few women stroll past, faces we've been seein' most every day. They wave and call out, "Cold this morning," as they pass. I know a few by name. Greg and Zeke always come together, leavin' from a trailer small enough to pass for a minivan. This morning, they stop to invite me and Daddy to stop by one evenin'. They'd be honored to feed us.

I leave it there. One evening, unspecified.

We're not in Baxter to sample the social life. In fact, though I don't care to admit it to my daddy, I'm beginnin' to lose heart. Minds slip as time goes by. Folk lose interest and we're in danger of becomin' pathetic if the nothin' of the past few days continues. Crawlin' home with my tail between my legs holds no appeal, but I've been through investigations in Iraq and Afghanistan both. Win some, lose some, that's the way it goes, like it or not.

◆

Charlie's spent the night away from his girlfriend in Norwood for the first time, and that's a break. It figures that he'd have a retreat somewhere, a place to rally or just hide out. In any event, he's holed up this morning in Oakland Gardens, not far from where Titus Klint and Stitch Kreuter took their final breaths. Later, maybe, we'll survey the location, but for right now my attention is captured by a man walkin' toward us. He's got to weigh two-forty, with a salt-and-pepper beard that hangs to the top of his chest. But the denim vest he wears is plain, with no club colors to indicate that he's a biker. He's half smiling, too, and when he removes his Cubs baseball cap, I see that his palm is thick with callus.

"Name's Ray Howland. Hope I'm not disturbin' you."

"No fear, Ray. I'm Maggie Miller and this is my daddy, Aaron." I watch him nod to Daddy, who doesn't look up. "So, what brings you to our doorstep?"

"I think I know something you should know. For your sister's sake. See, I lost a brother couple years back. Shot dead in the street. Collateral damage, you might say. Bullet wasn't meant for him, according to the cops. Hardly matters because they never did find the man who fired ten shots into a crowd of people. So, you have my sympathies."

"Thank you, Ray, but what is it I need to know?" My laptop begins to beep. Charlie's on the move.

"Well, these men, the mob is what I call 'em, they're in every bar hereabouts. *Every* bar. So, I'm sittin' at the Boomtown Sports Bar, enjoying a drink before I head back to my RV, when I overhear one of these mob guys talkin' to the bartender. Seems the women who work across the street?"

He gestures to the Paradise. "They're about to move on. Didn't say where, only they'll be leavin' Boomtown, with new girls coming in. The Paradise is closin', too. Man they call Charlie is puttin' it up for sale."

"These new women, you know where they'll be workin'?"

"Can't say, Maggie, but it won't be hard to find out. Like I said, they have people everywhere. They'll get the word out."

"And the women workin' here currently? Any notion where they're headed?"

The question's pretty stupid and I'm not surprised when Ray shakes his head before takin' his leave. Daddy waits a moment, then says, "The man's smart, baby girl."

Daddy's talkin' about Charlie, and he's right, in theory. Get the witnesses gone? There nothin' not to like from his point of view. But there's a worm in that apple. If any of the girls are feelin' a need to right the wrong that befell Corey, the threat of bein' dragged off could motivate her to pull the trigger. Knowin' it's now or never.

◆

I see it comin' before the first shot's fired. Charlie turns onto the block, parks, and gets out. A pickup on the far end of the block eases out of a parkin' space, then comes rippin' down the street. The rest lies somewhere between the terminally stupid and a syndrome I called wrong place, wrong time when I was still on the job. The pickup's more dent than smooth metal, the muffler a distant memory, but the tires squeal as the driver stomps on the gas. Charlie's head jerks to the left and I think I see him smile. His hand streaks beneath his coat, emerges less than a second later clutching a semiautomatic. At the same moment, the door to the Paradise opens and a woman steps out, unaware as Snow White biting down on that poisoned apple.

Charlie crouches, but that's as far as he's willing to go. He's sighting his weapon as bullets fly from the front and back windows of the pickup. I'm lying on my belly with my head turned toward the action. Daddy's propped up on one arm, the better to get to the .45 beneath his sweater should self-defense become necessary.

The world slows down, as it always does in combat, the seconds stretching out, one after another. They ooze by like sap on the trunk of a tree. Charlie begins to fire, the muzzle of his weapon sweeping left as the truck rolls by. I can't see or hear the bullets as they pass Charlie's body, but he keeps his cool, only a small tightness around the mouth and eyes indicating he's engaged in more than a morning stroll. He proves accurate too. A spray of blood fans out from the far side of the driver's head and the pickup swerves, first scraping against a parked car, then tracing a pair of revolutions before coming to a stop with the driver slumped over the steering wheel.

The passenger in the back leaps out, a large man, middle-aged, with carrot-orange hair and a beard to match. I expect him to resume the attack, using the pickup as a shield, but he takes off toward Main Street. Charlie watches him go for a second, then turns to the woman in the doorway. She's obviously in shock. Her mouth has formed a perfect circle and she's staring straight ahead. Blood runs in a steady stream from her right forearm, which she cradles in her left hand. Even from where I lie on my stomach, I can see shards of protruding bone.

"Gotta go, Daddy," I call as I jump to my feet and head across the road. Charlie watches me, his eyes merely curious. "Nice shootin', Charlie," I call as I pass him.

"Appreciate the compliment," he responds to my back.

I reach the bleeding woman a few seconds later. Like any Special Forces cop, I've been trained in the basics of battlefield medicine. In this case, that training boils down to a simple task. Control the bleeding before her blood pressure drops far enough to stop her heart. The only remedy is a tourniquet, in this case my belt, which I yank free and fashion around her forearm just above the wound.

"This is gonna hurt," I tell her. "Best prepare yourself."

She doesn't, and her scream when I tighten down seems louder than the gunshots of a moment before. "You just hang on now and you'll be all right. The bleeding's already slowed, see? The bleeding's slowed and your heart's beatin' fine."

"I don't wanna die," she whispers. "Please, please, please."

She pulls back, as if I was the one doin' the killing. I don't speak because reaching her at this point seems unlikely to me. But I'm holding tight as I drop to my knees and pull down.

"You need help?"

I look up to find Charlie standing next to me, still calm. In the distance, very faintly, I hear sirens. "Calm her down if you can. It's only a matter of holdin' on until the paramedics arrive. Her livin' or dyin'."

Charlie takes the woman by her shoulders. He whispers something in her ear, but I can't make it out."

"Okay, Charlie," the woman says, "but it hurts so bad."

"You just got shot, Mary-Anne. So, look at the bright side. You're alive and you're gonna stay alive. That's gotta be enough." He pulls her back against him and she doesn't resist. "Because it's all you're gonna get for now. Later on, we'll talk about later on."

Is Charlie comforting Mary-Anne? Or intimidating the woman? Because he knows she's goin' to a hospital in Baxter, knows she'll be there for days, at the least. Knows Mariola will have access whenever she wants. Me, too, for that matter.

◆

Mary-Anne's still conscious when an ambulance rolls up three minutes later. She's alert as she watches a paramedic, a young man with a buzz cut flat enough to land a C47, jump out of the ambulance. Without speaking, he pulls my belt from her arm and replaces it with a torniquet of his own. I finally stand up, my clothes and face speckled with blood. Blood drips from my right hand, but I'm still holding the belt. Charlie's standing beside me, smiling.

"Do you have any idea," he asks, "how good you look right now?"

CHAPTER THIRTY-TWO
MAGGIE MILLER

I retreat to the trailer and Daddy, who's back in his lawn chair. Daddy's humming some tune I don't recognize and I know where he's going. The cops have already arrived to secure the scene, which includes us. Daddy's gonna hide behind his infirmities. Seen nothin', heard nothin', say nothin'. Me, I don't have that option and I'm workin' on my story when Mariola shows up, accompanied by her sidekick, Detective Weber. Charlie's seated on our side of the street, cool as ever, but I suspect he's got a problem. If he's a convicted felon, as he's rumored to be, possessing a concealed weapon is a crime.

Mariola has a problem too. We're in Sprague County. The Baxter PD can respond to the emergency, of course, but the investigation belongs to Sheriff Fletcher. He's not here, but one of his deputies pulled up a minute ago. Tall and raw-boned, he's wearing a dark brown uniform and a matching Stetson with a curled brim.

I head inside, refill our mugs, then a third mug, which I carry to Charlie. "Got a feelin' you need this," I tell him.

"What I need is for us to have a little talk," he says as he takes the mug. "Got a proposition you might want to hear."

"We already did the bribe bit. No need to revisit."

"Not what I'm thinkin', Maggie. Just lay easy for now and maybe we'll both walk away from this mess."

"That a threat?"

"I like you, Maggie. Truly. But you've brought nothing but headaches since the day you arrived." He waves his arms at the action across the street. The dead man's still in the pickup, being examined by a man in a suit stretched tight across his round belly, as if there was some mystery to be unraveled. Meanwhile, caught and cuffed, the red-headed man's sitting in a Baxter PD cruiser.

"As you can see, my plate is full without you adding to the misery. And your sister? Corey's not comin' back. Not now, not ever. But if it's justice you're after, maybe we can work that part out. Just stay patient for a little while longer."

◆

"'Fraid I'm gonna have to join him, Captain. I believe I'll save my story for the agency that has jurisdiction. No offense meant." I pause long enough to point to the red-headed man. He's being removed from the back of a BPD cruiser, headed, no doubt, for the back of a Sprague County cruiser. "Wasn't for your quick work, he'd still be on the run. So, hats off . . ."

Mariola waves me to a stop. "Is that a compliment from one cop to another? Funny you never mentioned your role in the military when you filled me in on your background. How you were a detective. How you investigated crimes similar to the one that took your sister's life."

Charlie looks up at that point, a grin on his face that I find mischievous enough to be termed childlike.

"Wasn't relative to Corcy's passin', Captain."

"In your estimation."

"Yes, ma'am, in my estimation."

"Well, let me make one thing clear. If you plan on taking justice into your own hands, remember this. There's no place on Earth you can hide where I won't find you."

❧

It's not that I don't believe her, or doubt her competence. It's only that I don't care. I retreat to the front of my trailer, resume my seat beside Daddy, and open my laptop. Paramedics from Sprague County are taking the pickup driver's body out of the truck. The top of his head is simply missing, what's left of his brain a blood-soaked sponge. As blue as they are empty, his eyes are wide open.

They match the blue coveralls worn by the paramedics who load the body bag into the back of an ambulance.

I wait a moment for my laptop to boot up. Jay-Jay's installed the requested camera behind Stardust Jewelers and I access the camera first. It's motion activated and in sleep mode at the moment, but I'm able to set it running with a simple click. Nothing happening yet, but it's nearly time for the store to open. And past the time when Charlie usually arrives with the prior day's take. I call Jay-Jay, but he's already at work and can't get away. That leaves me and Daddy, and we're not going anywhere until Sheriff Fletcher's through with us. Fletcher's already on the scene, assessing the situation while the Baxter cops pack up. He's a large man, maybe six-six, with the kind of gut that makes a man (never a woman) appear all the more powerful. His weapon fits that persona well, a long-barreled revolver, probably a .357, in an elaborately tooled holster.

I watch Fletcher approach Charlie. I can't hear what they're sayin', but Charlie's cool never wavers. Fletcher's either. The sheriff's acceptin' whatever bullshit Charlie's sellin'. The conversation lasts only for a few minutes before Charlie breaks away. He heads for the Paradise, his stride as smooth and athletic as ever.

"C'mon, Daddy, we need to move."

I lead Daddy across the street to Sheriff Fletcher. I think his frown is habitual, the look of a man accustomed to his authority. Word out there is that his family has deep roots in Sprague County, along with a major investment in the county's farmlands.

I introduce myself quickly, then say, "My daddy has a doctor's appointment over to Baxter Medical Center. Took us more'n two weeks to make the arrangements. We didn't see nothin', so I'm hopin' we might leave the scene. Course, we expect to cooperate if you think you need us."

Fletcher's expression softens for just a moment. Whatever he has in mind, we're not gonna gum up the works. After all, we have no story to tell.

"Didn't see who did what?"

"No, sir, just hit the dirt. Scared, as you might expect. And I had my hands full with my daddy. He ain't right."

Fletcher registers the blank expression in Daddy's eyes, and I'm thinkin' I see relief in Fletcher's. He shouldn't let us go without taking a formal statement. The idea's to lock us into our story and he's cop enough to know that. But . . .

"Just leave your name with the sergeant over there. We need to speak with you, we'll be in touch."

Ever the cooperative citizen, I do just that.

◆

Daddy has no appointment. A medical exam is the last thing we want. We're here to take a look at the Stardust before Charlie finishes his collections and arrives to stash them, almost surely in the store's safe.

We don't stop as we drive north on Baxter Boulevard. No need. The shutters on the jewelry store are up and the shelves in the window are full. Charlie's manager has access to the store's safe.

"Good to know," Daddy says.

"And now what?"

"More waitin'."

I review the camera's data every day. It's not a lengthy task because there's not much happening in the alley behind the store. Except for Charlie's prompt arrival in the morning, Charlie and the package he carries. Day after day, a fat package going into the store. No surprise, that. Charlie's not about to leave the money under a mattress. No, what's a lot more interesting is what the camera hasn't recorded. The money going out.

CHAPTER THIRTY-THREE

CHARLIE

"**C**harlie, whatta ya doin'? Tell me what the fuck you're doin'."

What I wanna tell Ricky Ricci is simple. I'm doing my fuckin' job. The one you told me to do. But as I've never in my life considered suicide, I don't.

"Jeez, Ricky, we're makin' money hand over fist."

"For how long, asshole?" He pauses, but I have nothing to say. "An outright fuckin' war with a motorcycle gang? What kinda bullshit was goin' round and round in that little brain of yours? You take stupid pills when you got up that morning?"

Last time we spoke, just after me and Dominick visited the Horde in their canyon hideout, Ricky congratulated me. Now I take stupid pills. But that's how it goes in Thug-world. Your boss can disrespect you any time he wants. And you, no matter how tough you are, have to take it. You can't talk back, can't even raise your voice. And make sure your tone is wheedling.

"The Horde was established when we got here. In the trade. They pretty much controlled distribution in Baxter."

"You shoulda reasoned with 'em."

"I tried. I met with the club president, man named Zeb, but there was nothin' doin'. Their attitude, right? We were here first. This is our turf and we own it. I made the asshole a fair offer, but he wouldn't budge."

◆

"What's this I'm hearing about the dead whore?" Ricky abruptly changes the subject, a trick designed to throw his people off-balance. Unfortunately, he uses it too often and I don't react. "What's her name?" he asks.

"Corey Miller."

"Yeah, and she's got a sister makin' trouble."

"Maggie Miller."

"So, what's up with that?"

"You know the basics. An overdose. I had to get rid of the body . . ."

"You shoulda buried her."

"The ground was frozen solid, Ricky. We tried."

"Lemme get this right. You could blow up a hundred motorcycles, but you couldn't dig a hole in the ground because the ground was too hard."

"I had somethin' else to do that night, somethin' I can't talk about over the phone. Even encrypted, it's better you shouldn't hear this. And if you wanna say I'm wrong about how I dumped Corey's body, I'll go this far. I couldn't call 911. That would bring cops to the Paradise. But I should've left the body in some cornfield outside the Baxter city limits. That was my mistake and I own up."

Suckin' up 101. Admit you're wrong and beg forgiveness. Ricky takes his time processing my confession. I know he'll offer absolution, no matter what he plans to do. Better I shouldn't see it comin', if it's gonna come.

"Yeah, so what the fuck, water under the bridge. You take your lumps and move on."

"I hear that, boss, and I appreciate it, but as long as I got you on the phone, I could use your advice. See, the cops out here think Corey was murdered—"

"Old news, Charlie."

I have to wonder who's been whispering in Ricky's ear, but now's not the time. "Okay, check this out. I know who killed her."

"Who?"

"Bruce."

"Angoleri?"

"Bruce handed out the envelopes that night. He's the only one in a position to know which girl would get which envelope. And nobody else OD'd, not in the Paradise or the whole fuckin' city. Just Corey Miller."

"And for what? Because she was pregnant? And how the fuck did that happen?"

Again, I have to wonder what little canary has been twittering in Ricky's ear. "Corey had an IUD, but IUDs don't always work. And Bruce hasn't confessed. I haven't even put the question to him. But there's no doubt that Bruce passed Corey Miller the overdose. No doubt at all."

"If she was pregnant, why didn't she get an abortion?"

"Abortion's illegal in this state, and maybe . . . Look, I don't have all the answers, but maybe she waited too long for the abortion pills to work. I'd need to get in Bruce's face to answer every question. But the facts speak for themselves. One, Corey Miller was pregnant when she died. Two, the Baxter cops are investigating aggressively and they're not lettin' up. Three, if the cops get their hands on Bruce's DNA and it matches the embryo, he'll be arrested."

A long pause follows, a legitimate pause most likely. I look around my so-called office, thinkin' it's not a corner office on the fiftieth floor of some Wall Street tower. It's a cube, the only decoration a calendar with photos of vintage tractors. The tractors have iron wheels and look like props out of some post-apocalyptic Australian movie.

"You know Bruce is married to my cousin."

"I do, boss." I'm fully aware of Bruce Angoleri's status. If he's to be whacked, the order has to come from the boss. Meantime, the boss decides to change the subject.

"Look, I'm not worried about the cops. The sheriff, right? That's bein' handled. But the dirt our project's sittin' on? It don't belong to us, Charlie. It belongs to people who wanna keep life simple. Simple and quiet and smooth. No muss, no fuckin' fuss."

Now I get it. In this business, everyone pays up. The boys in Boomtown pay up to me. I pay up to Ricky. And Ricky also pays up to the powers behind Boomtown. That makes Ricky a contractor with his client threatening to cancel the job.

"I'm not seein' trouble ahead, boss, unless the cops grab Bruce. He's the wild card in our deck."

Whacking Bruce isn't the only option here. Bruce can be called back to New York and hidden out until the Boomtown operation grinds to a close. Or he could lawyer up and fight an order for a DNA sample, or extradition if he's indicted. It's up to Ricky.

"Okay, Charlie, here's what it is. A wild card in a deck is one too many cards. Handle it. Quietly, right? Very fuckin' quietly."

"Consider it done."

"And one more thing, the pickup's gonna be delayed. Edith Pinella had a stroke and Joe won't leave her bedside. I have another couple in mind, but it'll be a few days, maybe a week, before I get them out to you. In the meantime, make sure you hold onto that money. No slipups. The money's got places to go. Even the delay's givin' me fuckin' headaches."

◆

I head out to a Quonset hut on the southern edge of Boomtown where the ladies of the Paradise are currently housed. And where they're gonna stay until we find a place for them, a place far away from Boomtown and Captain Mariola. Me, I don't like the whole idea. Too much like pure trafficking, which wasn't how it started. But the orders come straight from New York. Nobody walks away until her debts are settled.

So, no more strolls to Baxter Boulevard, no more shopping for cosmetics, or a manicure, or lingerie. The women are confined and guarded, and my job this morning is to make them aware of the consequences sure to follow any act of defiance. Meantime, the place is a shithole. Lawn chairs, cheap mattresses on the floor, picnic tables, plastic forks and knives, takeout, takeout, takeout.

The women are not happy, of course, but I'm not expecting them to be happy. I'm here to drop the hammer, or at least raise it above my head. The stick first, then the carrot.

"We're slaves? That it?" a woman named Harley Johnson asks.

"Debtors."

"And how are we supposed to pay our debts if we can't work?"

Harley's generally enthusiastic and very popular. If it wasn't for a serious smack habit—I know she scores before work every day—she'd have earned her independence long ago. But the woman's not really interested in repayment. She's worried about that turkey, the cold one in the refrigerator.

Bruce Angoleri is in the room, along with Gene Casio, his second-in-command. Both are lookin' up at me like I'm a magician about to pull the magic rabbit out of the magic hat. Meanwhile, I plan to put Bruce in the hat, and the longer this bullshit goes on, the happier I'll be to perform the trick. When Corey revealed her pregnancy, Bruce should've come to me with his problem, not taken it into his own hands.

"I'm gonna do this much for you," I tell Harley and the rest of them. "I'm gonna freeze your debts until you can start earning again. No vig, no interest. Plus, I know some of you are hurting, so I've brought the magic cure."

I glance at Dominick, who produces a clear plastic bag filled with smaller glassine envelopes. The women's eyes jump to those envelopes.

"On the house, ladies, to make the time slide by. And more to come until we get you settled. Vegas is where I'm thinkin' right now." This is bullshit. I don't know where the women are going. But Vegas has to sound good after a couple months in Baxter. "So, I'm advising you to slow it down. Let the game come to you. Play cards, play Scrabble, watch television, and pretty soon this royal pain in the ass will be yesterday's news. But know this. What's happenin' here is a lot bigger than you. It's an avalanche. You get in the way of an avalanche, you get buried in the rubble."

I nod to Dominick, who quickly distributes the envelopes. There's smack in some, coke in others, meth in a few. Whatever, the goodies are snatched up, no hesitation. That's good, because any of these women can tie the dose that killed Corrie to Bruce. Which is all Mariola's waiting for. She'll arrest Bruce minutes after securing a witness, then extract a DNA sample. By force, if necessary.

Bad for Bruce, bad for Ricky, and really fucking bad for Charlie Setter.

CHAPTER THIRTY-FOUR

CHARLIE

I arrive at the Stardust ninety minutes later and come in through the back door. In the showroom, Adelyn's offering one of our gold pendants, a heart, to a young man wearing brown canvas pants stained with concrete. A couple, still teenagers by the look of them, are admiring the engagement rings on display. I'm reminded of a special order my parents filled for a hedge fund manager. The man wanted—no, demanded—a vivid yellow diamond, at least five carats, internally flawless. A year later, when my father located the stone, the hedge fund manager and his girlfriend decided to go their separate ways. So sorry.

"Would you like the pendant engraved?"

"How much does it cost?"

"Five dollars per word."

The workman's face brightens. "Yeah, sounds good. It's May-Lynn's thirteenth birthday." He laughs. "She's a teenager now and I wanna do something nice before she rejects me."

"I know exactly how you feel." Adelyn removes a plastic sheet from beneath the counter and passes it to her customer. "You can use any of these scripts. And you need to decide exactly what you want to say. The message can't be changed later on."

I watch Adelyn move to the couple examining the engagement rings. "Hi, folks, how can I help you?"

◆

There's nothing more to accomplish in the Stardust, but I leave with my impressions of Adelyn reinforced. She's a natural retailer and I'm going to help her if I can. Already, I've been taking her online for lessons in determining the quality and pricing of gemstones. Will the Stardust survive our stay in Boomtown? Probably not, but if I have the money, and I think I will, I'll back her somewhere else. In return for a slice of the profits. Successful investment is all about management. A great idea in the hands of a poor manager? Tits on a bull.

I stop for an early lunch at the newly opened Hilton Hotel. The menu in the Nissan Room is fairly extensive, and pricey by local standards. But I hear that a delegation from Japan will arrive within a couple weeks to evaluate the plant's construction schedule. They'll expect something better than McDonald's.

I don't go for the grilled octopus, Xtapodi, whatever that might be. But the hamburger I order is thick and juicy, topped with Gruyère, pickled onions, and a spicy aioli. The check's spicy as well, twenty-five dollars. Cheap by Manhattan standards, but on another level defiant. Baxter's on the way up. Nothing can stop us now.

◆

Unfortunately, there's something—or someone—who can stop Ricky Ricci. Her name is Mary-Anne Carlson and she's currently residing in Baxter Medical Center. That's where I head now, to comfort, if not heal, the sick. Construction fever's already made its way here and the featureless blue-glass hospital is adding a new wing. The Nissan Wing, surely.

I'm in a reasonably good mood as I grab an elevator, as I come out on the fifth floor, as I stroll into Mary-Anne's room. That ends abruptly when I find Captain Mariola standing beside Mary-Anne's bed. Mary-Anne's arm is in a heavy cast, from above her elbow to mid-palm. She's lying quietly, very quietly, undoubtedly because the docs have given her some drug to relieve the pain.

"You don't give up, Captain."

"Never."

"Despite her being in no condition to respond? Or maybe she'll mutter something and you can pretend she dropped a name."

"I've been at this business for a while, Charlie." Nothing in her eyes betrays a hint of what's going on inside. "And it's a funny thing. Thieves always think that everyone's out to steal from them. Liars believe the people around them lie every time they open their mouths."

"You think I'm being overly suspicious?"

"Charlie, when I take you down, I'm gonna do it fair and square. I won't have to make anything up."

That gauntlet thrown, Captain Mariola marches out of the room. I listen to her retreating footsteps sound on the polished stone floor, then turn to Mary-Anne.

◆

"She gone?" Mary-Anne asks.

The woman's groggy, yes, and clearly stoned. She's also a druggie veteran who can get off and still function. I've never spoken more than a few words to her. She's not my type. Too corn-fed, between the sandy hair, the freckles, and the pale blue eyes.

"Yeah, she's gone."

"I didn't tell her nothin', Charlie. Not a word."

I stroke the back of her good hand. It's carrot time for Charlie Setter. No sticks today. "I know you didn't. What are the docs sayin'? About the arm?"

"They're sayin' I'm gonna keep it." Her eyes flutter as she fights the drugs in her system. "Probably, right? Like it's not a guarantee. But the scar, it ain't gonna make me real popular with the johns. Unless they're some kinda freaks."

"I see your point, and I wanna tell you how bad I feel about what happened. It's not like I saw it coming, but I still feel responsible somehow. Meanwhile, I can't turn the clock back."

"So, what am I supposed to do?"

"I been thinkin' about that. See, it's complicated because you're a witness to a crime. You saw what happened. The two guys in the pickup shot first. I was defending myself."

"That's what the cop said."

She stops abruptly, her eyes squeezing shut. She's in pain despite whatever they're giving her, probably morphine. And she will be for a long time. Worse yet, Maggie Miller saved her life, which might lead Mary-Anne to divide her loyalties. There's a plastic cup filled with water on the table. I pick it up as I slip an oxy into her good hand. I don't have to tell her to swallow it.

"Here's what I can do, Mary-Anne, but we have to keep it to ourselves. Otherwise, the girls'll decide that I've gone soft and that's not gonna work out for anyone."

"Okay, I can deal with that."

"Good, good. So, are the docs treatin' you right? You need me to set up the TV?"

"No, it's already working."

"Excellent. So, here's the deal. Somebody's gonna come by every day with a booster to make sure you're not hurtin'. Plus, all debts are forgiven, from right now. You owe me nothing. And when you're ready to travel, I'll set you up wherever you wanna go, find you a place to live, and put maybe five grand in your kick. Or maybe the scar won't be all that bad. Maybe you can cover it up with some kinda long sleeves. If that's how it works out and you wanna stay, great. But whatever, I'm not gonna leave you to handle this on your own. I'm gonna take care of you."

I'm lying, partially. I want to make good on my promises, but I have no idea if I can. Forgiving her debt? Setting her up? I have to get Ricky's approval. Maybe I'll succeed, maybe I won't. It depends mostly on what kind of mood he's in when I call. That's for later, though. For now, I just wanna buy a little silence when Maggie Miller shows up, which I'm sure she will.

CHAPTER THIRTY-FIVE

CHARLIE

Dominick's wearing his great stone face, staring through the windshield as we leave Boomtown on the northern end. Baxter has no suburbs and we're riding between farm fields before we travel a mile. I'll have to explain things to Dominick, but I'm enjoying his inner turmoil. Dominick's lips move when he deals with two thoughts at the same time. In this case, there are numerous questions to be answered and Dominick's mouth is zipping right along.

I may be easily amused, but I'm not a sadist. Dominick won't come out and ask the first question. A matter of pride.

"I spoke to Ricky this morning."

"What'd he say?"

"Ricky's decided the only remedy for the threat against his empire is to eliminate the threat."

271

"You talkin' about Rita Lafayette?" Dominick's eyes narrow and his mouth screws down. I don't know if he's about to hit me or cry.

"What's up with you and women? First Corey, now Rita."

"I got a sister."

"I got a grandmother. So fuckin' what?" I glance over, but Dominick has nothing to say. "Anyway, you're not thinkin' straight. Rita's not the real threat. She's not the one who's gonna be arrested if the cops make a case. And they're gonna make a case, Dominick. Corey was pregnant. There's an embryo and the embryo has DNA that can be compared to . . ."

"Bruce Angoleri's DNA."

"Keep going."

"Bruce handed out the envelopes that night. He's the only one who knew what was in 'em."

"And he gave that fatal envelope to Corey Miller. Who just happened to be pregnant."

We drive past a small herd of buffalo, maybe two dozen animals grazing in a meadow. A peaceful life, idyllic, until the day they're loaded into cattle vans and driven to a slaughterhouse.

"So, what are we doin' in cow country?"

"They're not cows, Dominick. They're bison."

"Great; so what're we doin'?"

"Bruce has to disappear. I'm talkin' about his body. That way, it doesn't matter how much evidence the cops produce."

"Not like Corey."

I'm pissed now. "We're not to blame. We were led to believe that Corey died from a simple overdose. Why? Because Bruce told us she did. Look, and this is a lesson you should take to heart. Corey's pregnant with Bruce's kid. That's a problem, right? A problem Bruce should have taken up the ladder. To me, Dominick. But he didn't and now we got a problem, which I did take up the ladder. Bruce has to go."

"Yeah," Dominick says after a moment. "I could see that."

◆

We're an hour into the drive, more or less wandering from one country road to another, without coming upon a suitable place to conceal Bruce's corpse. The fields have been seeded but the ground cover is little more than green fuzz. From time to time we pass small abandoned farmhouses. Tempted though I am, I drive by. The houses—shacks, really—are close to the road and I can't chance their being used from time to time by druggies, or partying teenagers, or even desperate squatters. Tire tracks and crushed weeds are visible before several.

Bruce can't be found, at least until we're finished in Boomtown. Mariola's sharp, no doubt about it. Even without a DNA sample from Bruce, she might put together enough evidence to secure an arrest warrant. If Bruce is still around, faced with a long sentence, or even the death penalty, I'm pretty sure he'll turn. I made him for weak on the day I met the man, a prime example of the risks of nepotism. For Ricci and the rest of the New York guineas, hiring family reduces the risk that some punk will trade your time for his. But a punk is a punk.

The sun's dropping when we finally stumble on the perfect spot, an old barn about thirty yards off the road. Surrounded by planted fields, the roof has caved in on one side and the whole structure lists seriously to our left, ready to fall over any minute. Best, the only tracks I see were left by the plow that turned the soil and planted the seeds.

"Ya know—Bruce? He's gotta weigh two-thirty."

Dominick's right. Thirty yards might not seem like all that much, but dead bodies are hard to move and we're not gonna be able to come up with a stretcher. Not enough time.

"Whatta ya think we should do?"

Dominick looks at me. "We could drive to the barn, take him out there."

"And leave tire tracks that'll lead whoever farms this dirt right to his body? We have to carry him, Dom. Yeah, along with at least one shovel and maybe a pry bar to lift the floorboards. And we have to do it fast. And I don't want his blood all over the car. Or anywhere else, for that matter. So whatever way you plan to take him out, do it clean."

◆

Another problem that I recognize before I start off—we have to get back here and I have no idea where we are. There's only one thing I can do and it's gonna cost me a cell phone. I have a GPS app on my phone. I use it first to plot my way to Boomtown, then save the current location. Nice, right, but I'll have to lose the phone afterward, then download another navigation app on the new phone, maybe WAZE. New York cabbies swear by it.

So it's all good and I'm almost home when my phone rings and the GPS drops when I answer it. Technologically proficient I'm not. But it's Bruce and I know it's gonna be bad news, news that can't wait.

"Hey, boss, we got a problem."

"And what might that be, Bruce?"

"Rita Lafayette. She's gone."

"Corey Miller's roommate?"

"Yeah."

"And how did that happen?"

"She climbed through the bathroom window."

"With nobody watchin' out."

"Hey, boss, I can't be everywhere."

◆

I push into Maggie Miller's trailer. A man not given to foul moods, or moods of any kind, I'm in as foul a mood as I can imagine. All I can think about is dragging Bruce alive into that barn, about chaining him to a beam, about putting a round into that flabby gut, about watching him die in pain. And I'm not surprised when I find Maggie Miller and her old man sitting in loungers, or Rita Lafayette standing by a miniscule sink making coffee. Rita's a cop-hater from way back. No way she'd go to the police.

"Well, well, well," Maggie says, "the gang's all here."

I take a step toward her, but stop dead in my tracks when her looney father suddenly overcomes his mental afflictions. He flips the blanket in his lap aside to reveal the .45 auto in his hand. Gun and hand roll up, rock steady.

"Must be havin' one of his good days," I tell Maggie.

Maggie flips her chin at Rita. "Might as well know it. Cat's out of the bag. Rita named her a name. Bruce, which is what I already thought."

Now what? Because the bitch is right. Rita can't take the word back. So now what? Reason with the Millers, father and daughter? Threaten them, despite Daddy's gun? Leave quietly, head for our little armory, come back with a dozen AR15s? You could use the single wide to strain spaghetti by the time we finished.

I let my revenge fantasy run for another few seconds, then take a breath. It's only been a few hours since Ricky gave me a simple order. Turn the heat down. Pouring a few hundred rounds into a single-wide trailer isn't likely to meet Ricky's expectations.

"I like you, Maggie. Truly. And your old man? Let's just say he had me fooled and leave it at that. But you have to stay out of my business. There's no escaping that bottom line." I want to tell her not to worry about Bruce. That Bruce will get what's coming to him. I don't. I can't. "Now I'm thankin' you, sincerely, for not callin' Mariola. And I'm not holdin' a grudge against Rita, but I have her on the outside. Bad enough with Mary-Anne in Baxter Medical."

Rita speaks up for the first time. "Fuck you, Charlie. You don't own me."

"I may not own you, Rita, but you definitely owe me." I look at Maggie. "She tell you? How she owes me five grand? Which she mostly put up her nose? If we were talkin' about a straight loan, a street loan, I'd have broken her legs by now."

"Talk to me, Charlie. It ain't up to Maggie." Ms. Lafayette again, her hawk's face sharpened by anger. "I'm not goin' nowhere. As for what I owe you? Take your debt, and your ten-point-a-week interest, and shove 'em up your ass. You been paid back a hundred times over."

◆

It's natural, after a run of bad luck, to think it can't get worse. And that's exactly what I'm thinking as I leave the trailer. Alone. Then I see Dominick standing by the car. Instead of sitting in it. He's wearing his customary blank-page expression, but his head's going from side to side, over and over again, left, right, left, right.

"You ain't gonna believe this, boss," he tells me. "Gene Casio called a few minutes before you come out. Seems like Bruce Angoleri went out to buy a pack of cigarettes, maybe two hours ago. He hasn't come back."

"Anybody try callin' him?"

"Yeah. Went straight to voice mail."

CHAPTER THIRTY-SIX

DELIA

B lanche Weber jumps out of her chair and moves to intercept me when I come into the squad room. "I'm dying to know," she says.

"Know what?"

"About Fetchin' Gretchen." Her grin runs from ear to ear.

"Ah, Gretchen."

"No more Fetchin'?"

I lead the way into my office. "I've been feeling guilty all night, Blanche. The girl was so scared that I thought she'd faint. I didn't think I was that intimidating."

"I think it's more about Danny."

"Danny makes Gretchen afraid of me?"

"Danny's beautiful, Delia, seriously beautiful, and an athlete to boot. To a freshman, he's a stud, a perfect catch sure to draw likes on whatever social media kids are using these days." She stops, lowering her chin so that she's looking up at me. "There'll be others. Other girls. Gretchen won't keep him without a fight. Your boy-child is high status. Sit beside him in the lunchroom and he lights you up."

I lay a paper bag on my desk, carefully remove a latte and a toasted almond doughnut. "So, I should have asked her to prove herself worthy of my son?" I don't wait for an answer. "Gretchen's a nice kid, and very . . . very earnest. She wants Danny to keep his grades up, to get more sleep, to eat healthy foods. And Danny, he lapped it up like a kitten at a bowl of ice cream. Her concern, her motherly attitude, crap he'd never take from me. And it feels like only a week since I was teaching him to read."

Blanche takes a seat and we sit in silence for a moment while I get started on my latte. I'm determined to close the Corey Miller investigation with an arrest, but I'll have to move fast. Charlie's smart. Smart, analytical, and ruthless. And Bruce? Let's say he's a loose end and leave it there.

"I want a search warrant for the Paradise Inn. Get on it right away."

"The grounds?"

"Corey Miller almost certainly died there. That makes the Inn a crime scene."

"What are we looking for?"

A good question. Search warrants have to be specific. No fishing expeditions. "Fentanyl or any object that might have held fentanyl."

"That a real long shot, Delia. Corey was killed two weeks ago."

"True enough. But I'm really after Bruce Angoleri's DNA. We can't include that in a search warrant, but if we get inside, maybe we'll find an excuse to grab his toothbrush or a comb. At worst, it'll give me another chance to brace the women who work there. Now, off you go. I've a doughnut to savor, the same doughnut I promised myself I wouldn't buy when I left home this morning. I intend to enjoy every nibble and crumb."

◆

An hour later, caffeinated and caloried, I head for Baxter Medical Center and its star patient, Mary-Anne Carlson. She's where I left her, in bed with her arm in a hard cast. She's looking miserable and I have to suspect that whatever they're giving her to kill the pain isn't enough to feed the habit she brought with her.

"Hey, Mary-Anne, how're you feeling?"

"Shitty." She presses the little button that controls the flow of morphine. Twice. Unfortunately, the little button is programmed to work only every four hours. I know because I checked at the nurses' station on my way in. When Mary-Anne's effort comes to nothing, she looks up at the clock. "So, whatta ya want?"

"I'm afraid I have some bad news for you."

"Just what I need."

"Probably not. See, you witnessed a homicide that's still being investigated."

"I told you what happened."

"Did you? Until our investigation's completed, we can't be sure. Like we can't be sure you'll stick around. You know, in case we need you to testify. Face it, you're a flight risk on steroids. So, we're moving to hold you as a material witness."

"You can't do that."

"Sure, I can. Can and will. Plus, until a judge signs off on the application, I'm posting a uniformed officer to make sure you stay where you are. Visitors will be screened, of course, with the officer in the room during visits. To keep you from conspiring."

May-Anne's so pissed, her freckles light up. I half expect them to blink on and off.

"You fuckin' cops are all the same. Doesn't matter what you got between your legs, you're all the fucking same."

"I can't argue the point. We all wear the same uniform. But I have a question, let's call it hypothetical. A man named Bruce kills a woman named Corey. He does it because she's pregnant with his child and won't get an abortion. My question is this, Mary-Anne. Given the nature of Corey's employment, how does he know the child is his?"

Mary-Anne responds quickly. "Condoms. With the johns. That was the rule. Condoms or go home and jerk off."

It's a last-piece-of-the-puzzle moment. I step back and give her some room. My threat to detain her as a material witness? If it holds any water at all, it can't be more than a spoonful. But in the short run, before she can lawyer up and get into a courtroom, there's nobody with the authority to stop my posting a cop to make sure no visitor slips her a little something in a glassine envelope.

"So, what do you want from me?" Mary-Anne continues. "What crime did I commit?"

"No crime, which is why I haven't read your rights to you. You're a witness, like I already said."

"I told you what happened, I swear."

"I'm not talking about the shootout, Mary-Anne, and we both know it. The other day, I made an appeal to your conscience. To you and the other women. Me, I'm a realist. My appeal didn't work. Time to move on. Which I'm doing, here and now."

I take out my phone, punch in the number of the reception desk at headquarters. A minute later I'm speaking with Lieutenant Aaron Levanche, the duty officer. My request is quite specific and I make sure that Mary-Anne hears my instructions. Visitors are to be constantly monitored.

"Tell me what you want," she says when I hang up.

"The drugs at the Paradise. Who handled them on the day Corey died, who distributed them?"

"I don't know who coulda handled the coke and the smack. Why should I? Me and the girls, we weren't interested in where they come from. Only where they'd end up, which is in our bodies. Trust me, Officer . . ."

"Captain."

"Trust me, Captain, after a night at the Paradise, you need something to make you feel better. Need it bad."

"I'm not here to critique your lifestyle, Mary-Anne, so get to the point. The fentanyl overdose that killed Corey didn't materialize out of thin air. Somebody put it in her hand. Who?"

Mary-Anne isn't ready, but I don't back down. I wait fifteen minutes until her police-officer guardian arrives, then promise to pay a second visit later in the day. I don't blame her for clamming up, though. She's afraid of Bruce, Charlie, Dominick, the entire crew. As well she should be.

◆

One more courtesy call before I return to the house. I head to Mount Jackson and Zack Butler's manicured brick colonial. Miranda opens the door as I raise my hand to knock, then steps back to allow me inside. I'm guessing Zack has a security system that allows him to identify his visitors as they approach the front door.

"Morning, Captain." Zack's seated where he was last time, in a coffee-colored armchair with his oxygen concentrator to one side.

"Good morning, Zack. How are you?"

"Still breathing air." He turns to his health aide. "Miranda, please. Coffee, and perhaps two slices of that pound cake." The smile never leaves his face as he comes back to me. "Did you know I'm good friends with Jack Harmon, your son's baseball coach?"

"I didn't."

"Jack and I are invested together. And before you indulge your suspicious nature, he's investing money inherited by his wife." He crosses his legs. "Well, if you know Jack at all, you know how much he talks about the kids on the team. Truth be told, I believe the man would exchange his entire investment for a trip to the state championships."

Miranda returns to the living room carrying a tray with the goodies on top. I sip at the coffee, but leave the cake where it is, despite an alluring glaze speckled with orange zest.

"Your son, believe it or not, is Jack's golden ticket. Or so he believes. Jack thinks Danny will be throwing in the low nineties by the end of the season."

"Great, Zack, but I'm not here to chat. I've got a busy day ahead."

"You disappoint me."

"Sorry. Or not sorry. Not sorry because I believe that you, meaning the Boomtown investors, invited the New York crew to exploit the chaos. In return for a piece of the action."

"Captain . . ."

I wave him off. "I'm not here to conduct an investigation. I'm here to ask a favor. You have influence in the capitol. I want you to turn up the heat on Sheriff Fletcher and the Sprague County Board of Supervisors. If we're given the authority to patrol Boomtown, we'll restore order." I lean forward, staring straight into his eyes. "You made a mistake inviting these New York assholes to prey on the construction workers. Too gung ho. Too violent. Titus Klint, Corey Miller, Stitch Kreuter, a fifteen-year-old runaway? Talk about overkill. So, how many more until the state police step in hard? Until they take a close look at the grid in Boomtown, the sewage disposal system, the water supply? And one more thing, if Gloria Meacham knows about your connection to the Shearson Investment Group, you didn't cover your tracks all that well."

CHAPTER THIRTY-SEVEN

DELIA

I'm like a kid in a fight, blindly throwing punch after punch, hoping one of them will connect. But I've no more punches to throw at present and I drive over to Lillian Taney's for an early lunch. I haven't seen Emmaline for a few days and I've been missing her. She's playing in the backyard when I arrive, swinging on a rope swing hung from the branches of a white oak. Lillian's stirring the coals in a charcoal grill. Next to the grill, on a folding table, a plate of stacked hamburger patties, sliced cheddar and seeded rolls, accompanied by a bowl of potato salad. Heavy on the mayo.

"Push me, Aunt Delia."

After exchanging a quick hug with Lillian, I comply. Emmaline's full of herself today, chattering on about her new boyfriend, Freddy, who lives a couple blocks away. Emmaline met him at a playdate, where he gave her a toy airplane, an F35.

"It's a stealth fighter," she solemnly declares.

"And what does 'stealth' mean?"

Emmaline gives me one of her now-you're-cheating looks. "You can't see it because it goes so fast. That's what Freddy says. It's invisible." Before I can ask any more stupid questions, she starts in on her favorite cartoon characters, the Minions. I tune out, as adults tend to do, but I'm still here, laying my hands on Emmaline's back, pushing her forward. I need this break, this slice of normal existence to keep the horror in check.

We all need it, all my cop brothers and sisters, and I've witnessed rapid post-divorce declines when bar and bottle replaced home and hearth. Maybe, when I think of Danny leaving to start his own life, that's what I fear. I have Zoe, true, but I've never been able to sustain a close relationship, the longest gone after a mere six months.

The burgers come off the grill a few minutes later and the conversation shifts to Danny and Mike while Emmaline stuffs her face. Our kids, our domestic lives, all those personal ties that make it possible for me to do my job. I soak it up, eager as a junkie in need of a fix. Still, I don't have a lot of time, which is why I'm not upset when Blanche calls from headquarters. We now have a search warrant for the Paradise Inn. I instruct Blanche to assemble a small team, no more than five cops, including her. I want as few people as possible looking over my shoulder.

◆

Blanche and her team are in place when I reach the Paradise. I'm not expecting trouble, but we're prepared, six armed cops, four in uniform, as we march up to the front door. Only to find the door unlocked and the trailer's interior empty except for a few odds and ends.

"Stand down for a moment," I tell my crew as I place a call to the office of our district attorney, Tommy Atkinson. Tommy isn't available and I have to settle for a line prosecutor named Sheila Giannis.

"If the occupants have moved out, anything left behind is considered abandoned," she explains. "Similar to trash left at the curb."

"Our warrant is fairly specific . . ."

"Forget the warrant. Look anywhere you want at anything you want to look at. Abandoned means abandoned. Private property rights no longer apply."

◆

I order Patrolman Frank Baxter to video the entire trailer, every room, every closet, the interior of every drawer, empty or not. There's no rush, what with the place empty. Or so I conclude until a Sprague County patrol car turns onto the street. It's going too fast, and stops too short, to be part of any routine patrol.

The deputy sheriff inside dons his Smokey Bear hat before getting out of the car. A voice of authority in Sprague County, he pulls himself up to his full height and raises his chin so high that he looks at me along the length of his nose. If it wasn't for the Coke-bottle glasses, I'd be intimidated.

"Before you get started, Deputy, we have a warrant to search the domicile in furtherance of a homicide investigation. I can't let you go inside."

Hearing this, the four cops standing outside, come to full alert. This is not lost on the deputy, who still hasn't introduced himself. Or told me what he wants. Not that I need to hear it from his lips. The simple fact that he showed up being proof enough. Somebody made a call to Sheriff Fletcher. Fletcher dispatched this deputy, with more to come.

Which means I can't wait. I leave the deputy and my team outside as I plunge into the double wide. I've got my phone out, ready to record the location of anything that might contain traces of Bruce Angoleri's DNA. Maybe a used handkerchief with his initials embroidered in a corner. Not happening, but I do find two rooms once occupied by men. A pair of socks in a corner of the only closet in one of the rooms. A torn shirt, possibly soiled, on the floor of the second. Soiled underwear beneath a bed. Hair in a small comb with broken teeth. As it stands,

I've secured Charlie's and Gene Casio's DNA through a federal database. Neither impregnated Corey Miller. That leaves Bruce.

You only have to get lucky once. I order Frank Baxter to video every inch of the room, but not to recover any evidence. That job I assign to a patrolwoman named Bonnie Lammister. Just in time too. Sheriff Pickford Fletcher arrives only a minute later. He's too big to slide out of the marked patrol unit. He has to unfold, one limb at a time, but when he rises to his full height, the man is truly imposing, a giant.

Imposing or not, I'm on the phone to Vern before Fletcher saunters up to me, taking his time, his authority preceding him like a shock wave. In rural counties like Sprague, the sheriff is the law. And that goes double for sheriffs like Fletcher, whose family has been prominent for generations. Unfortunately, Vern doesn't answer his cell phone.

"You are?" he asks, as if he hadn't met me a couple days ago.

"Captain Mariola."

He doesn't respond and I know he expects me to explain myself. Maybe even to apologize. For my part, I want to call him a hillbilly asshole just to see if he'll reach for his weapon, the six-shooter tucked into its tooled holster. In fact, I don't say anything, forcing him to speak first. Whatever we're doing, it's ongoing, so if he wants it to stop, he can't wait around.

"May I ask what you're doing in Sprague County?"

"Executing a search warrant pursuant to a homicide investigation."

Fletcher likes to intimidate, obviously, and I think he'd be at it now if he had the manpower to back him up. "Let me see it."

I resist the urge to make him say please. The only items of significance from Fletcher's point of view are the address to be searched and the judge's signature. Still, he makes a show of examining the warrant as he considers his position here. He should be aiding the investigation into Corey Miller's death. That's not happening, but does he really have the nerve to impede it? Corey's been all over the local news for days, the same stations, newspapers, and websites that Sprague County residents go to for their news.

The tension dissolves in an instant when a battered Jeep turns onto the street. Basil Ulrich of the *Baxter Bugle* is behind the wheel. He guides the Jeep to a halt and hops out, followed by a photographer.

Sheriffs are elected, not appointed, and Pickford Fletcher's a seasoned politician well into his fourth term. His transformation from brooding hulk to affable giant seems effortless, a conditioned reflex. "Well, Basil, how're you this fine afternoon?"

"Eager for news, Sheriff." Basil nods to me. "Afternoon, Captain."

Fletcher jumps in ahead of me. "Had a report of a break-in." He jerks his chin at the Paradise. "Turns out the

Baxter PD's executin' a search warrant. Signed by a judge."
Another grin. "Good enough for me."

◆

Good enough for me as well. Fletcher and his deputy desert
the scene. He can't stop the search, but he's not prepared to
embrace it either. Basil presses me, but I refuse to comment.
Ongoing investigation, the usual disclaimer.

"C'mon, Captain, this has to be about Corey Miller.
Everybody knows she worked at the Paradise."

"If everybody knows, Basil, what do you need me for?"

In truth, nobody needs me. Not here, anyway. I leave
Blanche to supervise the activity and cross the street to
where Maggie and her dad sit in lawn chairs, enjoying the
show.

"Afternoon, Captain."

"Good afternoon, Maggie." Out of the corner of my eye,
I detect movement inside the trailer, a shadow behind
a tiny, curtained window. "You have company? Am I
interrupting?"

"No, ma'am."

"That's good, Maggie, because if I conclude that you're
obstructing my investigation, I'll put you in a cage. That's
not a threat. It's a promise."

"Now, see, takin' that attitude? Makin' enemies? And
just when I was goin' to offer a tidbit sure to advance that
investigation."

I can't help it. I smile. "Let's hear the tidbit, Maggie. Please."

"The ladies who toiled in the Paradise? You drive down to the southern edge of Boomtown and make a left, you'll find a Quonset hut, pretty good size. The ladies are bein' held prisoner in that hut."

"And how do you know this?"

"Word come to me from a member of the community with a conscience."

CHAPTER THIRTY-EIGHT
MAGGIE MILLER

M e and Daddy cool our heels outside, allowing time for events to unfold. My news caught Mariola by surprise, but I'm not deludin' myself. She won't cut me any slack, tip be damned. The woman's a true believer in law and order, that policin' belongs to the police. There ain't no room for street justice in her worldview. Guess that's modern. Guess my own origins are as primitive as city folk take them to be. Hillbilly primitive, family honor primitive. The police are not your friends, not in Redmond Lake. In the back hills of Kentucky, the police belong to whoever holds the power, political and economic. They're a blunt instrument ready to smash any threat to those powers. The police, the prosecutors, and the judges, all feeding from a trough provided by the politicians.

Sometimes, maybe most of the time, humans base their decisions on educated guesses. Having been a detective, I claim an educational advantage. So, what would I do if faced with the info I fed to Mariola? Women imprisoned? A murder suspect currently missing and likely to be minding those prisoners? I'd hightail it to that Quonset hut is what I'd do. And if I was Charlie and got a call informin' me that Captain Mariola's at the front door, I'd surely follow.

◆

Charlie's on the go an hour after my conversation with Mariola, a black dot traveling east from his girlfriend's home in Baxter. Three minutes later, the dot slides across the southern boundary of the construction zone. It continues straight onto First Avenue and that Quonset hut. God, how I love bein' right.

Time to go.

◆

Me and Daddy head inside where Rita Lafayette sits on our love seat watching a reality TV show. The woman's workin' something over in her mind, has been since she got here. I can see the wheels. They're still turning, relentlessly, and I suspect she's reached a state of near paralysis.

"You got any plans, Rita? Folks who'll put you up? Maybe someplace far, far away? We can drive you to Sheldon, drop you at the Greyhound."

"You throwin' me out?" Rita's angry and bitter all the time, far as I can make out. Now she's feelin' a hundred percent betrayed. I can see it in her eyes.

"Wouldn't think of it. But me and Daddy are leaving now and I don't expect we'll be comin' back. You can stay here if you want. Rent's paid through the month. But if I was in your shoes, I'd run for it while I still can. Charlie gets his hands on you, he ain't gonna be in a forgivin' mood." I give it a couple ticks. "And what you brought with you in your handbag? It's not gonna fill your nose forever."

A pile driver in the construction zone starts up at that moment, the crash of metal on metal reminding me somehow of the church bells in Redmond Lake. I don't think Rita's hearin' it that way. Her mouth is tight and her eyes are spewin' rage.

"Don't know where you come from or what you hope to accomplish," I finally tell her. "But there's a loaded Glock in the top drawer of my bureau. I was you, I'd keep it close to hand."

◆

Early on, me and Daddy found us a hidey-hole up in Oakland Gardens, the devastated neighborhood in the northeastern part of the city. The little house we rented looked ready to give up the ghost, what with the mold on the walls and the buckled floorboards. But neither's been a problem for us because we've kept our distance, the house bein' more about findin' that private space when privacy was called for. Which it is now.

We do make one stop before we reach the house, the parking lot of a strip mall. The lot's fairly crowded and I have to search for a few minutes before pulling into an open space next to a Toyota Highlander with tinted windows.

"You prepared, girl?" Daddy asks we get into the Highlander.

"Yessir, I am. Been prepared since I first saw Corey's face on the television. What happened to her wasn't right, and I'm not just talkin' about her murder. The women who worked at the Paradise are currently bein' held prisoner. Maybe their lives are sinful, accordin' to some. But they did nothin' to merit bein' enslaved. I don't believe whining helps, and I'm not expectin' justice in this world either. Not while there's men like Bruce and Charlie roaming through it. You have to settle for fightin' back the little bit you can, for takin' justice one piece at a time, knowin' you'll never get to the bottom of the pile. That new demons are born as fast as the old ones die off."

◆

Jay-Jay's in the house when me and Daddy come through the door. He's sitting on a hard bench, legs crossed, smoking a cigarette. The furniture in the room is sparse, to say the least. A scatterin' of cheap pine chairs, a table that's propped up in one corner, a lamp with a torn shade, unlit, on the table. The only item still new lookin' is a mattress on the floor. Bruce Angoleri's lyin' on the mattress, his wrists and ankles secured with zip ties. His head jerks up when me and Daddy walk into the house. Maybe he didn't know Jay-Jay from Santa Claus, but he's figured it out now.

"He give you a hard time, Jay-Jay?" I gesture to a bleeding wound just behind the ear on the left side of Bruce's head. As scalp wounds go, this one isn't as bad as it is scary, at least from Bruce's point of view. There's a line of blood that runs along his neck, from the wound to the soaked collar of his shirt.

"He was reluctant at first, Maggie, but we come to an understanding."

"Listen—" Bruce speaks for the first time, but I'm not ready.

"Later, Bruce. We'll have plenty of time later." I turn back to Jay-Jay. "You didn't gag him."

"Didn't wanna chance him chokin'. But when I told him to stay quiet or I'd beat him till he cried, the man chose Plan A."

I'm feelin' warm now, warm toward Jay-Jay, who left his wife and two daughters to uphold the family honor. The man never faltered, laboring day after day at the construction site, helping with whatever needed doin'.

"Jay-Jay, words are failin' me . . ."

"That's a first." This from Daddy, standing with his feet apart, starin' down at Bruce.

"Now, Daddy, I know you're not one to polish another man's shoes, but this time you need to back off. Jay-Jay's a hero in my book and that's the way we're gonna tell it when we come home. Jay-Jay, you packed?"

"Packed and the trunk loaded."

I kiss him on the cheek. "Then go home to Janny and your girls. Go be a father again."

As I watch Jay-Jay's Tahoe roll down the block, then turn south toward I-70, I find myself wishing I was finished here. We have what we come for, me and Daddy. We have the man who almost certainly murdered Corey and the baby growin' inside her.

Still, there's questions to be answered. Not on Daddy's part. Quick judgment's been a way of life for him, maybe startin' from birth. Heavy hands too. Heavy enough for me and Corey to spend as much time away from his company as possible.

It's evenin' now, with the sun just above a row of girders at the construction site a couple blocks away. I'm seein' this because the houses in between have been demolished. Some long ago, some recently. There's construction all around us, too, though not on this block. Seems no part of Baxter's immune from development. The city's reinventing itself, still not sure of the outcome but movin' ahead anyway.

Little by little over the next couple hours, the construction sounds die off. The shadows deepen rapidly, this bein' early May, then disappear as the dark settles in. Standin' at the window, I can see a few scattered streetlights, but most have been out for a long time. The infrastructure's in need of a serious upgrade, but development marches on. If Boomtown wasn't lurkin' on the border, Baxter would probably be called Boomtown. It has that feel.

◆

I can't say the waitin' was comfortable with only those hard-backed chairs to set on, but I'm grateful when the neighborhood grows quiet enough for me to hear a gusty wind as it pushes through the weeds and shrubs around the house. It's time now, but I'm feelin' a reluctance. Maybe I'm not as tough as I think I am. Maybe I can't make myself believe that murder justifies murder.

"Okay, Bruce, let's get you sittin' up."

Between me and Daddy, we drag Bruce off the mattress and prop him up against the front wall, with the window to his right. I need to focus on Bruce and keep watch at the same time.

"You know why you're here, Bruce?"

"Why don't you tell me?"

He manages a defiant tone, but I'm staring into his large brown eyes and reading deer-in-the-headlights. The defiance part doesn't bother me in the slightest, it being so common in the initial stage of an interrogation. Only this isn't an interrogation.

"Me and Daddy are puttin' you on trial, Bruce."

"For what?"

"For murderin' Corey." He starts to speak, but I shake my head. "This trial, it's not like trials you get here in America. There ain't no courtroom, and no judge to keep things honest. No lawyer, neither. This trial, it's more like you might find in China or Russia. In this trial, you're guilty until you prove yourself innocent."

CHAPTER THIRTY-NINE

DELIA

Gene Casio's not happy to see me walk through the door. Or Cade Barrow, for that matter, who I collected along the way. Or two members of Cade's SWAT team, Howard Castle and Sal Grigorio. They're in uniform, without the RoboCop SWAT gear, but all three are large men. And no more in love with human trafficking—which should be called slavery—than I am.

Released on his own recognizance after being arraigned on the gun possession charge, Casio decides to make a show of it.

"What do you want?"

"Get out of the way, Gene."

"Not unless you got a warrant."

Without speaking, Cade steps forward and slams the heels of his hands into Casio's chest. Casio flies back, loses his balance, and lands on the floor. His blue eyes light up. The man's been pushing women around for a long time. He's no doubt concluded that preying on the weak equates to power in the real world. A genuine badass. That a number of those women are there to witness his humiliation does my heart good.

"You have a gun on you, Gene?"

Howard Castle's already drawn his weapon. Is he looking for an excuse? Back in Florida, I taught a course in de-escalation. That's not where I'm going today.

"Answer the question, Gene."

"Yeah," he admits.

"Roll onto your stomach and extend your arms." When he hesitates, I add, "Patrolman Castle, are you in fear of your life?"

"Gettin' that way."

Criminal mentality has always been a mystery to this cop. I recognize it, can predict it, but I don't understand how a man charged with possession of a firearm will commit the same offense a day later. I watch Casio roll onto his belly, as ordered, and extend his arms. Cade pats him down, recovers a Browning auto, finally stands up.

"He's clean."

◆

The Quonset hut's interior is beyond primitive. Metal walls, metal roof, some kind of composite floor. A dozen lawn chairs, most occupied, are clustered at one end of the room. Against a wall, folding picnic tables hold soft drinks, playing cards, scattered paper plates, and a small flatscreen. A kitchen counter barely five feet long includes a sink and a tiny prep area. A refrigerator alongside the counter is small enough to bring on a camping trip.

Hanging from a rope that runs across the building, sheets partition a smaller part of the hut. Cade's already on it, crossing the room to yank one of the sheets off the line to reveal eight or nine scattered, very narrow mattresses, each with a crumpled sleeping bag on top. There's another room, this one with a door, a bathroom no doubt. Cade checks it out.

"All clear, Captain."

"Great. Gene Casio, you're under arrest. You have the right to remain silent, but if you decide to shoot your moron mouth off, anything you say can be used against you in a court of law. You also have a right to a lawyer. Free if you can't afford one, which I'm sure you can. Do you understand these rights? You should, you asshole, because they're the same exact rights I read to you a day ago." I gesture to my team. "Take him out of here. Yourselves too."

I'm not going to charge Casio. For one thing, he hasn't committed a crime. The statute only applies to concealed firearms carried in public. I'm looking for privacy here, a few words with Charlie's women.

"Anybody wanna tell me what happened to Bruce?"

"Gone." This from a tall woman with a pair of shoulders to match. Her name—or the name she gave me last time out—is Gretta.

"Gone where?"

"Left to run an errand. Never came back."

Bruce on the run? It makes sense. We're close to making an arrest and Charlie knows it. If Charlie knows it, his boss in New York probably knows it. Gangsters aren't all that complicated. They prefer simple to complex solutions. The simplest way to deal with their Bruce problem? Execution. That would make sense to Bruce. As would acting first, before Charlie executes his orders by executing Bruce.

There's a third possibility out there, one I don't want to consider. Maggie Miller. She didn't flinch when I threatened her, but I don't believe she dismissed my threat either. A dangerous woman, surely.

"Why don't you tell us what the fuck you want?" This from a slender woman whose name I can't recall.

"The real question is what *you* want. All of you. The real question is whether you want to be enslaved. Because that's exactly what's happening. At any minute you can be sold off to the highest bidder and taken anywhere in the country. Just pack your clothes, get in the car."

"Listen up, Officer—"

"Captain."

"Great, Captain. But if you think we're gonna rat on Charlie, you need to think again. Hard as our lives may be, suicide's not on the table." This from Gretta, who's taken a step forward. She's asserting a right to defend her sisters, with her body a psychological barrier. To get to them, you've got to go through her.

"I know that, Gretta." I watch her flinch at the use of her name. "But it's pretty obvious, with the Paradise shut down, that you're gonna be shipped out like so much excess inventory. Has anyone told you where you're going?"

"Charlie said something about Las Vegas."

"Something about? Look, I've already spoken to Rita, so I'm not makin' it up as I go along. Charlie and his people are holding your debts. You can't leave until they're paid in full. That's the way it's supposed to work, but we all know that shylocks swap debts. It happens every day and there's nothing to stop Charlie from selling your debts. And yours, and yours, and yours. Nothing."

One sure way to get folk to pay close attention? Tell them what they already know. The women, all of them, are listening now. "Take a second to consider what Charlie's dealing with here. Corey Miller was murdered. Corey Miller was pregnant. Bruce Angoleri gave her the mix of fentanyl and heroin that caused her death. You're all potential witnesses. For example, Corey was pregnant? How many of you did she tell? Did she name the father of her child? Charlie doesn't know the answer and he doesn't know what you know either."

"Okay, we get it, Captain." Gretta draws the last word out. Captainnnnnn. "But what the fuck can we do about it?"

"That depends on how you want to spend the rest of your life, Gretta. Do you want to wake up in the morning and learn that you're headed to an iron mine in Minnesota, where the January temperature drops to fifty below zero? Or a copper mine in Idaho? Or an oil field in Alaska? Remember, Charlie wants you as far away as possible. He wants to be certain you're not around to testify. The farther away, the better."

"You haven't answered my question."

"I'll answer it now. Pack your clothes and leave. I'll arrange transportation to the bus station, even pay for tickets to whatever destination you choose. You get that? A destination you choose, not Charlie. And I'll make sure the cops who escort you keep Charlie and his thugs well away."

"Suppose they come after us?"

"You've been watching too much television. You know, where some twelve-year-old clicks a keyboard and your whole life appears on the screen. Charlie's not gonna find you. Most likely, he won't even look. Yeah, he wants the money he claims you owe him, but he also wants you far away. Which is exactly where you're going. Far, far away."

I look from one woman to another. They're teetering. They know I'm right, but they've been dependent for years and years. Time for my closing argument. "You don't need tea leaves to read your futures. You'll never be out of debt. Charlie or some other pimp will make sure of that. They'll use you until you can't earn, then dump you on the street with the clothes on your back and a habit you can't feed.

Better to get out now while you're still young enough to have a chance at life." I glance at my watch. "We don't have a lot of time, me or you. Once I leave, Gene Casio's gonna walk back into this pitiful excuse for a house. He's gonna make sure you don't have another chance to get away before Charlie decides your fate."

◆

A commotion outside draws my attention. I hear Charlie first: "You can't keep me out of my home." I want to laugh until I hear Cade's reply: "One more step and I'll kick you all the way back to New York."

"I need to attend to this," I tell the women. "Those of you who want out, now's your chance."

About half the woman begin to move toward the back of the hut as I reach the door. By the time I get back, they'll be ready. Outside, Charlie's standing a few feet away from Cade Barrow. His eyes are wild as he fights for self-control. Can't blame him. His plans are falling apart.

"You got no right to force your way onto private property."

He's correct. But as we're not about to make an arrest, what's he gonna do about it? Sue the Baxter Police Department?

"You lost, Charlie," I tell him. "This is the beginning of your end and what you need to consider is how your bosses in New York are gonna react to your failure. But not here and now. Here and now you're gonna back off. You and Gene. Like across the road, at the very least."

Casio and Charlie look at each other for a moment, eyes darting back and forth as they consider and reject every choice except compliance. Finally, the pair cross the street to lean against Charlie's car.

"This ain't over," he tells me. "Not even close."

There's nothing to be gained by responding and I don't. I turn to brief Cade on the situation.

"You want me to order up a van? Drive them to the bus station?"

"Yeah, and make sure nobody interferes. You see any of Charlie's people around the station, warn 'em off." I wait for Cade to nod, then step back inside the building to find eight women, every one of Charlie's indebted workers, packing bags.

"I owe Charlie nine fat ones," Gretta explains. "This is an offer I can't refuse."

CHAPTER FORTY

CHARLIE

First thing, a van shows up, the kind used to transport cops to some event, maybe a parade, maybe a riot, wherever they're needed. My heart sinks because I gotta figure the girls have turned. They're gonna rat, gonna sell out the whole operation. Given enough witnesses, Mariola can bust me and half the crew. Then the girls march through the door carryin' suitcases. They're leaving, but it's not the worst outcome. Sure, we'll lose the debts, but we've already made our money back ten times over. Meanwhile, gone is gone, for me and Mariola. And it's not like there's a whore shortage. It's not like I'm gonna have a hard time finding replacements.

There's still Ricky, of course. He's not gonna be happy—the guy's cheaper than Scrooge McDuck—but

Ricky's for later. There's too much happening now for me to worry about the future. Assuming I have one.

Next to me, Gene's goin', *motherfucker* this, *motherfucker* that. I put an elbow in his ribs. The women are leaving, that's one problem solved, with many still to go. Including Rita Lafayette in Maggie Miller's trailer, Mary-Anne Carlson in a hospital bed, and Bruce, Bruce, Bruce.

"Get on the horn, Gene. I want to see everyone at La Mina in an hour. No excuses. Everyone."

Gene's a follower, always has been. Now he looks at me through watery blue eyes, seeming grateful. True, his pimp world is falling apart, but my tone is firm and he's reassured. Someone's in charge.

"Get in the car, Gene. Make the calls."

"Okay, Charlie."

"Everyone, Gene. No bullshit."

◆

Mariola has to get in a final shot. Naturally. She's turned this into mano a mano, me against her. Gonna run me out of town. I've been warned. See you on Main Street at high noon, or inside the OK Corral, or maybe Wild Bill Hickok taking one to the back of the head.

"Get out, Charlie, while you can," she tells me. "Pack up your thugs and hit the road."

"Jeez, Captain, that's harsh, really harsh. And just when I was startin' to feel at home. By the way, tomorrow morning a lawyer's gonna show up by Mary-Anne's bedside. You know, to explain her options."

It's weak, but it's the best I can do for the moment. And I'm not a fool. Mariola's right. The odds are growin' steeper by the hour. The odds against makin' this operation a success. Mariola's hoping that matters, that I'll evaluate my position on the battlefield rationally. That I'll conclude that retreat is my only option. It's a joke really.

If we shut down, Ricky's gonna suffer massive losses. The cost of establishing the operation, all the debts, all the zeroes he hoped—no, expected—to flow into his hands. He's not gonna take his frustration out on Gene Casio, or any of the other foot soldiers. Foot soldiers are too valuable. But lessons have to be taught. Bruce, for one, if Ricky ever got his hands on him. And me, the man he trusted to execute his Boomtown project.

So it's all in for me. If I can't restore order, there's no goin' home to Ricky. I'll have to get in the wind and hope he can't find me. But, again, that's for later. We're not finished yet. And maybe, just maybe, Bruce is truly gone, no longer in Boomtown or Baxter. No Bruce, no arrest, no headlines, no wrath of the righteous visited on the unrepentant.

I can do hope. In fact, I've always been optimistic. But I'm smelling a rat here. Bruce hasn't shown much anxiety up to this point. No reason he should, because I haven't gotten in his face, haven't threatened him, haven't even whined about his betrayal. Plus, he's married to Ricky's niece, who comes to Ricky's house with her two kids every Sunday. So why'd he run?

I have a name for this smelly rat. Maggie Miller, the queen of chaos. Her interference has to end, simple as that. As for me, I have nothing to lose. Or everything, depending on how you look at it.

◆

They dribble inside, two or three at a time, including two women. I guess the times really are a-changin'. I don't have a problem with either of the women. In fact, I would have put them in charge of the Paradise if Ricky hadn't reserved the part to his niece's husband.

My people are wearing their great stone faces, which means they're worried. Our meetings have generally been congenial. Lots of gossip about the folks back home, a stiff drink to smooth the way. The worry part worries me, but at least I won't have to spend much time bringing everyone up to date.

"Listen close, because I don't want to repeat myself. Bruce Angoleri murdered Corey Miller. He handed her the overdose, knowing it was an overdose, because she was pregnant with his child. Now Bruce is gone and that's what we're gonna deal with tonight."

Sam Lobosco raises a hand. Very predictable. Sam's in his fifties. He's been with Ricky almost as long as Dominick. "Corey Miller was a whore. She took on maybe six or eight guys a night. It coulda been any one of 'em."

"No, Sam, it couldn't be a john because the Paradise had a rule. Ironclad, right? Condoms only. That was me giving the order and the women were glad to hear it. An STD can take a whore off the count for weeks." I wait for Sam to nod acceptance. "We have to move fast because Bruce is nowhere to be found and the whores are off to God knows where. That last part, the whores, is good news. At least they won't be talkin' to the cops. As for Bruce, if he's gone, that's also good news. But if he's not, if he's holed up in Boomtown or Baxter, we have a problem that can't be ignored. Understand? If the cops get their hands on Bruce, if they charge him with murder, he can put all of us away."

Kenny Duro raises his hand. He's on Tony Carbone's drug crew, a quiet guy with a confident attitude. You give him a job, he does it.

"What's up, Kenny?"

"Bruce, I'm pretty sure he had a buddy." Kenny scratches the top of a bald skull the shape of an egg. "Not one of us."

"Like who?"

"Like a dealer named Mack Killian."

"Does Killian buy from us?"

"Yeah, always. Mack's good people. Reliable. He lives toward the top of Boomtown in one of those cab-over campers. A local, right? Grew up in Sprague County, but moved here because it's a lot safer. No cops. Anyway, I saw Bruce's car parked in front of Mack's camper. Twice, I saw this."

"You might have told me before, Kenny."

"I know. I was thinkin' about it. Ya know, thinkin' it over. I mean, Bruce has his thing and we have ours."

I stop him right there. "Forget what I said. It's not blame time, right? It's find Bruce Angoleri time. Tell me, what does Mack buy from us?"

"Smack. Strictly."

"Does he cut it with fentanyl?"

"I can't speak to that. Mack pays for the product and I go home. What he does afterward is his business."

CHAPTER FORTY-ONE

CHARLIE

Mack Killian's little camper is parked two blocks from Boomtown's northern boundary. There's a trailer to the right, its windows dark, and a vacant lot to the left. The sun has disappeared and darkness all but settled in, a darkness the block's one streetlight, a hundred yards away, barely penetrates. Dominick and I take positions on either side of the door as Tony Carbone knocks twice.

"Hey, Mack, it's Tony Carbone. Open up."

The door has a small window covered by a curtain. When the curtain's pulled aside, light from inside the camper illuminates Tony Carbone. A former boxer with the facial scars to prove it, Tony's thin lips are parted in a completely unconvincing smile.

"Whatta ya want, Tony?"

Tony holds up a paper bag. "I got a package I need to off in a hurry. You been good people, Mack. Good people right along." He gives the bag a little shake. "Hey, we don't wanna talk our business on the street. Open up, man."

After a short pause, Killian does just that. A big mistake because we push our way inside and close the door behind us. Killian's eyes widen, but his pupils remain mere pinpoints.

"What, what . . ."

The interior of the camper is tiny, with barely enough room for the four of us. There's a bed at one end, a small couch, a kitchen counter with a TV on top, and a sink. A small door hides what must be a bathroom.

"I'm not gonna beat around the bush," I say. "I don't have the time. Tell me about you and Bruce."

"Bruce?"

I slap him across the face and he falls back on the couch. Dominick yanks him back to his feet.

"Better listen up, Mack. I just told you I don't have time for bullshit."

Killian raises a hand to the side of his face. He's relatively sober now, the adrenaline flooding his body a counter to whatever drugs he's put in his veins. Both arms are scarred.

"Yeah, Bruce comes over from time to time."

"Why?"

"Look, I didn't know it was some kind of secret. Like he was sneakin' out."

"I asked why, Mack. Why does Bruce come over? What does he want?"

Tony Carbone chimes in. "Maybe it's sex. Are you and Bruce fucking, Mack? Who pitches, who catches?"

Killian's offended, and pissed. I can see that much. Only he's half Tony's size and not stupid enough to raise his voice. Or stoned enough.

"Bruce likes to get off, okay? It's no big thing. I'm like a dealer, right? Nobody comes for the conversation."

"Good, now we're makin' progress," I say. "How often he show up?"

"Maybe five, six times total."

"He ever take somethin' home?"

"Couple times."

"See, that's what I don't get. Bruce could've bought smack from our people. Just like you, Mack, just like you buy from us. So, it doesn't make sense that he'd buy our smack from a dealer who's probably cut it to shit."

Tony gives Killian a little shove. "Answer the man."

"He didn't ask a question."

"Yeah, Tony, he's right. I didn't ask a question. So, I'll ask one now. You cut the smack we sell you with fentanyl? And think carefully before you answer. If you say no and we find any fentanyl in this camper? I don't think I need to explain what happens next."

For dealers like Mack, fentanyl is about profit. Manufactured in Mexico, fentanyl can be purchased readily, and cheap, on the dark web. Start with an ounce, 28.5 grams, of reasonably potent heroin. Add a third of a gram of fentanyl, then cut the pile with an ounce of some neutral chemical like sucrose. Now you have two ounces of reasonably strong heroin at a tenth of what two ounces should cost you. There's still the risk, of course, that the mix is uneven, or the fentanyl is more potent than you expect. Then addicts end up dead.

"Yeah, I cut with fentanyl, but so do a lot of dealers. I mean, like everybody."

"I'm not here to question your ethics, Mack. I want to know if you sold or gave fentanyl to Bruce."

Mack's death sentence is written on his face. Bruce used the fentanyl he got from Mack Killian to murder Corey Miller. For me, it's not a moral issue. No, for me, Mack Killian's another way for Mariola to tie Bruce to Corey. He's a loose end. I nod to Dominick, who takes a quick step toward Mack. When Mack turns to face him, I slide my right arm around Mack's neck, locking my bicep on one carotid artery, my forearm on the other. Yanking on my right wrist with my left hand, I lock the hold down.

The flow of blood to his brain interrupted, Killian instinctively reaches for my arm, only to have Dominick grab his hands. Then he's kicking and twisting from side to side, the anticipated response. I take a step back, pulling him off balance without loosening my grip.

Twenty seconds later, Killian passes out. His eyes bulge now and his lips are turning blue. He's limp, a rag doll, arms hanging straight down, a dead weight. Only he's not dead, not yet, and I hold on tight. I'm not feeling much of anything at the moment, and neither is Tony judging from the relaxed set of his mouth. Only Dominick's animated. He's nodding away, still holding on to Mack's hands.

"Another minute, boss," he explains. "Just another minute."

The minute passes and I lower Mack Killian to the floor while Dominick checks for a pulse in his throat.

"Nothing."

Time to go, but I take a moment to check the scene. Given Killian's livelihood, his body will be discovered fairly soon. What will Sheriff Fletcher and his deputies make of what they find? There are no marks on Killian to indicate foul play. No ligature marks, no bruising, no crushed bones in his throat. Killian's brain was deprived of oxygen until it shut down. That stopped his heart, ending his life. In the same way that an overdose depresses respiration, depriving the brain of oxygen. Given that Pickford Fletcher is as lazy as they come and wants no part of what's happening in Boomtown, I have to believe he'll take the easy way out.

"So what now?" Tony wants to know.

"Now we take care of our Maggie Miller problem. Once and for all."

◆

I've got the boys jacked up, but my goals fall short of killing Maggie and her old man. What I want, most of all, is Rita

Lafayette. Present when Bruce put the overdose in Corey Miller's hand, she's a final nail in Bruce's penal coffin. At the moment, I don't know what's happened to Bruce.

I have no desire to harm Rita Lafayette. I just want her away from Baxter. I have no real beef with Maggie Miller either. But if we can't come to an agreement, I'll kill Maggie and her now-recovered father. Not me personally, but I'll see that it's done. I can't have the woman constantly stirring the pot, because Sheriff Fletcher will have to act if the chaos continues. I mean, keeping things cool was the entire reason me and Dominick attacked the Horde in that canyon. Instead of arranging an ambush in Boomtown.

◆

An air horn sounds only a few hundred yards away as we leave the car. Tonight's deliveries have already begun. I listen for a moment to the faint rumble of diesel engines idling at the south end of the construction zone, then a quick hiss of escaping air as some trucker eases up on the brakes.

"All right, let's do it."

Maggie's windows are dark. I can see that much from the corner. Fine with me. The locks on these cheap trailers are flimsy enough. Let's be waiting inside when she comes home.

Good idea, but it's not to be. Back in the shadows against the trailer, a woman sits on a lawn chair. Quietly waiting. Her expression doesn't change as we approach to within twenty feet. Next to me, Dominick stirs, his first instinct predictable. In a way, I can't blame him because Rita Lafayette raises a hand—a hand holding a gun—then lowers it to her lap.

"Cool it, Dom." I hold my hands apart. "You, too, Rita. We're not here to hurt you."

"Then what do you want?"

"Maggie Miller."

"Gone."

"Gone where?"

"Don't know. Just packed up and left." Back in the shadows, Rita's dark eyes are black holes, no pupils, no iris. "Advised me to do the same."

I take a second here. The street is quiet, but for how long? Maybe, with the Millers gone, we should back off, live to fight another day. Or at the least, drop the temperature a few degrees.

"Why don't you take the advice, Rita? Why don't you leave, too? The other girls? Mariola escorted them to the bus depot. They're headed for parts unknown, their debts in the past. Every single girl, free to start over again."

"They're not girls, Charlie. They're women. Anyways, I'm waitin'."

"For who?"

"Waitin' for Bruce, mostly."

Alongside me, Dominick's again sliding his hand toward the gun tucked beneath his belt. I lay my fingers on his elbow, but keep my gaze on Rita. "That ain't gonna happen, Rita. Bruce is gone, or missing, or something else. Maybe he'll turn up, but it won't be here. Not at Maggie Miller's trailer. You have to know that."

Rita shakes her head, very slowly, and I can't help but think she's slipped over some edge I can't name. And I realize something I might have considered before. All along, I've heard rumors that Corey and Rita were lovers. I didn't dismiss these rumors. I didn't care, because it didn't matter at the time. It matters now.

"Look, Rita, I know Bruce was the father of Corey Miller's child. I know he killed her. I know he did it deliberately. But you don't have to worry about justice. If I get to Bruce, I intend to execute the bastard."

"Only he's gone, like you said."

"And he's the one who killed Corey. Not me."

"But you dumped her, Charlie. You dumped her out like she was so much garbage."

"Gimme a break, Rita. I had no choice."

"But we're not, we're not garbage." Something between a wail and a snarl obscures the words, and the repetitions that follow. "We're not, we're not, we're not garbage. We're not, we're not, we're not. We're not garbage."

Rita Lafayette comes out of the chair as though yanked upright by a higher power. Her eyes are wild and impossibly wide as she begins to fire. Her first two shots hit Tony in the chest. Both pass through his body, expelling twin jets of blood. He totters for a moment, hands rising to his chest, then falls back, his head crashing against the ground hard enough to be heard.

The shock stops me for a moment, but not Dominick. He yanks at his gun as Rita turns to face him. Then they're standing twenty feet apart, firing over and over again, the roar of gunfire engulfing me like a shroud. It doesn't stop until a bullet takes off the back of Dominick Costa's head, until his body slowly folds in on itself, until knees, waist, and shoulders collapse, until he drops, headfirst, to join Tony on the ground.

Rita turns to me, her blouse red with blood. She's finished, her gun empty, though she continues to yank at the trigger. The woman's taken everything from me, even my dreams. There'll be no more boom in Boomtown. The carnage will force the hand of governments in both counties, and in the capitol as well. And for what? For a fucking overdosed junkie whore? For a nobody? For nothing?

"We're not, Charlie," Rita tells me, her tone earnest, as if her sincerity will somehow convince me. "We're not. We're not garbage."

"No, Rita, you're not garbage," I explain before I pull the trigger. "What you are is fucking dead."

I spin around to find a dozen witnesses, including the born-again bitch who lives on the other side of the road. I don't threaten them. There's no point, because there's a double-barreled shotgun coming for Charlie Setter, the first trigger to be yanked by Mariola, the second by Ricky. And only one door open. Run for your life. That's the sign over the open door, plainly written, no mistakes. Run for your life.

CHAPTER FORTY-TWO
MAGGIE MILLER

Me and Daddy spend the night concealed by a dumpster. The dumpster's off to one side in the alley behind Stardust Jewelers. We didn't plan to come out until shortly before dawn, but given the craziness by our trailer, we figured we needed a head start. Charlie Setter's the issue. You'd assume the man's gonna get his sorry butt out of town as fast as he can. That's just human intuition, what with the cops already lookin' for him. But myself, I can't imagine Charlie gettin' all that far with little or no money to back his play. Can't imagine him leavin', either, if all the money he's been deliverin' to the Stardust every mornin' is still inside.

"I believe," Daddy said before we left the house, "the issue here isn't if, but when."

Meantime, we've been waitin' all night, to no good effect, and my thoughts have turned gloomy. It's possible that Charlie beat us to the punch. He might've drawn a straight line between the gunfight at the trailer and Stardust Jewelers, might be Charlie's been and gone. Not a happy thought.

◆

As it turns out, one member of the team is still playin' by the old rule book. The woman managin' the Stardust day-to-day pulls into the alley at seven thirty, right on time. I can't imagine she's heard the news, because she gets out of her car like she doesn't have a care in the world, lookin' neither right nor left. She's conservatively dressed in a white sweater and navy skirt that traces the contours of her butt and hips without being crude. Just another workday.

"Don't scream now," I tell her as I slide my left arm around her waist and push the muzzle of a 9mm Glock into her rib cage. "We're goin' inside, no muss, no fuss." Behind me, Daddy's still unfolding his fifty-plus body. "Tell me your name?"

"Adelyn."

"Okay, Adelyn, we're not here to hurt you, or anyone else for that matter. So, what you're gonna do, right now this second, is take one of those keys you're holdin' in your hand and open the door."

"No worries."

Adelyn's tone is cool and smooth, her knowing eyes calculating. Whatever the path that led her to Baxter, it wasn't mainstream. She unlocks the door, steps inside, and turns on a ceiling light. Me and Daddy follow.

"You know who we are?" I ask

"I do, Maggie." She smiles. "Hell, you're a Baxter celebrity."

"Great. Now lock the door."

She looks at me for a moment, then smiles. "You've been watching all along."

I assume she's referring to the fact that Charlie has to unlock the door with his own key when he arrives because the door's never unlocked. I point to a tall, combination safe.

"Open it. Just the clock, not the door."

She complies without hesitation, then steps back. I pull the door open, revealing trays of jewelry on narrow shelves. But no money.

"There's another door behind them shelves." Daddy says. "Figures."

"I see that. Now, Adelyn, I'm gonna speak plain as I can speak. We been steady watchin' the store and we know that Charlie comes every mornin' without fail. We know he comes through the back door with a package in his hands, a package he ain't totin' when he comes back out. We also know that he visits his properties before he makes an appearance, the Paradise, the casino, the bars. You hear me, Adelyn? There's no use pretendin'. Where's the money?"

Adelyn points to the solid steel sheet behind the shelves. "Back there. Like a safe within a safe."

I tug at a shelf. Nothing moves. "How do we get back there?"

"There's a keypad under the bottom shelf. On the right. Only I can't open it."

She reaches up to smooth her hair, though I can't see a hair out of place. "And before you start with the threats, you can skip to the chase and just shoot me because I don't know what I don't know."

There's a flaw in Adelyn's claim. I can't know what Adelyn does or doesn't know until I put her claim to the test. She appears a hundred percent sincere, but maybe she's just a good liar. I've been in too many interrogation rooms to still believe I can't be fooled.

"Can we get through that lock?" I ask Daddy.

Daddy's wearin' a small backpack. He drops the backpack to the floor, removes a flashlight and a screwdriver, finally drops to his knees. "Gettin' through the lock won't open the door. Just leave it locked permanent. We'd need a blowtorch, which we don't have. And don't have time to get."

I step behind Adelyn and push the gun's muzzle in the soft space just below the edge of her skull. I don't intend to pull the trigger, murder for money bein' on the far side of my ethical boundaries. But just like I don't know what Adelyn knows, Adelyn can't know what I might or might not do.

"I need you to unlock that partition," I tell her.

She stiffens, but doesn't break, her voice steady when she speaks. "I can't help you, Maggie, so if you're gonna pull that trigger . . ."

◆

A small leather couch rests against the wall opposite the safe. I put Adelyn on the couch next to Daddy and open my tablet. A moment later, I'm monitoring the camera in the alley behind the store. The screen is empty at the moment, because the camera's motion-activated and there's nothing moving.

"I knew her," Adelyn says out of nowhere. "Corey, I mean. She liked jewelry and she came into the shop a couple times a week. She'd bring coffee. Coffee and a smile. Corey had the greatest smile. Mischievous, right, like she just got over on someone? She'd tell stories about . . ."

"Go ahead, Adelyn. You ain't gonna offend us." This from Daddy.

"She told stories about the johns. Mimicked them perfectly, right down to the Midwest accents. I could laugh at her stories because I was in the life. Not that long ago, either." She sweeps her hand from left to right. "This store, it ain't much. The jewelry is mostly crap, real low-end. Only I like . . . no, I gotta say liked. I liked chatting up customers. I liked putting some cheap necklace around a girl's neck and telling her she looked great. That's gone now. It's over."

I'm sympathetic, but there's a question on the tip of my tongue, one I'm afraid to ask. I ask anyway.

"Did Corey ever talk about family?"

"Yeah, sure." She hesitates for a moment. "One time she came in about four o'clock, maybe an hour before she was due at the Paradise. We had a drink together. Jim Beam, neat. Corey told me she'd fucked up so bad in life, most likely her folk wouldn't want her back. But she'd go anyway, sometime, someday. Just show up. Here I am."

◆

I'm not locked on the monitor when my tablet lets go with a long beeeeeeep and a car I don't recognize pulls into the alley. It stops alongside the Stardust's rear door and Charlie slips out. He looks from side to side, shoulders hunched as he walks to the door, keys in his hand. The man's taking a big chance remaining in town, and he's expecting a big payoff. What he's not expecting is Daddy standing to one side of the door. What he's not expecting is the muzzle of a .45 Colt jammed into his rib cage. What he's not expecting is Maggie Miller coming through the door leading to the salesroom. Holding a semiautomatic in her own hand.

"Mornin', Charlie."

I'm not expecting resistance, and not really prepared when Charlie explodes. There's no real plan, no strategy to his madness. Charlie stomps his right foot into the ground, hands curled into fists, and looks up at the ceiling, his eyes mere slits now. The sounds coming from deep in his chest are guttural, a sound I associate with strangulation, with empty lungs screaming for breath. Then he spins, just as suddenly, and attacks Daddy, reaching for the Colt in Daddy's hand.

In the course of his life, my daddy's faced off against every weapon short of a chainsaw. He steps back, then to his right, leveling the Colt, but he doesn't shoot for the reason I've stated before. Here and gone before anybody knows we left. At least anybody with the power to detain us. But Charlie's too crazy to intimidate. It's as if he'd just as soon be dead, a man watchin' his life swirling round and round before it heads off to a septic tank. Whatever's hidden behind that safe wall is the key to him makin' a getaway of his own. Now he doesn't care. Now he's decided that he's dead anyway and he'll go down fighting. Me and Daddy, his boss in New York, Captain Mariola? Without money, he might as well find a coffin and lie down.

◆

I need to alter that way of thinkin'. I need to make Charlie understand that escapin' into the next world ain't on the table. I start by slamming the muzzle of my Glock into the side of his head. He staggers to one side, and blood starts to flow from a long tear in his scalp, but he doesn't go down.

I correct that oversight by smacking him again. This time he hits the floor hard enough to stay put. Behind me I hear Adelyn repeat herself, again and again.

"Holy shit, holy shit, holy shit."

"The duct tape, Daddy." In the service, I dealt with numerous brawls. First rule, bring the situation under control. Second and third rule, too, come to think on it. Charlie's eyes are open, but they're not seein'. He's tryin' to roll over, but can't. These are temporary conditions and we need to take advantage.

Daddy finally gets in gear. He pulls a roll of gray duct tape from the backpack and together we bind Charlie, his wrists and forearms first, behind his back, then his legs, from his ankles almost to his knees. Charlie Setter's not goin' anywhere until we set him free.

◆

"Adelyn," I ask, "you have shoppin' bags out front?" Charlie's eyes are still rollin' around in his head.

"By the register. What do you need them for?"

I'm tempted to respond with something like Charlie's body parts, but restrain myself at the last minute. "Time for you to move on, girl. Ain't nothin' for you in Baxter. But I'm thinkin' about what you said before, about likin' the jewelry business. So why don't you pack up this jewelry and hit the road? Should be sufficient to buy you a head start wherever you end up."

Adelyn only hesitates long enough to flash a broad smile before going to work, filling three large shopping bags with maybe half the Stardust's merchandise. On the way out, she stops to kiss my cheek. "Corey was good people. Didn't have a harmful bone in her body."

◆

Charlie's come awake by the time the door closes behind Adelyn. I watch Daddy lock it, then turn on my prisoner.

"Charlie, do you believe that a small chance, even a tiny chance, is better than no chance at all?"

"Fuck you."

"I want you to give me the numbers to open the lock."

"Fuck you."

"Thought you might take that attitude. Daddy, tape Charlie's mouth. It's best if no one hears him scream."

Charlie manages a few more obscene comments before his mouth is securely taped, and I believe he means to resist us. I also believe that beneath this momentary lapse, Charlie's a rational man. He just needs remindin'.

"Daddy, you have a hammer in that backpack?"

"Sure do." He removes a standard claw hammer and passes it over.

"Okay, Charlie, here's the way it's gonna go. I want you to give me the numbers for that keypad. If you do, I'll cut the tape before we leave. That's a chance, Charlie, and small as it might be, it's better than no chance at all. As for us, me and Daddy, if you hold out, we'll still head home. Not rich, true, but safe in the bosom of the family. Not you, though. Not you, Charlie. See, forty minutes after we clear the city, I'm gonna call Captain Mariola and tell her I've left a wrapped-up present for her in the Stardust Jewelry store. Not in the best of conditions, true, but still serviceable."

"Damn, girl," Daddy says, "you do go on. Get to the point."

"Now, Daddy, I know what I'm doin' here. It's important that Charlie should understand what's at stake. No confusion, two possibilities only." I raise the hammer so Charlie can't help but view the head. "What I'm gonna do is smash your right kneecap." I touch his knee and he jumps, pulling it off to the side. "Daddy, would you mind holdin' Charlie's knee down?

"Ain't no knee replacement gonna fix the damage I plan to do, Charlie. Hope you understand that. A gimp on crutches don't stand much of a chance doin' life without in a maximum-security prison."

Charlie's lips move beneath the tape as I raise the hammer. I can't hear what he's tryin' to say, but I get the message. How's he supposed to reveal the code if his mouth is taped?

"Your eyes, Charlie. When you're ready to communicate, indicate the numbers with eyeblinks."

I tap his knee with the hammer, hard enough to hurt without doing any real damage. But that's enough for Charlie. He blinks four times and I walk over to the keypad and push the four button.

"Next number, Charlie."

Our route takes us south onto I-70, then east. Daddy's behind the wheel, cruisin' down the middle lane as he keeps a respectful distance from the car in front.

"I think we're good, honey."

"Guess so." I punch the number of the Baxter PD into my phone. A man answers and I ask for Captain Mariola. A moment later, I'm speaking to a woman, who wants to know what I want with her boss.

"Tell her it's Maggie Miller callin'."

The wait is very short. "Maggie, it's Captain Mariola. How are you this morning?"

"I 'spect it's been a long night for both of us."

"Long, but productive. And for you?"

"Equally so, Captain."

"Good to hear. Now, what can I do for you?"

"I'm wonderin' if y'all are still lookin' for Charlie Setter?"

"You're a wonder, Maggie Miller." Her laugh is genuine. I believe, if it were possible for me and Daddy to remain in Baxter, we might become friends.

"Charlie's in the back office at the Stardust Jewelry store," I tell her.

"When did you see him last?"

"Forty minutes ago."

"Do you think he's still there?"

"Yes, ma'am, I believe he'll be tied up for a while."

"And you, Maggie?"

"Here and gone."

◆

Usin' the Google map, I plotted the distance from Baxter to Redmond Lake at 480 miles. A bit short of seven hours if we don't stop. And we won't, except to buy gas. We can't risk some bored trooper takin' a notion to have a look-see at the car we're drivin'. And I do know that the odds against a search, given how ordinary me and Daddy look, are very long. But the stakes are as big as stakes can get for ordinary folk like us. If a trooper were to raise the trunk, he'd find three suitcases restin' on a blue tarpaulin. One of those suitcases is filled with money, over a hundred thousand dollars, at the least. Be a hard business explainin' the money to that nosy trooper. Be harder still if he found Bruce Angoleri's body underneath the tarp.

I'm sitting alongside Daddy in the front. Behind us, on the back seat, an urn contains my baby sister's ashes. The Millers have a family plot holdin' stones set in place three hundred years ago. Time and weather have done their work and the oldest ones can't be read. They're no less regarded for that. Nor will Corey Miller's grave be ill-regarded. Corey was—is, really—a Miller after all.

On the other hand, Bruce is headed for a dark place. Our piece of Kentucky is pocked with mine shafts, some runnin' hundreds of feet below ground. Tunnels that deep have to be serviced by vertical air shafts. You drop a stone into one of these shafts, you mostly don't hear when it hits bottom.

Funny thing about Bruce Angoleri. I don't believe he really understood our concern, mine and Daddy's. In his mind, he was the victim. Corey just wouldn't listen to reason. Wanted that baby and where it'd go from there was anyone's guess. Maybe she'd declare him the father and demand child support. And how would that work out, what with Bruce married to his gangster boss's niece.

No, Bruce couldn't let word of his impending fatherhood get back his boss. Surely, I could understand that. "I hadda do it," he told me, "Corey forced my hand."

We're approaching the Kentucky border when Daddy asks me a question I'm sure he's been holdin' back. "Did you mean it, baby girl, when you told Charlie you were gonna smash his knee?"

"Don't know exactly. Maybe yes, maybe no. Don't matter anyway. It ain't the truth of what you claim that matters, it's whether or not the individual on the other side believes you. But I'm not thinkin' about Charlie. City of Baxter, neither. I'm thinkin' about roasted chicken fresh from Harmon Renfrow's smoker and Aunt Mary's peach cobbler. I'm thinkin' about comin' home."

CHAPTER FORTY-THREE

DELIA

All in all, I'd rather storm a drug house armed with a peashooter in my underwear. I keep looking through my bedroom window at a sunbaked yard. Hoping for rain. This afternoon, two hours from now, I'm going to attend Mayor Vern's annual picnic, this year to be held at Goldman High's football field. Danny's school.

Not my first rodeo. I've been attending, Danny in tow, every year since I became Vern's partner. Chat and eat, chat and eat, chat and eat. Schmoozing is what they called it when I served back east. No sweat.

"Delia, are you out of the shower?"

The voice belongs to my lover, Zoe Parillo. Zoe and I plan to attend the party as a couple. If I don't chicken out.

"Yeah, I'm done."

We pass each other, me on the way to the kitchen, Zoe headed for a quick shower. Danny's sitting on our living room couch, engrossed in a textbook. Finals are fast approaching and Gretchen's been giving him a hard time about his already acceptable grades. Truth to tell, I think Danny's growing tired of the nagging. Gretchen means well, but Danny's a teenager and one mother's enough. In fact, it's one too many.

"Mom, you look like you're walking on eggs."

"I'm nervous, no question." We've already spoken about the picnic and how much I hate being stared at.

"Well, don't worry, Mom. If you need support, I'll be on the other side of the field. Or maybe under the grandstand."

I laugh. I have to. And Danny's right about one thing. Everyone knows. That's what he told me. Everyone knows you're gay. It's true, for sure, but walking onto the field with Zoe by my side? It'll be like wearing a hat with little flashing lights: LESBIAN, LESBIAN, LESBIAN.

And what will I—we—do if we're snubbed? Baxter is pretty much ground zero for the Midwestern Bible Belt. I've met most of the preachers, priests, and our one rabbi without incident. But was their civility based on a mutual understanding? Don't force my hand and I'll keep my bigotry in my pocket?

I won't know—I can't know—until I get there.

◆

An hour later, Zoe wanders into the living room. The dress code for the mayor's annual picnic is defiantly casual. We're not, after all, Eastern elites attending a gala at the Met. We're solid, salt of the earth, just plain folk. Zoe's wearing a summer-weight teal dress specked with pink blossoms, probably tea roses. The dress flares below the waist, which somehow emphasizes a slender body that sharply contrasts with that of her chunky partner. I'm wearing white jeans and a blue top I designed myself. Heavier than a T-shirt, lighter than a sweatshirt, the sleeves are elbow length. Letters arranged in an arc across the top read: BAXTER. At the bottom, in a straight line: POLICE DEPARTMENT. Between them, a facsimile of my detective's gold shield.

I head for the coffeepot, Zoe trailing behind. She puts her arms around me and leans forward to whisper in my ear. "You're a fucking hero, Delia. You cleaned up Dodge and drove the Clanton gang out of Tombstone. Adulation is what they call it. Baxter loves you."

◆

Dominick Costa and Tony Carbone were pronounced dead at the scene. Rita Lafayette was shot three times, but she's still alive, twelve days after the gunfight. Minus a spleen, her left lung, and a piece of her liver.

The ordeal did little to soften her attitude. When I dropped by the hospital, she shook her head as I entered her room. Her greeting was even more emphatic.

"Fuck off, pig."

◆

Six people witnessed parts of the shootout, though none witnessed the buildup, their attention only drawn to the scene after the first shot was fired. From that point forward, however, they were riveted to the unfolding drama. Still, like most witnesses, they disagreed about many details, even who was the first to fall.

"I think my heart stopped," a workman told me. "It was a blur, like I'm not sure if it took two seconds or a week before it was over."

Bertha Framm, who lives across from the Miller's trailer, was the most coherent. She'd just come out of her trailer to walk Stonewall, her German Shepherd, when the first shots were fired.

"The one on the right dropped first. Don't know his name, but he fell straight back. The one on my left, I seen him around with Charlie Setter. Charlie was the third one, standin' a little behind the other two. Anyways, the one on the left and the woman—don't know her name, but she worked at the Paradise—shot at each other and I believe the woman was wounded." Here Bertha paused for just a moment, swallowing hard before she continued. "The other one, Charlie's friend, the top of his head just blew off and he was gone, finished."

"And that left Charlie and Rita?"

"That's her name? Rita?"

"Yes, Rita."

"Well, Rita, she turned on Charlie, but her gun was jammed, or maybe she was out of ammo because she kept pullin' on the trigger, but nothin' happened."

"And Charlie?"

"Charlie didn't fire right away." Again, she hesitated. "Okay, so all along, Rita was screamin', 'We're not garbage.' Like, over and over again. Me, I gotta figure Charlie was listenin' close, because he took a step toward her and said, 'No, you're not garbage. What you are is dead.'"

◆

Bertha Framm was the only witness to report the dialogue, but several others confirmed two of her assertions. First, that Rita Lafayette was attempting, but unable, to fire her weapon after Dominick Costa fell. Second, that Charlie hesitated, then took a step toward Rita before firing.

That was enough, even without knowing how the confrontation began, to arraign Charlie Setter on a charge of attempted murder. It was enough for my favorite law-and-order judge, Millicent Jordan, to hit him with a $100,000 cash bail.

And that should have been that. Out of sight, out of mind.

No such luck. Three days later, two FBI agents, contacted by Charlie's attorney, showed up at Vern Taney's office. I wasn't present at the meeting, but they left satisfied. Charlie had agreed to cooperate in a RICO investigation targeting a New York gangster named Richard Ricci. The morning after the meeting, Charlie and his FBI handlers left Baxter for parts unknown. They would produce him, of course, if our case went to trial, but in the meanwhile, Charlie would be held at a secure location of the federal government's choosing.

◆

The remainder of Charlie's crew, those still breathing air, fled to New York after they learned that an arrest warrant had been issued for Bruce Angoleri, charging him with murdering Corey Miller. Bruce has also vanished, but the arrest warrant's been uploaded to a federal database. If Bruce is arrested anywhere in the country, he'll be returned to Baxter. Myself, I don't think he's alive. If his own crew didn't take him out, then Maggie Miller probably did. I can't imagine her leaving Baxter otherwise.

With the enemy off the field of battle, the victors can hardly be blamed for taking a collective bow. Doesn't matter whether you read Basil Ulrich's stories in the *Baxter Bugle*, or listen to Katie Burke at WBAX. The Detective Division of the Baxter Police Department closed the Corey Miller homicide without incurring the expense of incarcerating or trying a defendant. As Zoe said, we're heroes. And there's more to come. The Sprague County Board of Supervisors finally agreed to allow the Baxter PD to co-patrol Boomtown. As of yet, we've made no arrests. Harassment is the order of the day, the message simple enough. Whatever you're up to, find a private place to do it.

This see-and-hear-no-evil policy came from the top. From Mayor Venn and City Council President Gloria Meacham. For them, and for most of Baxter's gentry, the bottom line remains constant. The plant must be built and the temporary workers here to build it will never confine themselves to church socials or pickup softball games. Keep the vice outta sight. That's the gist of their message.

Fortunately, the headaches accompanying this approach don't really touch the Detective Division. We don't prevent crime. We punish perpetrators after crimes are committed. It's a different story for the Patrol Division.

◆

"Mom, you ready?"

"As a matter of fact . . ."

Zoe dangles the car keys in front of my face. "Time to go, girlfriend."

I feel like a condemned prisoner being led to her execution as we drive the few miles to the picnic, as we park two blocks from the field, as we thread our way between haphazardly parked cars, SUVs, and pickup trucks. It's a beautiful day, warm and breezy with no hint of the oppressive summer heat soon to follow. Later on, by midsummer, the grass on the field will dry and brown. For now, it's a shade of green I associate with photographs of the Irish countryside.

The edge of the eastern side of the field is lined with food stations. Baxter BBQ will never compete with the BBQ industry in St. Louis or Kansas City, but as a matter of tradition, our local pitmasters come out in force on Picnic Day. The mingled odors of woodsmoke and roasting meats, chicken, pork, and burgers, greet me as I cross the street and step onto the grass.

That's when Zoe takes my arm.

We're noticed, of course, and I find myself wondering which one of our proud citizens I'm gonna punch in the mouth first. The best defense being a good offense. Then I hear a scream from across the field, followed by the joyous shout of a little girl.

"Aunt Delia! Aunt Zoe!"

Emmaline runs across the grass, wobbling but determined. She's dressed in pink, pink shorts, pink top, pink bow in her hair. I glance at Zoe to find tears in her eyes. I won't go that far, but I drop to one knee and wrap my arms around this child. I want to hold her for the rest of the afternoon, but I only have the girl for a few seconds before she wriggles free and grabs Zoe. Then it's Danny's turn.

I keep my eyes on Emmaline as I stand. She's taken Danny's hand and they're walking off to join Mike. As I watch, she turns suddenly, a huge smile lighting her face, and waves.

"Delia, Zoe."

I turn to find Gloria Meacham standing a few feet away. Gloria is Baxter royalty. Born into a farm family that can trace its roots to the first settlers in the region, her ancestors arrived within a few years of the Revolutionary War's end. Now she steps forward to bestow faux kisses, on my cheek first, then Zoe's, before stepping back.

"Congratulations, Delia."

"For what?"

"You're being promoted to Inspector."

I think it over for a moment, then ask the only relevant question. "Does it come with a raise?"

"Afraid not."

◆

Lillian approaches a minute later, working to keep a struggling Cora under control, then Vern carrying two bottles of beer that Zoe and I eagerly accept.

"Big news," Vern tells me. "The city's new budget includes money for a real Medical Examiner and a facility to go with him." Vern has always been quick. In this case he quickly notes the frowns on the faces of his audience, then adds, lamely. "Or her."

After a few minutes of small talk, Zoe and I begin to circulate. We remain together for a short time, then drift away from each other. Some of the picnickers keep their distance, including Pastor Gotrick, but there's nothing overt, no outright snubs. As for myself, I'm drawn to smiles like iron to a magnet. Baxter is an overwhelmingly Republican city, but if Republicans aren't big on gay rights, they're gigantic on law-and-order. And there's no calculating their commitment to Nissan and its plant. Though I can't see Nissan canceling its own commitment in light of the investment they've already made, the craziness in Boomtown had them afraid.

I'm something of a hero, nevertheless, and nobody I speak to is concerned with the ongoing vice in Boomtown, or seems to realize that it's simply gone to ground. And I know there's trouble coming down the line. The New York mob has been replaced with a dozen independent entrepreneurs, all vying for market share. Violence will surely follow.

◆

That's for later. For now, on this beautiful spring afternoon, only a step away from a blazing prairie summer, the mayor's invited guests have locked themselves into the present. I join them, gladly, wandering about until I reach the BBQ pits, where I pick up a brisket sandwich and another beer. I'm still working on the beer when I approach Zack Butler. He's in a wheelchair, attended by the ever-faithful Miranda. There's a paper plate in his lap with a skewer of grilled veggies on it. Cherry tomatoes, zucchini, cauliflower, slices of pepper. Zack's staring at the skewer, but he looks up as I approach.

"Have I ever mentioned that Miranda's early career was spent as a prison guard in Baghdad?"

"You on a diet, Zack?"

"In the interests of a health that deserted me ten years ago. But never mind, congratulations are in order, Inspector Mariola."

I have to laugh. Most likely, Zack knew about the promotion before anyone told Vern. Just now the man seems to be everywhere.

"Big happenings in the works," he tells me. "The City of Baxter's in line to expand. A decent slice of Maryville and Revere Counties. Maybe fifty square miles." He looks down at his food for a moment, then back at me. "The Nissan plant won't run without an executive branch on top. They'll be specialists of every kind, including high-priced mechanics to maintain the robots. Where will they live? Mount Jackson won't hold 'em. Them or the kind of stores they'll want to patronize. Or the schools they'll want their kids to attend. No, if we're to host all Nissan's higher paid executives and workers, along with all of Nissan's subcontractors, along with all of their families, we'll have to expand."

"And build, Zack. Don't forget build."

Zack's mischievous smile reminds me of Danny's smile, back when he was five years old. "And build, Delia. And build, and build, and build."